6/2

D0344411

SUMMERSET ABBEY

Center Point
Large Print

**This Large Print Book carries the
Seal of Approval of N.A.V.H.**

SUMMERSET ABBEY

T. J. BROWN

CENTER POINT LARGE PRINT
THORNDIKE, MAINE

This Center Point Large Print edition
is published in the year 2013 by arrangement with
Gallery Books, a division of Simon & Schuster, Inc.

Copyright © 2013 by Teri Brown.

This book is a work of fiction.
Names, characters, places, and incidents either are
products of the author's imagination or are used
fictitiously. Any resemblance to actual events or locales
or persons, living or dead, is entirely coincidental.

The text of this Large Print edition is unabridged.
In other aspects, this book may vary
from the original edition.
Printed in the United States of America
on permanent paper.
Set in 16-point Times New Roman type.

ISBN: 978-1-61173-681-6

Library of Congress Cataloging-in-Publication Data

Brown, T. J.
    Summerset Abbey / T. J. Brown.
    pages ; cm.
    ISBN 978-1-61173-681-6 (library binding : alk. paper)
    1. Sisters—Fiction. 2. Household employees—Fiction.
    3. Social classes—Great Britain—History   19th century—Fiction.
    4. Great Britain—Social life and customs—19th century—Fiction.
    5. Large type books. I. Title.
PS3602.R22893S86 2013b
813'.6—dc23
                                                    2012046413

I dedicate this book to the father of my heart, Lyle George Foreman, who was born in 1916, during World War I and lived to see a man on the moon, the World Wide Web, and his rebellious, youngest daughter become an author. I'm not sure which one he found most shocking. I love you, Papa.

ACKNOWLEDGMENTS

First and foremost, I have to give all props to my amazing agent, Molly Glick, who didn't even bat an eye when I sent an email out of the blue saying we should pitch an Edwardian. She not only rolls with the punches, she makes magic happen out of nothing. Next, I must acknowledge Lauren McKenna, editor extraordinaire, who knows exactly what she wants and how to bring out the best in me, and the equally hardworking Alexandra Lewis, who spent hours going back and forth with me via email to whip this book into shape. It's a far better book because of her insight. My most gorgeous cover is due to Lisa Litwack and a heartful of thanks goes to production editor John Paul Jones and copyeditor Jane Elias, for her copy editing savvy and comma knowledge.

Gratitude to Art Braccioforte, who read the first few chapters and told me it had merit. Huge props to Dianne Cooke, freelance editor who helped me clean up the messes I kept making and sending her way, and more sparkly props go to fact checker and amazing Edwardian author Evangeline Holland.

And then there is my crazy, wacked-out, one-of-a-kind family to thank—my husband, who takes care of me, as I haven't the first clue as how to do it myself and, in fact, tossed women's lib back forty years in order to get out of doing the bills, maintaining the cars, repairing all the house stuff, and going to the store. My wonderful children—Ethan, who makes me laugh and finishes my sentences, and my daughter, Megan, who makes up for my lack of sense by learning how to work on cars and look beautiful doing it. There are no words to express how much I love you three. I could survive almost anything, including cancer, editorial letters, and a zombie apocalypse, as long as I always have you guys by my side.

CHAPTER
ONE

Prudence Tate paused before the arched doorway to allow Victoria time to regain her composure. In front of her, the sanctuary was so filled with black feathered hats, it looked as though a flock of ravens might have overrun the church. The scent of stale incense, decaying flowers, and ancient prayers permeated the foyer, but Prudence barely noticed these things.

Next to her, Victoria's slight body trembled with grief and exhaustion. "Do I really have to do this?" Victoria asked, her voice more of a wish than a whisper.

Born too soon to a dying mother, Victoria had always been frail, but what she lacked in health and vigor she more than made up for in temperament. Only the death of her father had lately diminished the audacious glint in her china-blue eyes.

"We have to." Prudence slipped her arm lightly around the younger girl's shoulders. Tears slid down Victoria's face and Prudence feared she would fall apart completely before they made their way down the aisle.

Funerals were as scripted as coronations, and custom dictated the familial order of the church procession. Rowena, as Victoria's older sister, had gone ahead of them on her uncle's arm and was no doubt waiting for Victoria at their pew. Sir Philip Buxton's closest contemporaries, all men in fussy black mourning coats, stood behind them, waiting to go in. They fidgeted, looking at anything but the two girls.

Tradition dictated that Prudence, as the governess's daughter, wait in the back of the procession with the staff, but Sir Philip's bohemian household had never given a fig for tradition.

Looking at Victoria, Prudence felt her chest squeeze around her heart so tightly that she couldn't breathe. Recent weeks had taken such a toll on the girl that even though the woolen, crepe-trimmed mourning dress had just been fitted, it hung on her as if there were nothing of substance underneath. Victoria had never been conventionally pretty; her face was too thin and her eyes were too big, but she usually displayed a vivacity that, in spite of her weak lungs, made her the most arresting person in the room. Today that vibrancy had dimmed and dark circles bruised her eyes.

Prudence reached down and took a firm grip of Victoria's hand. "Come. They're waiting."

Victoria cast her a wobbly smile as they walked through the doorway and down the aisle to where Rowena and their uncle, the Earl of Summerset, waited.

When they reached the pew, the Earl gave Prudence a look so disdainful that she almost stumbled. His nose twitched with contempt, as if she were one step away from an Irish peasant with dung still clinging to her shoes.

Before she'd died, Prudence's mother had gently warned her that even though she'd been raised as one of Sir Philip's girls, there were many who would think of her as nothing more than a cheeky and presumptuous servant. Evidently, Lord Summerset was among that group.

Rowena, on the other side of her uncle, looked beautiful in a stylish silk crepe mourning gown that skimmed her ankles. A cunning little toque perched atop her upswept dark hair, and she wore a gold locket clasped around her neck. Rowena held out her hand and, relieved, Prudence reached out and clasped it with her own. Without letting go of either girl, she and Victoria scooted past the Earl to join Rowena.

They stood as the rest of the procession solemnly made their way to their proper places, but Prudence, thankful to be tucked firmly between the two people she loved best in the world, took no notice.

A lump rose in her throat as she caught sight of the ornate casket, draped with a full spray of lilies, carnations, and palm fronds. The only reason she was here, clutching Rowena's and

Victoria's hands in hers instead of shrinking into the background with the other servants, was the kindness of the man who lay inside. After Prudence's father had died, her mother, who had worked at Sir Philip's estate as a girl, had been sent to attend to Rowena and Victoria's ailing mother. When his wife died, Sir Philip asked her to stay on to help raise the girls, and Prudence, exactly between his daughters in age, became part of the family. Prudence, who volunteered her time at several different poorhouses in the city, knew exactly what happened to young girls left alone in the world. She would forever be grateful to Sir Philip for not allowing that to happen to her.

She blinked away her tears and occupied herself by looking at the rest of the congregation. Only a few looked familiar. Among them were Rupert Brooke, the high-strung and handsome young poet; Ben Tillett, the iron-jawed union leader; and Roger Fry, the controversial artist responsible for bringing London's shocked attention to post-impressionism some years prior. These were some of Sir Philip's friends, a motley collection of artists, intellectuals, and misfits.

Because the Earl had arranged the funeral, most of the people in attendance were his peers, men from the House of Lords and others from the cream of London society.

Sir Philip would have hated it.

The beautiful gold arches and polished marble of St. Bride's Church gleamed, just as they had the few times the family had attended church. Sir Philip had chosen St. Bride's because, as he used to say, "Sir Christopher Wren built the kind of church that God might actually enjoy."

Gradually, Prudence became aware of a young man staring at her from across the aisle. Her eyes darted in his direction, then away. Moments later, unable to help herself, she glanced back to see whether he was still looking at her. He was. She turned slightly and stared fixedly at the bronze candelabra to the left of him, her cheeks burning.

Victoria leaned around her to whisper to Rowena. "Look, Lord Billingsly has noticed our Prudence."

"I'm right here," Prudence whispered, and gave both their hands a hard squeeze for emphasis.

She didn't look his way again.

Once the service started, Prudence sank into a well of grief that threatened to drown her. The waves of it lapped at her from all sides, covered her head, and made sight almost impossible. Inside, her heart broke and a waterfall of sorrow poured from the cracks. On one side, Victoria sobbed quietly, while Rowena's stiff resolve buoyed her from the other. She clung to their hands as the service passed in a blur of speeches.

They remained that way until it was time to get into the ornate black and gold funeral carriages that would take them back to their home in Mayfair for the reception. Behind the carriages stood a line of motorcars; most of the wealthy guests had long given up their carriages for the convenience and speed of automobiles. The Earl himself had several, and Sir Philip's sleek Eton-blue Belsize sat idle in the carriage house, but the Earl insisted on traditional horse-drawn carriages.

"Miss Tate will ride in the staff carriage." The Earl's voice brooked no opposition and his square jaw firmed. Prudence knew that look. Rowena's pretty face held the same expression when she got all stubborn about something.

Victoria's eyes widened. "Prudence rides with us."

"Nonsense. The Duke of Plymouth wishes to join us and there isn't enough room."

Prudence placed her hands on Victoria's shoulders. Tension vibrated through the young girl's slender body and Prudence's stomach knotted, sure that Victoria was going to throw a fit, the kind she used to throw when the family still called her baby and she wanted the biggest sweet in the shop. Even at eighteen, Victoria wasn't above a tantrum or two if she thought the situation warranted it. But her waiflike face suddenly fell and her lower lip trembled.

"It'll be all right," Prudence whispered. "I'll go back with the staff and meet you at home."

But upon arriving at the house, Prudence found herself so busy helping Hodgekins, their butler, and Mrs. Tannin, their housekeeper, that she barely got to see Rowena and Victoria, who were stuck in some kind of morbid receiving line in the marbled foyer. After the guests offered their hushed condolences, they went either into the pale green and white sitting room on the right, or to the formal dining room on the left to gobble up indelicate amounts of food.

Prudence slipped adroitly through the crowd, making sure there was enough port, brandy, and mulled wine. Carl, their footman, served oyster patties and croquettes, while the sideboard held silver platters of ginger biscuits from Biarritz and fine Belgian chocolates.

The hothouse flowers had been delivered and arranged earlier in the day. Black beribboned vases of lilies stood on every table and the enormous silver bowls on the dining room table overflowed with white chrysanthemums. The scent made Prudence's stomach churn and she wondered whether she would ever again enjoy the smell of flowers.

As she busied herself with mundane tasks, Prudence noticed that except for a few of Sir Philip's closest friends, who offered her their heartfelt condolences, the guests looked through her as if she didn't exist. When one pinched-faced woman wearing a black velvet turban handed her an empty glass, Prudence realized why she was invisible.

The Earl's friends considered her staff.

She stood in the middle of the wide marbled hall, holding a Waterford wineglass, tears pricking at the backs of her eyes. She didn't know whether to laugh or cry.

Prudence set the glass down on the nearest table and slipped away from the crowd into a small alcove near the curving mahogany staircase. She placed her hands on her heated cheeks and drew in several deep breaths.

"I know the daughters, of course," a female voice said, quite close to where Prudence was secreted. "They attended a house party at Stanton last summer with the Earl's family, but I don't know the girl who sat with them at the service."

"That was the governess's daughter," said a second woman. "Sir Philip raised her like one of his own and kept her on even after her mother died several years ago. Can you believe it? He had such liberal ideas. The girls practically ran wild in London."

The voices drew nearer and Prudence shrank farther back into the alcove.

"How bizarre. They seemed like very nice girls."

"Oh, they're nice enough. But I've heard the eldest is a member of the National Union of Women's Suffrage Societies, and the youngest says the most startling things. She has the tendency to bring up in conversation bizarre subjects young girls shouldn't even think about—strange talk of plants and herbs and such. And she's delicate, you know."

"I've never seen the girl at Summerset or at any balls during the season."

The second woman tittered. "Well, of course not. You don't think Sir Philip would push the Earl that far, do you?"

The voices moved away and Prudence leaned her back against the wall, almost upsetting a small occasional table with a marble statue of Circe on top. She reached out and steadied it with one hand, her cheeks burning. What did the woman mean about Sir Philip not wanting to push the Earl? Prudence wished she could hide away forever, but it wasn't fair to leave Hodgekins and Miss Tannin with all the work. They were grieving, too.

Pushing the conversation from her mind, Prudence hurried to the larder and pulled two extra bottles of port from the shelf, where they'd been sitting upright, ready for the occasion. She dusted them off and took them to the butler's pantry for Hodgekins to decant.

That done, she decided enough was enough. She may not be a daughter of the house, but she *was* a part of the family and she desperately needed Victoria and Rowena's comforting presence to erase the hurtful words still ringing in her ears. She turned the corner and stopped just short of running into a man putting on a black serge overcoat.

"I'm so sorry." She was about to step around him when she realized it was the same man who'd stared at her during the service. Her breath caught as she stared up into the obsidian darkness of his eyes.

"No, I'm sorry. I thought I could just leave through the back." He looked down at her and colored when he realized who it was. "I'm sorry. I only meant that I didn't want to trouble the family further. I didn't know Sir Philip very well."

"Then why are you here?" Her cheeks heated at her rudeness. Why did she say that? She couldn't think, couldn't breathe with him so close. She took a step back.

"My mother is ill and she wanted me to pay our respects. My parents know the Earl well and I'm good friends with Colin, the Earl's son."

"Oh." She risked a glance up at his face. Burnished brown curls fell over a high forehead and he regarded her steadily beneath quizzical brows. They stared at each other for a long moment and she wondered whether he felt as dazed as she did. Her heart sped up as the moment lengthened. She finally broke eye contact. "Thank you."

She moved to go past him and he caught her by her elbow. "Wait," he said, his voice almost urgent. "I don't even know your name."

"Prudence," she said, before pulling her arm away and moving down the hall.

"But who are you?" he called after her.

She couldn't tell him, for at that moment she didn't know.

Prudence found the girls still standing in the marble foyer, greeting guests. Alarm spread through her as she spied Victoria on the other side of a potted palm. She hurried to the Earl, who was speaking to a gaunt gentleman in a top hat.

"Excuse me, sir," she whispered.

He continued talking, though she'd seen him glance her way.

Pressing her lips together, she tugged on his arm. "Lord Summerset, I must speak with you."

He turned to her, irritation written all over his face. "What?" he snapped.

"It's Victoria. I think she should be excused from the receiving line. She doesn't look well."

"I'm sure she's fine." He turned his head to where Victoria stood and his jaw tightened. Victoria's skin had paled to muslin white and she swayed on her feet. He sighed.

"Take her upstairs and sit with her. Rowena can do the receiving by herself."

She hurried to Victoria's side without the courtesy of a reply.

Slipping her arm around Victoria's waist, she whispered, "Come with me. You're done for the evening."

Victoria, always on guard against being coddled, stiffened in annoyance. There was nothing she hated more than being babied for her breathing affliction, but Prudence could feel tremors running up and down her slim body.

"I'm perfectly fine," she started to say, and then gave Prudence a wry smile as her legs trembled. "I guess I could use a break." She leaned against Prudence and let herself be led away.

"I'm just so sad and that's what makes me tired," Victoria said, as they slowly climbed the stairs to her bedroom.

Prudence kissed her cheek. "You'll feel better after some sleep."

"Do you really believe that?"

Prudence hesitated, her very bones aching with sadness. "Not really. But what else can we do?"

Rowena watched them go, Prudence's dark head leaning against Victoria's blonde one, and wished she could join them. But someone had to play hostess and it was a duty she'd been taking on more and more as she got older, though rarely at occasions as formal as this. Her father had never stood much on formality. He could trot out the pomp and ceremony when he needed to, but his taste ran more to last-minute late suppers with friends, or hearty sandwiches in the sitting room with a couple of bottles of good wine. The kind of guests they usually entertained appreciated the generous simplicity of her father's hospitality.

She turned quickly to the stout woman in front of her as the tears locked behind her eyes threatened to spill over. If she began crying, she might never stop, and she still had hours until this ghastly reception was over. "Thank you so much for coming . . ." Her mind blanked as she desperately tried to come up with a name.

"Your father was a good man, dear." The still nameless woman patted her hand and moved on.

When the tide of mourners coming through the door waned, she was finally able to leave the foyer. Snatching up a glass of brandy, she gulped it down, ignoring her uncle's frown from across the room. She needed something to help her get through the rest of the evening.

That done, she wandered from room to room, looking above people's heads so she wouldn't have to make the obligatory society chitchat. Her father had been contemptuous of that sort of empty nattering and Rowena shared the sentiment. Aristocratic prattle made her contrary and apt to say things like "Beastly weather, isn't it?" even if there wasn't a cloud in the sky.

So she avoided it, plumping the pillows on the winged-back sofa and wiping away a water ring on a Chinese bamboo side table. Before her parents had moved into the stuffy old Victorian home, her father had gutted it, making the rooms larger, adding a glass dome above the staircase to let in more light and plastering the walls in a creamy white. From the sash windows in the front to the gleaming mahogany floors dotted with Oriental rugs, everything about her house was beloved. Her mother had decorated it for comfort rather than show and had ended up creating a spacious, airy home that was both supremely comfortable and pleasing to the eye.

Her uncle came to her side. "As soon as the crowd thins out a bit, I need you to meet me in the study. Your father's solicitor wishes to discuss the details of your father's will with us."

"Will?" she asked stupidly. Perhaps the brandy hadn't been a good idea.

"Of course. You didn't think he would leave you and Victoria without means, did you?"

Without means? She turned the phrase over in her mind. Well, no. She had never thought about money at all. Her father took care of household expenses. She suddenly realized that he wouldn't be able to do that anymore. Her throat tightened. Wouldn't the solicitor take care of that? Or the bank?

Her uncle continued. "We need to discuss your future. He never spoke about any of this with you?"

She shook her head, bewildered, and her uncle

awkwardly patted her shoulder. "Never mind, dear. We will talk about it with Mr. Barry."

He moved away, leaving her to ponder his words. Her future? The thought of her future had always filled her with a certain anxiety. Her girlfriends or their parents always had so many plans regarding their futures, while hers remained a frustrating blank. She just couldn't seem to make up her mind as to what she wanted to do, despite her efforts to fill the void. One summer, on the advice of a friend, she had thrown herself into sports until she could play lawn tennis with a vengeance and golf as well as any man, but once she realized the void was still there, her racquet and clubs were relegated to the attic. Finally, at her father's gentle nudging, she'd dedicated herself to the National Union of Women's Suffrage Societies. Because she wanted to please her father, she remained involved long after she would have drifted away on her own. The women there made her uncomfortable. Confident and self-reliant, they were all charting their own paths, while her own remained a mystery. She supposed that someday she would marry, but it wasn't really a priority and she had yet to meet a young man who interested her. Most of the girls she'd grown up with thought marriage was the epitome of their life ambitions, while many of the women at the suffrage meetings decried marriage as a form of slavery.

Though her father never agreed with that sentiment, he wasn't keen on the idea of her marrying young either. "Plenty of time for that," her father always said. So Rowena had drifted, strangely apathetic about her own future.

How quickly things changed. Her father had been in excellent health until he had caught cold several weeks ago. The cold rapidly turned into pneumonia, and then he was beyond talking to her about her future or anything else.

Rowena took another brandy for good measure and made her way through the throng of people to the upstairs library.

Once inside she stopped, the scent of worn leather, pipe tobacco, and dried foliage triggering thousands of memories. No room in the house was more her father's than this one. Part study, part library; she, Victoria, and Prudence had spent many hours reading or playing quietly while her father worked, categorizing and recategorizing the dozens of plant specimens he collected or grew in the conservatory. A noted botanist, he never grew tired of discussing his work, and she often asked questions just to hear the warmth and excitement of his voice as he answered.

Swallowing, she avoided the captain's chair behind the polished wooden desk and sat in a comfortable chenille chair facing one of the four dormer windows lining the wall.

She sipped her brandy, letting the warmth slowly

course through her body, calming her nerves.

"I'm sorry your wife couldn't accompany you," a voice said behind her. Rowena recognized it as her father's solicitor.

"She was feeling poorly and I thought it prudent that she remain at home. London in the fall is rife with illness," her uncle said.

"Very wise."

Rowena leaned forward to announce her presence, but her uncle continued.

"Besides, she always disapproved of the way our nieces were raised. Poor Philip was a bit of an individualist, I'm afraid. It's a wonder both girls aren't raging suffragists."

She'd best put a stop to this immediately. She coughed discreetly and stood, facing her uncle.

Both men startled. "I'm sorry," she said. "I must have dozed off."

"And it's no wonder," Mr. Barry put in quickly. "It's been a trying day for all of us. My deepest condolences, Miss Buxton."

"Thank you." She turned to her uncle. "Have the guests left?"

"The last of them are leaving now. The servants are taking care of it. Shall we be seated?"

She liked Mr. Barry, who wore his thin, hawked nose like a badge of honor, a contrast to the untidy tufts of white hair now freed from his hat. He went to her father's desk and opened a valise. As he sat at her father's chair, Rowena looked away and took one of the seats in front of the desk. Her uncle sat at the other.

Mr. Barry cleared his throat. "There are really no surprises here. Your father not only had the allowance from the family estate, but he received a good sum of money when he was knighted. He invested well, and you and Victoria are the only beneficiaries."

She nodded. Who else would there be? As the youngest son, her father had no precious title to bestow on a male heir.

"However, he did appoint your uncle as guardian of your financial trust until you reach the age of twenty-five or marry an appropriate man, whichever comes first."

She frowned, drumming her fingers on the arm of her chair. "What does that mean, exactly?"

"It means that your uncle or his solicitor will pay all of your expenses and oversee your investments until you are old enough to inherit. It was your father's way of protecting you and Victoria from common fortune-seekers."

On the surface, it seemed reasonable, but underneath, the first stirrings of unease niggled. Did that mean her uncle would be in charge of her life for the next three years? Or that hc had to approve of her choice of husband before she could marry? Not that marriage was imminent, but the thought of having to consult with her uncle on expenditures . . .

"So really, nothing will change, correct? Our household expenses and bills will simply be sent to my uncle instead of my"—she choked slightly on the word—"father?"

Mr. Barry nodded. "Exactly."

Her uncle cleared his throat. "Your aunt and I discussed the matter and we feel it best if you spend the winter at Summerset."

She chose her words carefully. "Thank you for your offer, Uncle, but I think it would be beneficial for Victoria if we did not make too many changes all at once. We should stick as closely as possible to our regular routine . . ." Her voice trailed off, knowing how impossible that would be with her father's absence.

"Would you please leave us, Mr. Barry? This is family business now," Uncle Conrad said.

The solicitor nodded. "Again, my condolences, Miss Rowena. Your father was a good man and a good friend."

She nodded, unable to speak.

When Mr. Barry had gone, her uncle turned to her, his eyes kinder than she had ever seen them. The family resemblance to her father took her breath away. They had the same firm jaw and aquiline nose and the same green eyes. No, not the same, she decided. Her father's eyes were warm and humorous, whereas her uncle's were somber, no doubt from years of carrying the responsibility of the family estate and title.

"Don't you think it would be better to make a complete break with the past? The house will be full of sad memories for you and your sister. Besides, your aunt Charlotte and I aren't sure we will even keep the house. The house in Belgravia is much larger and better located."

Her head jerked up. "What do you mean, not keep our house? Of course we're keeping our house! This is our home!"

"But for how long? When you and Victoria are married, you both will have homes of your own. I'm not entirely sure I want to have the expense of maintaining two London houses."

She leaned forward, gripping the arms of the chair. "Why should you have to maintain it? The expense will come from father's money, surely?"

"The house did not belong to your father," he told her gently. "It belongs to the estate. My father bought it for him as a wedding gift, but retained the deed."

She glanced around her father's beloved study, which wasn't his after all. And because it wasn't his, it wasn't hers.

"Please don't sell it," she pleaded. "What about the furniture? The servants?"

He patted her hand.

"I did not wish to upset you," he said, placating her. He stood as if the conversation was over. "These decisions do not have to be made today.

But I must insist that you and Victoria accompany me home. We will be laying your father to rest in the family crypt. Surely you wish to be there for that. And Victoria loves Summerset."

She leaned back into the chair, trembling with anger and loss. "Of course. When do you wish to leave?"

"Decency demands we do it as soon as possible, but I have business to attend to in the morning. We can leave the day after."

His voice sounded relieved that she wasn't making more of a fuss. But why would she? She wasn't a child and his arguments were reasonable. She would deal with the house issue at a later date. She could not allow him to sell their home. But right now, she just wished to escape to her room to think.

"Very well," she said. "I will have Victoria and Prudence pack their things."

Her uncle had turned to the door, but now he paused. "There is no need to bring servants. You'll be well cared for at our home, as always."

She stiffened. "Prudence isn't a servant."

"Of course she is. She was the governess's daughter. It's only because of your father's generosity that she was kept on after her mother passed."

"My father loved Prudence, as do my sister and I," she flared. "She is part of the family."

Her uncle blanched. "I'm afraid your father

allowed you and your sister too much latitude concerning this girl. She certainly is *not* a part of the family."

"She is! She's been a member of our family for almost as long as I can remember. He treated her no differently than he treated Victoria and me. She was educated with us, went shopping with us, and—"

"Your father was a good man, but he had dangerously liberal convictions. I allowed him that privilege because he never disgraced the family name. Though not formally introducing you to society came perilously close."

Rowena stood and faced her uncle. "We were so suitably introduced to society! Both Victoria and I were presented to the Queen, as is proper, but neither one of us wanted a coming-out ball. We detest that kind of showy, excessive waste. Did you know you could feed one hundred families for a year on the money spent just on the flowers for one ball? We did our duty by attending the occasional society or charity function, but we simply weren't interested in that sort of thing. Our father respected that."

His jaw tightened. "That is precisely what I am talking about. How are you to find a suitable husband if you don't enter society? Your aunt especially has been worried about the both of you. I should have stepped in years ago. Never mind that now. You and your sister will accompany me to Summerset and Prudence will remain in London."

His voice was implacable and Rowena stilled, her stomach coiling into knots. Instinctively, she knew she would get nowhere if she defied him outright, but leaving Prudence behind was unthinkable. She took a deep breath and, keeping her voice steady, tried a different tactic.

"Prudence has been like a sister to us, but more important, she has always been Victoria's companion. No one can settle Victoria as she can, and Victoria is so delicate . . . With our father's death, I'm afraid one more loss would be harmful to her health." She paused, letting that sink in. To deny his sickly niece her companion would seem heartless. Besides, even her uncle had a soft spot for Victoria. "If you will allow us to take her as our lady's maid, it would be beneficial for Victoria, as well as being perfectly appropriate. Surely you wouldn't deny us our lady's maid?"

She pressed her hands in front of her and lowered her eyes. Inside she seethed.

Her uncle's jaw worked. They both knew she'd backed him into a corner. "Of course, if you insist. But just remember, she is coming as staff, not a guest in our home."

He inclined his head and left the room. Trembling, Rowena fell back into the chair and covered her face with her hands. The enormity of her responsibilities choked her. *Father, what*

31

have you done? A man who had raised her to independence had essentially shackled her to a man who didn't believe women should be independent at all. She could lose the house, Prudence . . . everything.

Drawing in a deep breath, she collected her thoughts. How independent had she been, really? She knew nothing of finances and had never bothered to ask. She'd had all of the freedom, none of the responsibility, and stupidly she'd never even know what to ask for. She'd been selfish, thoughtlessly flitting from one whimsy to another, never learning anything useful. No wonder her father had given financial responsibility to his brother.

It was a mistake she couldn't afford to make again. Not with Prudence and Victoria depending on her, even though the thought of having people depend on her for good decisions terrified her. Decision making had never been her forte.

She stood, glancing about the room, at the wooden telescope by the corner window, the globe she and the little girls had played with so often, pretending to be world travelers, the lamb's wool rug she and Prudence had lain upon, their toes pointed toward the fire as they read.

It was up to her to keep this precious room and her little family intact. There was no one but herself to do it.

CHAPTER
TWO

Victoria had a secret.

It was the first thing she thought of in the mornings and the last thing she thought of at night. She hugged it to her breast like a treasure that was hers and hers alone. Of course, her father had known her secret, as did Katie, the parlor maid, but since he was gone now, it really, truly was her very own.

Papa.

Again, the overwhelming feelings of loss clawed at her insides and she curled up into a ball, pulling the coverlet tighter around her chin. The early morning sun streaming through the gaps in the curtains glanced off the French bird's-eye maple headboard, causing it to shimmer and gleam as though it were a living thing. She traced the inlaid floral pattern of the wood, her finger leaving a smudgy trail in the wax.

Papa.

Restlessly, she slipped out of bed, kicking her legs to untangle them from the fine cotton nightgown that covered her from neck to toe. It often wrapped itself tightly around her in the night, making her feel as though she were in a burial shroud. Next to her, Prudence sighed and slipped further down under the covers to make up for the loss of Victoria's warmth. Victoria didn't like to sleep alone. Nightmares plagued her sleep and Prudence's warm presence comforted her.

Katie had already started a fire in the cream-tiled fireplace, and it burned cheerfully behind the brass screen, fighting off the autumn chill. Victoria's dressing gown and knitted slippers had been placed on the ottoman in front of it to warm. She wrapped the dressing gown around her, frowning at the satin pink ribbons and rosettes adorning the sleeves and yoke. Rowena had bought it for her last Christmas, and though Victoria hadn't told her, it always made her feel like a child.

Rowena had come into her room last night to tell her they were shutting down the London house and moving to Summerset for the winter. She loved Summerset, but there was something Rowena wasn't telling them, she could sense it.

The only secrets Victoria enjoyed were her own.

Frowning, she curled up on the velvet window seat and opened the curtains just enough to see out. Below, the dairy truck was delivering milk, cheese, butter, and eggs. At every stop, kitchen maids would meet the deliveryman at the door for their goods so that when their employers arose, there would be fresh cream for morning tea or coffee. She knew the servants would bolt their own breakfast sometime between when their employers awoke and when they came downstairs for their meal.

Victoria knew that servants had secrets, too. For instance, she knew Katie sometimes stole food from the larder and sent care packages to her mother in the East End. She'd always suspected her father knew about it, too, and chose to turn a blind eye.

She watched until the dairy truck disappeared down the street and then returned to her thoughts. What could Rowena be hiding from her? And worse, how would moving to Summerset affect her own secret? She glanced toward her closet where she kept her beautiful new Underwood Number 5 typewriter hidden, deep in the back where Rowena and Prudence would never find it. For several months, instead of going to piano lessons every week as the girls thought she was doing, she had joined Katie at Miss Fister's Secretarial School for Young Ladies to learn typing and shorthand in secret. She hugged her arms about herself. Perhaps Miss Fister would let her continue the course by correspondence? She would go and ask her this morning while the girls were busy packing. She would think of some excuse to get out of the house.

Of course, now that her father was gone, Victoria's secret studies had lost some of their appeal. She'd originally taken the course so she could help him with his work. The ability to type would come in handy when cataloging various plant species, and shorthand would make taking notes as he worked on his lectures much easier. As a child, she'd sworn that she would never marry, but stay with him forever so they could travel the world together, looking for exotic plants in faraway places. He'd laughed at that but agreed, and kept her secret. He knew how dearly she loved secrets.

But now, even though all that was gone, she still wanted to keep her secret. It was the last thing she'd shared with her father. The plan would just have to be tweaked, that was all.

Perhaps she would go on to the university and study, though how one went about going into the university, she wasn't sure. But she was sure she could do it. In fact, she was sure she could do almost anything, in spite of having a body that tired much too easily and wouldn't breathe when she wanted it to.

The door opened quietly behind her and Katie brought in a tray that held a steaming pot of hot tea and two cups for her and Prudence. "Thank you, Katie," she whispered. "And I think we should go out for a walk today." Katie set the tray down on the ottoman and poured the tea. Handing a cup to Victoria, she nodded solemnly, understanding her meaning. "That's a good idea, miss."

Victoria moved to the vanity. Like the bed, it was made of bird's-eye maple and had been polished so that she could almost see her reflection in it. Katie quickly took the plaits out of Victoria's hair with deft fingers and brushed until it fell like a sheaf of wheat down her back. "Thank you, Katie."

"Can I get you anything else, miss?"

"That will be all, until I need to dress. We can go out after breakfast."

The girl shot her a conspirator's smile and left the room. Smart as a whip, Katie had picked up shorthand faster than she had. She wouldn't be a maid for long.

Victoria heard Prudence stirring behind her and took her a cup of tea. "Wake up. We have lots to talk about."

Prudence yawned and sat up in bed. Her hair had come out of its plait in the night and tumbled down her shoulders in a fine, dark cloud. Victoria plumped up the pillows behind her and Prudence sat back, taking an appreciative sniff of the cup. "And what would we have to talk about this morning?"

Victoria picked up her own tea and sat on the edge of the bed. "Rowena. She's hiding something."

"I don't know what you're talking about," Prudence said, but her green eyes slid away from Victoria's.

Victoria gave a little bounce, almost upsetting both their cups. "Oh, you do!" she cried.

"Be careful! You're going to make me spill! And I don't either know what she's keeping from us."

"But you do agree she's keeping something from us, right?" Victoria persisted.

"I'm sure there are many things she and your uncle talked about that she didn't tell us. We were all exhausted last night. That doesn't mean she's purposefully keeping things." Prudence looked at her sharply. "Do you feel all right? Your color is high."

Victoria flounced off the bed. "I feel as well as I can. Stop fussing so. I'm not a child."

Honestly, it was no wonder she never got any stronger the way everyone babied her. Prudence and Rowena treated her like she was still in the nursery even though she'd turned eighteen last spring.

"I'm going to bathe and dress," she said in her most dignified tone. "No, don't get up. I can draw my own bath and Katie will be up in a bit to help us dress."

After a breakfast of scones, honey butter, fresh fruit, and kedgeree, during which they all pretended to eat but no one did, Prudence and Rowena rushed off to begin packing and do all the work necessary for their move. No one asked her to help, and for once Victoria was grateful to be left out. She wouldn't have to think up an excuse to disappear, after all.

Their uncle was staying in his own Belgravia monstrosity of a house, so she was on her own. Before putting on her coat and collecting Katie, she tiptoed up to the study. One of the advantages of being so small and pale was that she could often sneak about unnoticed. It was one of the many reasons the household could never keep secrets from her. She knew every shadowy nook in the house and effortlessly spied on the servants as well as her family.

So she knew exactly where her father kept the key to the safe secreted behind the strange painting his friend Picasso had given to him. Running her fingers along the back of the top desk drawer, she triggered the mechanism that opened the secret compartment. She snatched the key and paused, listening for any noise in the hallway. Satisfied, she took down the picture and opened the safe. Her father kept a folder full of old papers there, along with the extra household money. She grabbed the pound notes and then hesitated. Perhaps she ought not to leave his papers here when they closed up the house? Well, she could decide on that later. Carefully, she shut the safe and returned the painting to its proper place, tucking the notes away in her purse and slipping the key back into its hidden compartment. Then she tiptoed back upstairs to her room, pulled her new Lucile wool coat out of the wardrobe, and went to find Katie.

The pale autumn sun shone as they walked down Brook Street, and the sidewalks were crowded with people wanting to enjoy the last bit of warmth before the rains. Children, the girls in their enormous hair bows and boys in their knee breeches, scampered about on the sidewalks, hindered only by their stiffly starched nannies. Harried housekeepers and maids ran errands, hoping to get back in time for their afternoon tea. In the streets, hansom cabs, broughams, and victorias vied for room among the ever-increasing multitude of motorcars. The acrid scent of exhaust now competed with the good, clean, grassy smell of horse manure.

It was an obscenely beautiful day for having just lost her father, and Victoria remained silent as she and Katie walked slowly down the street to Miss Fister's school. It wasn't a long walk, but as always, Victoria was winded by the time they reached their destination. She and Katie sat on a bench near the school to rest.

"Are you all right, Miss Victoria?"

Victoria smiled at her friend and concentrated on breathing in and out slowly, as the doctor taught her to do. "I'll be fine." She took a few more careful breaths.

"I'm desperately sorry about your father, miss. He was a good man, the way he paid my way to the school and all." Katie's freckled face puckered as if she was trying not to cry.

Victoria's throat tightened, which didn't help with her shallow breathing. She patted Katie's hand in answer.

Having recovered, she told Katie to sit tight and entered the old brick office building where Miss Fister's school resided. Miss Fister wasn't in and Victoria was disappointed that she wouldn't be able to say good-bye to her teacher, but she wrote a short note explaining the situation and left her address with the clerk, along with the remainder of her and Katie's course fees.

"Is everything all right, miss?" Katie's dark red brows knitted together when Victoria rejoined her in front of the school.

"Yes, I just wanted to make sure you were taken care of after I'm gone. I've paid the fees off for both of us." Her generosity buoyed her step as they headed toward home. No wonder her father had been so giving. It felt wonderful.

"Oh, thank you, miss!"

On impulse, Victoria linked arms with Katie. "You've been a good friend, keeping my secret."

Katie's eyes widened. "Well, it's my secret, too. Hodgekins would say I didn't know my place if he knew."

"You'll make a good secretary someday."

"I hope so. That day may come sooner than we think."

"What do you mean?"

"Well, on account of your uncle selling the house and all. The staff is all in a dither about losing their jobs."

Victoria stopped and clutched Katie's arm. "Where did you hear that?"

"From Hodgekins, of course. Your uncle told him that the house will probably be sold by next summer. He wanted the staff to have time to look for other employment."

Victoria's knees buckled and Katie caught her around the waist. "Miss!"

Black spots appeared in front of her eyes and her chest got the hollow, tight feeling that meant she was about to lose her breath completely. She gasped, fighting for air. The black spots knitted together, becoming a tunnel, and she knew she would faint if she couldn't get a breath of air soon. Katie backed her up against the brick wall of a millinery shop and she leaned against it gratefully. She pressed her lips together and counted, one, two, three, and took a little breath.

"Miss! Do you need your nebulizer, miss?"

Victoria heard Katie's panicked voice as if it were traveling from a great distance. She shook her head and continued counting. One, two, three, little breaths. One, two, three . . . bit by bit her pulse slowed and her chest opened.

"Is everything all right, miss? Is this girl bothering you?" A man dressed in a posh flannel jacket and waistcoat hastily approached them.

Victoria's eyes flew open, aghast at the man's assumption that Katie, in her worn woolen uniform, was accosting her. "Certainly not. Mind your own business," she gasped. "How dare you make such presumptions based on our attire. You should be ashamed of yourself!"

The man's eyes widened as he tipped his bowler and backed away.

"Are you all right now? Was it something I said, miss?"

Victoria shook her head. "No. Of course not. It was just . . . just an *episode*. The same as always." Though her new doctor called her an asthmatic, Victoria hated the word "asthma" and refused to use it or any variation of it. It sounded so . . . sickly.

Katie's face scrunched up, but she said nothing as she helped Victoria stand upright and they began walking slowly down the street.

Victoria's fingers and toes tingled and she wasn't sure if it was the aftereffects of her experience or the anger building at her core.

So that was what Rowena was hiding from her. They were selling her home! Their lovely house with its countless windows, bright, clean lines, and years of treasured memories. How could Rowena let it happen?

Prudence kept her eyes closed. Each little jolt of the carriage grated against both her bones and her nerves. When they had started out yesterday, she'd felt a stirring of excitement underlying the grief that still lingered on her skin like a film of powder. But that had been early in the day, before the endless green fields and autumn-lit trees had lost their novelty. By the time they'd stopped at the inn in Bedford last night, she'd been stiff and more than a little sore. Now every muscle screamed at her enforced confinement. She wished they'd waited to come down until the next week, when the driver would be delivering Sir Philip's new motorcar to Summerset, but the Earl had insisted on a traditional funeral procession. He rode in the carriage in front of them, while the black mahogany coach carrying Sir Philip's coffin led the way.

Often, when they met a motorcar, the coaches had to stop to settle the horses, which made her want to scream. It felt as if they'd never reach Summerset.

Rowena and Victoria had barely said two words to each other since their quarrel the other day. Victoria had been in such a huff, she'd had to be put on the nebulizer on and off for the rest of that afternoon. For Prudence, the sulky silence between the sisters made the never-ending ride even more unbearable.

Her mind still reeled from the revelation that Rowena's uncle was going to sell their home. Rowena promised she wouldn't let it happen.

Prudence had no idea what she could do to stop it, but she had to trust Rowena.

Next to her Victoria stretched. "How long now, Ro?" Her voice sounded contrite and Rowena answered in kind.

"It shouldn't be too long. Look, we're going past the kissing mill."

"Why do you call it that?" Prudence asked as both she and Victoria craned their heads to look out the carriage window.

"The locals have a legend that if you ask your girl to marry you by the water wheel, she can't say no," Victoria said.

Rowena snorted. "I think it's just a private place for couples to get away to kiss."

"I think it's lovely," Victoria said. She turned to Prudence. "We're on Summerset land now. The manor is over the next hill. I can't believe you've never been here before."

"It does seem strange," Rowena agreed. "Victoria and I have spent almost every summer here since we were children."

Prudence looked down at her hands. "My mother was happy with the holiday to Bath your father gave us every year. She said there would be time for visiting later on."

"But you never did," Victoria said.

"No. I never did."

"Weren't you born in the village?"

She nodded.

"Well, you could have family here."

Prudence had never thought about it, but it was entirely possible. So why had her mother never come back to visit? Most women can't bear to be parted from their families, but her mother's family was never mentioned. For that matter, her mother had rarely spoken of her girlhood and never about Summerset Abbey. Could it have something to do with the Earl, as those women at the funeral had suggested?

"So tell me about Summerset," she said, partly to change the subject and partly to pass the time.

"It's lovely, imposing, and terrifying," Victoria said immediately.

Prudence raised her brows. "Terrifying how?"

"It's a bit intimidating because it is so large and some parts of it are rather frightening. But it's lovely, too."

As Victoria warmed to her subject, Prudence learned that Summerset was built in the early 1600s on the site of an earlier home that had been built on the ruins of a castle constructed in the eighth century. It sat on a park of over a thousand acres, with three formal gardens, a kitchen garden, its own lake, and several ponds. The house itself had over a hundred rooms and was staffed by a small army of sixty servants, which included not only housemaids, footmen, and gardeners but also a carpenter, a stonemason, and a mechanic to keep the motors in top shape.

"I think you'll like it, even if it's very different from our house," Victoria finished. "You'll especially love the library, which has over five thousand books."

Rowena cleared her throat in a very nervous, I-have-something-to-tell-you way. Prudence and Victoria looked at her expectantly.

"I'm afraid I wasn't completely forthright about my discussion with Uncle Conrad."

"You mean about something else besides him selling our home from underneath us?" Victoria murmured, and Prudence hushed her.

Rowena glanced at Prudence and then away. Prudence clenched her hands in her lap and tried to smile as a sense of foreboding shivered through her. "Out with it, Ro. You look as if you've swallowed a lemon."

"I feel a bit as if I have." Rowena bit her lip. "He didn't want you to come, you see. I don't know why."

Prudence felt her smile slip from her face and her body tense. "Yes, you do," she said quietly. "He feels you are far too familiar with the daughter of a governess who was a former parlor maid."

"That's nonsense," Victoria burst out.

Prudence ignored her. "If he didn't want me to come, why am I here?" she asked.

"Because I couldn't bear to part with you. Not now. We need to all be together." Rowena gave her a pleading look. "So I made a deal with him.

47

I said you would be our lady's maid, and of course, he couldn't deny you then."

The knots in her stomach tightened. "Well, that's not so bad." She tried to laugh, but it came out as more of a yelp. "I look after you both anyway."

The fine line of Rowena's jaw clenched. "I'm afraid he was very adamant about your being staff and not a guest. I'm not sure what he meant by that, but it sounded rather ominous."

Prudence licked her lips with a tongue suddenly as dry as parchment. "Is there any reason why you are just now telling me this?"

Rowena looked at the floor. "I was afraid you might not want to come if you knew."

Next to her, Victoria gripped her hand. "You would have come anyway, wouldn't you have, Pru?"

She gave Victoria's hand a reassuring squeeze. "Of course I would have. It'll be all right."

"Of course it will. And it won't be forever. I'll think of something."

Rowena tried to sound confident, but Prudence could detect the uncertainty in her voice. She turned to the window. Would she have come anyway? Probably. She'd always had one foot in each world. On one hand, she was Pru, racing through the house with her friends, studying at Sir Philip's feet, traveling with the family to the seaside. On the other hand, she helped her mother keep the schoolroom clean, and occasionally helped with some of her other duties when it was needed. When Sir Philip was alive, the arrangement had worked and they were all happy. But now everything had changed and she didn't know where she stood anymore.

The carriage turned a corner and Victoria called out excitedly, "There's Summerset Abbey, Prudence, look!"

Prudence craned her neck and her heart sank. Slender Italianate spires seemed to reach for the sky, rising from an imposing structure so massive it took up more than a London city block. The grounds around it were so immaculate and severe that Prudence couldn't imagine a leaf or stone daring to shift out of place. This was no comfortable home where little girls played hide-and-seek in cozy alcoves, or giggled while they devoured savory meat pies. Poets and artists wouldn't dare argue over their ale while lounging in front of the fire in this household. At this castle, for it was far more of a castle than a manor, everyone knew his place and stuck to it.

When they finally reached the front entrance, Lord Summerset leapt from his coach and came around to open their door. Prudence's knees ached as she stepped down first. A tall, thin woman in a billowing, old-fashioned black wincey dress stood stiffly before her. Prudence gave her an uncertain smile. Surely this wasn't

Lady Summerset? She jumped when Lord Conrad took her by the arm.

"Prudence, this is Mrs. Harper, our house-keeper. Mrs. Harper, this is Prudence, my nieces' lady's maid. Please show her to the servants' quarters and help her settle in. Her things will be brought up later."

"Yes, sir."

The woman took a firm grip of her elbow and led her around the corner of the building. Prudence glanced back in time to see Victoria and Rowena staring at her, their mouths open.

One of the footmen, waiting to help Rowena and Victoria down from their coach, also watched the scene unfold with his mouth agape. He almost started after Prudence but the footman next to him gave him an elbow and he fell back into his stance.

"Where is Mrs. Harper taking Prudence?" Victoria asked, a sense of urgency to her voice, just as Prudence was escorted down a steep set of stairs and through a small side door.

The servants' entrance.

If she didn't know where she'd stood before, she certainly did now.

CHAPTER
THREE

*L*ady Summerset Ambrosia Huxley Buxton
watched the arrival of her new charges from
the privacy of her boudoir. Her mullioned
window overlooked the front courtyard, giving
her the advantage of seeing all the comings and
goings at Summerset. She watched as her
husband dispatched that troublesome girl with
due haste. As he should. It was his fault they were
in this mess in the first place. She didn't like
assigning blame, but in this case it was all too
clear.

She leaned closer to the window, but the
fuzziness around the edges of her sight still
wavered. One of the many treats of old age that
no one warned her about. Of course, it wasn't as
though one could do anything about it. The
alternative to old age was dying young, and while
some may think it romantic to die with an unlined
face, Lady Summerset had too much common
sense to believe it to be true.

"Hortense! Bring my spectacles." She extended
her hand without lifting her gaze from the
window. She knew that Hortense had been
standing behind her with her eyeglasses the
whole time. Of course, Hortense had too much
tact to ask her mistress whether she needed

51

them, one of the many reasons why Hortense was one of the most valuable lady's maids in the British kingdom.

Lady Summerset put on her spectacles, then frowned. It looked as if Victoria was going to cause a commotion. The child had always been melodramatic, but she would let her husband deal with that. Served him right, actually.

Lady Summerset sat down in a side chair in front of the window, and held out her hand. "May I please get a cup of tea? Thank you, Hortense." A self-satisfied smile crossed her otherwise elegant face. The smile came with the knowledge that the scene below her was one hundred percent not her fault. She had warned, pleaded, threatened, and cajoled all those years ago, but her wisdom and foresight had been discounted as if she were just some "silly" woman. Now here it was in their laps and the danger was too dire for her to even enjoy a moment of comeuppance. She had to find a way to fix it.

Lady Summerset craned her neck to see whether Rowena had exited the carriage yet, for Rowena truly interested her. Every summer, she would await the child's arrival with bated breath to see whether her earlier promise of true beauty had been ruined by a bad complexion, an unseemly growth spurt, or the plumpness that had plagued Elaine's childhood. But no, Rowena had grown lovelier with every passing year. Lady

Summerset knew that beauty was one of the few powers afforded to women in their world, and she dearly wanted to teach Rowena how to use it. She had begged her poor misled brother-in-law to allow her to turn Rowena out, but the man had balked and had taken the girls abroad when Rowena should have been reigning over her first season. Odious man. Then he had done the same with Victoria, though the younger child, being pale and delicate and prone to outlandish and inappropriate remarks, was not nearly as presentable as her graceful sibling.

But to see such promise wasted was just too frustrating. The situation wasn't completely unsalvageable, though at twenty-two, Rowena's freshness was a bit worn, but as she hadn't been a fixture at all the collective events that made up London's society, she would still be somewhat of a novelty. And since her Elaine hadn't been offered for yet, the girls could attend balls together.

Rowena was bending over Victoria with the nebulizer. The little chit had gotten herself into such a state over the maid, she had given herself a breathing attack. Lady Summerset shrugged. She had little patience for Victoria's histrionics.

She turned from the window, irritation rippling across her shoulders. How like Philip to leave her with a mess such as this. What was she to do with two spoiled young women who were raised among aesthetes, bohemians, Marxists, and God knew who else? It would be a task to marry them both off well, even for someone of her caliber and connections. Of course, after spending all that money on her own daughter's Swiss finishing school, she had fully expected Elaine to be married in her first year out—but not only had she finished her season without an engagement ring, she professed to having a marked disdain for the institution. A philosophy that seemed to be shared by many of her contemporaries' children today. She and her friends spoke of it often when they got together—their children's disinclination for matrimony. Well, never mind that. They thought they were so clever, but soon the young swains would be looking at their partners in practical jokes with new eyes, and the Buxton girls—Elaine's playful good looks and breeding, Rowena's ravishing beauty and modern sensitivities, and even Victoria's delicate countenance and razor-sharp mind—would garner much attention from the opposite sex. Perhaps Catherine Kittredge's impossibly spoiled boy would be taken by Victoria. Thank God Colin was such a well-liked young man—the fellows were always happy to spend time at Summerset.

The girls had so little awareness of how important a good marriage was. Along with beauty, it was one of the few avenues to power a woman had. Let these suffragettes scream and fight for the vote, Lady Summerset knew that beauty and a good marriage—preferably to a man with means—were the only ways a woman truly could be safe from the horrors the world had to offer less fortunate women.

But the most important matter was to get rid of the maid as quickly as possible. The girl herself obviously didn't know what kind of scandal she could cause; otherwise she wouldn't have come here under any circumstances. Her eyes narrowed. Unless she did know and thought she might profit from it? Lady Summerset shook her head. The Buxtons would not stand for being blackmailed no matter what kind of scandal it would cause.

But how could she get rid of the girl without raising the curiosity of her nieces, not to mention her own children? If she took an interest in a mere maid, she would be arousing suspicion. Damned men; they got into these muddles but rarely knew how to get out of them.

"Hortense, I think the blue silk with the cream ruching will do for dinner tonight," she told her maid.

By not wearing mourning clothes, Lady Summerset was making a very pointed statement to her husband. She would wear black the day of the service, of course, but not a moment before. In all her years of marriage, she'd discovered that matrimony was not so much a partnership as it was a campaign. There were moments of complicity when she and her husband wanted the same thing, but they were rare. She took a deep breath. At least they were of like mind on getting rid of this troublesome young woman.

She held her arms up as Hortense settled her chemise down over her. "The girls have brought their own lady's maid with them, so you should have no extra duties. Of course, a new servant in the home always disrupts things just a bit."

Hortense gently turned her mistress toward the mirror to put the corset on. Lady Summerset had a theory that if she *watched* how much difficulty Hortense had in lacing it up, then Lady Summerset wouldn't be tempted by the raspberry ice or éclairs.

Now Lady Summerset could see her maid's face. It was oftentimes difficult to tell whether her words made any impression on Hortense at all—it seemed as if nothing she said could change or alter Hortense's thin, impervious features. Truth be told, Lady Summerset was just a touch intimidated by her impossibly correct, screamingly chic French maid. But she comforted herself with the fact that no other maid had been as pursued as Hortense, and her loyalty was unquestioned. Once, while Lady Summerset was playing bridge with poor Bertie and desperately trying to lose to his highness without detection, Countess Featherington was busy in the upper hall, trying to steal Hortense out from under her nose with a salary so generous that it made even Lady Summerset blink. Hortense had declined the offer and after Lady Featherington had told her of her maid's loyalty (right in front of Hortense, no less!), Lady Summerset had no choice except to give her a raise.

She watched Hortense carefully. "Of course, you will tell me how the new maid is settling in and if she is carrying out her duties adequately."

Hortense pulled lightly on the laces and her black eyes flicked up and met Lady Summerset's in the mirror. "Of course, my lady."

"Just keep an eye on her. We don't want her to get the idea that just because she's new to Summerset the expectations surrounding her work and behavior are any different than they are for any other lady's maid here at the abbey."

Hortense smiled automatically, but the smile didn't reach her eyes and Lady Summerset's shoulders twitched with displeasure. Really, Hortense ought to be more *grateful*.

"I will make sure your nieces' maid has the right qualifications, do not worry," Hortense put in quickly as if sensing her lady's displeasure.

Lady Summerset's good humor was restored. "What a dear you are. Thank you, Hortense. I wouldn't want the poor girl to think she wasn't welcome here, but a new addition to staff always stirs up such trouble and she is rather unique."

Hortense caught her eye in the mirror. "How do you mean, my lady?"

"She wasn't brought up in service. I'm sure the poor girl would find some other kind of work outside Summerset more fulfilling. Perhaps you could get the others to watch her, too?"

"Of course, my lady."

She watched as her maid expertly buttoned up the side of her underskirt, and sat back down to watch Hortense's nimble fingers work their French magic with her hair. From the knowing look in Hortense's eyes, Lady Summerset knew she had made herself quite clear without having to spell it out—make trouble for the newcomer.

What she didn't tell Hortense was that the future of their entire family rested on getting rid of this girl, posthaste. And if her husband couldn't do it, then she would have to.

As Victoria ingested the medicine that would help her breathe again, she couldn't help but think about how much she hated, no, *detested* the sickness that rendered her helpless when she most needed to act. When she had tried to defend Prudence in her moment of need, a fit had overtaken her, leaving her as helpless as a child. How could she ever hope to be an adult when she couldn't right a simple wrong?

When at last she could breathe again, she handed the nebulizer to Rowena.

"Very well played, girls."

Victoria's head jerked up at her uncle's caustic tone.

"But I've already been manipulated into bringing the girl here," he continued. "Don't be fooled into thinking I can always be so easily swayed. Victoria, you should go to your room and rest before dinner. Rowena, please make sure the trunks are sent to the proper rooms."

With his jaw tight, he turned on his heel and strode away without affording them another glance.

"Why didn't you stop him?" Victoria asked, once she could speak.

Rowena stood and straightened the skirt of her black traveling suit. "You don't understand. He has complete control of our estate until I am twenty-five."

"You mean we have no money until then?" She frowned.

"Oh, we have plenty of money." Rowena gave her a grim smile. "We just have no control over it, and we're in *his* home. Do you really want to defy him in his own home?"

"If Prudence can't stay with me, I would rather just go home," she grumbled, taking Rowena's proffered hand. She struggled upright, her muscles stiff from riding in the coach and her legs still trembling from the medicine.

Rowena sighed. "Oh, Vic. I think this might be

the best place for us right now," she said softly.

The girls stood hand in hand, staring up at the imposing front facade of the manor their father—and generations of Buxtons before him—had been raised in. The Bath stone facing had been weathered to a soft, warm honey color, which lent it the look of an Italian villa rather than an English manor. Gargoyles perched high above the front doors, guarding the entrance from inter-lopers. When the girls were small, their father had told them the gargoyles' names were Gog and Magog, and made up stories of their adventures when the sun set and they were released from their guard duties.

As she had told Prudence, most people found the home imposing, but Victoria had always loved every inch of it. "Maybe . . . but what about Prudence?"

Before Rowena could reply, the front door opened and a modish young woman with golden brown hair appeared. She ran lightly across the gravel and gathered Victoria in her arms. "I am so sorry about Uncle Philip. You both must be so desperately sad."

Victoria let herself be hugged, then stood back and eyed her cousin in shock. "Elaine! Look at you, all stylish and pretty."

Elaine laughed. "I can't believe it's been over a year since we've seen each other!"

Victoria couldn't stop looking at her cousin.

Elaine had always been an appealing dumpling of a girl, with pretty blue eyes and a sweet smile, but her shyness had rendered her practically invisible. This freshly polished Elaine, with her hair piled in pretty curls around her face and her newly slender figure encased in a striped, slim-skirted afternoon dress, hardly seemed like the girl she'd played hide-and-seek with two summers ago.

Elaine linked her arms with Victoria's. "Come, you must be exhausted. Why Papa didn't just take the motorcar, I have no idea. He's so old-fashioned."

Rowena hung back. "I'll stay here and make sure our things are unloaded properly. I'll be up in a bit."

Victoria's throat tightened. She knew Rowena was going to separate out Prudence's trunks to be sent to the servants' quarters. Bewildered and heartsick, Victoria let her cousin lead her into the house.

As always, Victoria was struck dumb by the domed rotunda shape of the Great Hall's entrance. It ran down the center of the house, a reminder of a feudal society where the lords and ladies greeted their visitors at the very end—the longer and more ornate the hall, the more important the occupants. At the end of the hall one could see into the grand salon. High above rose the coffered dome ceiling, the crown jewel of the hall, which was decorated with gilded rosettes and was the highest section of the entire building. There was a circular skylight at its zenith letting in light that danced and sparkled off the marble columns lining the room. Giant frescoes covered the upper walls, depicting angels floating above acts of violence and warfare.

"Mother is resting now, but said she will see you at dinner. You're staying in the Rose Room again? I moved to the Princess Room, right near yours."

Victoria let her prattle on. The long trip, her attack, and her worry over Prudence had exhausted her. She barely listened until she heard Prudence's name spoken.

"Pardon?"

"I was saying that you could have your maid draw you a bath before dinner. It's that girl, Prudence, right? The one you lived with? I didn't know she was your lady's maid."

Victoria stiffened at the curiosity in Elaine's voice. She didn't want to talk about it, but Elaine clearly expected an answer. "She isn't. She is just helping us for the time being."

"Well, if she's not your maid, who is she?"

Victoria didn't want to tell her anything more.

"Oh, look. You've got electricity!" Victoria pointed to a row of lights along the main stair-case at the end of the hall.

"Well, yes." Elaine seemed momentarily taken aback by the change of subject. "Papa had it installed last summer on the lower levels. We don't have it in the upper rooms yet."

They climbed the stairs, turning left, away from the guest rooms that overlooked the Great Hall, and went back toward the south wing, where the family rooms were. A giant portrait of the Eighth Duke of Summerset, their grandfather, dominated the end of the hallway, casting an ominous pall over the long corridor. Victoria stopped short when she saw it, and a shudder ran through her body. Elaine paused and noted what she was staring at.

"Ah yes. Father moved it from the dining room. He said it gave him indigestion just looking at it."

Victoria's eyes widened and Elaine nodded. "Whenever I complained to my mother about my father, she said I should be grateful. He's a thousand times better than the old duke was."

"Frightening," Victoria murmured, prompting Elaine's laughter. Victoria hadn't meant it as a commentary on her uncle's skills as a father, but upon the painting itself. Like most of the Buxtons, the Duke had thick, black hair, a strong jaw, and green eyes, but whereas the living Buxtons' eyes were as changeable as the ocean, the artist had caught the Duke's eyes exactly as Victoria remembered them. Flat green, like a lizard's, with no emotion whatsoever.

"I only met him a few times when I was very small and don't remember him much at all. Was he as frightening as I recall?" she asked Elaine.

Elaine had drawn closer to her as they studied the portrait and now leaned in to whisper. "Worse. Mother used to take me to his rooms after he became infirm. It's funny how she would never let my nurse or a governess take me, but always did it herself, and she stood right next to us the entire time. He really had as little use for us as we did for him, but Mother was determined to do her duty. I don't think she ever went to see him other than that, which is odd considering how ambitious she was."

Elaine slipped her arm through Victoria's and they turned toward the Rose Room. "Don't tell anyone, but that old man used to pinch Mother's backside whenever she got too close."

Startled, Victoria laughed at the mental picture and banished the disturbing portrait from her thoughts as she entered her bedchamber. It was actually a suite of three rooms, a small sitting room in the front with a large dressing room and bathroom on one side and the bedroom on the other. The room got its name from the border of painted blue roses running just under the highly detailed crown molding on the ceiling. An Empire dressing table and ornate mirror sat between two enormous windows on the back wall, while a pair of blue-and-white-striped chaise lounges sat in front of a small white fireplace. A soft Axminster rug softened the parquet floors, and fresh flowers from the conservatory stood on the tables.

Victoria unpinned her hat and took it into the bedroom. The blue and white color scheme continued into this room with the French blue coverlet and crisp white eyelet embroidered pillows. She'd spent many lazy summer days reading and dreaming in this delicately feminine space. If she couldn't be in her own room at home, there was no place she would rather be than here.

"Is there anything else I can do for you? I can ring the maid for some tea if you like."

Victoria laid her hat on the vanity and faced her cousin. "That would be lovely, but first I want you to take me to the servants' quarters."

Elaine blinked. "The servants' quarters? Whatever for?"

Victoria stared her down and Elaine had the grace to blush, letting Victoria know she had been right. Somehow Elaine knew more about Prudence's situation than she was letting on. Did that mean her uncle had sent a telegram about it? She wasn't sure what was happening at Summerset, but Victoria intended to find out.

CHAPTER
FOUR

Prudence followed Mrs. Harper's bony, disapproving back through a dark maze of hallways. "That's the servants' hall right there," she said, indicating a long, narrow room where the only light came from small windows just below the ceiling. "The kitchen is on the other side, but you won't need to go there very often unless your young mistresses require tea at odd hours." A cacophony of pots and pans banging and raised voices sounded from the kitchen. "I will show you the kitchen later. They're busy preparing dinner. Here is the sewing room." She opened another door to the right. The windowless room had a long table in the middle, a sewing machine off to one side, and the shelves lining one wall were stacked with bolts of cloth. "You'll find everything you need to mend your mistresses' dresses and underthings."

Prudence was surprised into replying. "Oh, I don't know how to sew."

Mrs. Harper looked down her long nose at Prudence. "Well, you'd best learn. Hortense is too busy with Lady Summerset and Lady Elaine to do your work, too."

Suitably chastened, Prudence followed Mrs. Harper up a steep staircase. Gaslights lit the cramped stairwell and countless feet had worn dips in the center of each step. How many servants spent their entire lives treading up and down these stairs?

After climbing for what seemed like forever, and passing several landings, they came out into a narrow, dark hall with doors on either side. The hallway smelled of mold, human sweat, and, oddly enough, vanilla.

"We call this petticoat hall. It's for the female house servants. The men's quarters are on the other side of the wing, and they are not allowed here. If you are caught fraternizing with the opposite sex, you will be dismissed without notice. You will receive thirty-two a year and will draw your wages monthly."

Mrs. Harper paused in front of a door and took a large brass ring of keys out of her oversized pocket. She fiddled with it until she found the right key and then opened the door. Moving aside, she waited for Prudence to enter.

Swallowing, Prudence stepped inside a room that could not have been more than eight by eight feet. After the lovely home she'd just left, its starkness struck her heart like a physical blow. Old green paint flaked off the iron bed in the middle of the room, and the mattress sagged under the thin quilts. The one small window in the room was covered with coarse yellow burlap. Under the window stood a rickety chest missing several knobs. Its matching table sat next to the bed and held a chipped plain white bowl and pitcher for washing. Above the table was a small, cracked mirror. There was no closet.

On the bed lay two black-and-white-striped calico blouses and two plain black bombazine skirts.

"The cost of the uniforms will, of course, come out of your pay. I have a list of rules for you to be aware of. Please go over them as soon as possible. Mr. Cairns and I pride ourselves on how smoothly this house runs and there is always a risk with a new servant."

A chill ran up and down Prudence's spine, one that had little to do with the cold draft coming from the window. What was she doing here in this cramped room with this sour-faced woman? This was not her life. Her life was with Vic, Ro, and Sir Philip in a warm, gracious home filled with the sound of music and laughter. But Sir Philip was gone and it had never been clearer to her that that life was over.

Mrs. Harper rooted around in her pockets again and handed Prudence a sheet of paper and a key hanging from a long chain. "The key is to your room. Wear it around your neck. I always tell young girls who spend most of their time looking at their reflections to put the rules up next to the mirror until you have memorized them."

Numbly, Prudence took both the key and the

paper. Outside in the hallway, they heard a muttered oath and the stamping of feet. Mrs. Harper poked her head out the door. "Are those her belongings?"

Prudence had never thought she'd hear anything in Mrs. Harper's speech except disapproval, but now her voice elevated in surprise.

Prudence and Mrs. Harper had to flatten themselves against one wall as four men, two in their bright velvet footman livery and two in rough work clothes, hauled the trunks into the small room. Prudence recognized one of the footmen as the one who had been so shocked at her being hauled out of the coach. He was a nice-looking young man, with plain features and friendly, greenish eyes.

The trunks, made of gleaming oak, were the most beautiful objects in the room. The men smirked, looking at the trunks, until Mrs. Harper shooed them out. The footman gave her another friendly smile before leaving the room.

Prudence waited for a moment before realizing that Mrs. Harper wasn't going to leave until she got a peek into the trunks. Reluctantly, she knelt and opened the first trunk under Mrs. Harper's critical eye. Because Prudence knew they were going to be at Summerset for an extended stay, she'd brought mementos she couldn't bear to leave. Childhood books she couldn't part with, the shining jewelry box Sir Philip had given her for her twentieth birthday, and the silver brush and comb set that were her mother's. She could almost smell Mrs. Harper's disapproval as she stacked the books on the dresser alongside her jewelry box and placed her comb and brush next to the washbasin. They looked garish in this painfully bare room, like orchids among thistles. She added a small photograph of her mother, set in an ornate silver frame and taken when she was younger than Prudence was now. Mrs. Harper's nostrils flared as she picked up the photograph. "Who is this woman?"

"That's my mother."

Mrs. Harper gave Prudence a sharp look and her lips tightened.

Prudence looked down at the clothes she had brought. Like Rowena and Victoria, she'd had several new mourning dresses made up, but even though they were a plain black, the high quality of the material and their modern style were completely inappropriate for her new position. She reached for her underthings. A princess combination made of fine cambric material with Valenciennes lace at the bust, several chemises with blue silk ribbons threaded through the top, and a soft batiste nightdress with embroidered scalloped edges.

Mrs. Harper sniffed. "I've never seen such absurdity. I don't know what you did before coming here, but you'll *not* receive such gifts at Summerset."

With that, Mrs. Harper whisked out of the room, while Prudence's cheeks burned with shame. Apparently, Mrs. Harper thought her someone's spoiled and indulged mistress. Apparently, the pursed-mouth woman had no idea that Prudence had been treated no differently than Rowena and Victoria only hours before. Prudence gave her door a hard slam and momentarily felt better. Then a wave of complete and utter loneliness hit again.

She sat heavily on the bed, crumpling the paper Mrs. Harper had given her. Smoothing it out with her hands, she read:

Never allow your voice to be heard by the ladies and gentlemen of the house.

Answer politely when addressed, but do not speak unless spoken to.

Step aside if you meet one of your employers or betters on the stairs, remembering to look down as they pass you by.

Never talk to another servant in the presence of your mistress.

Never call from one room to another.

Only the butler may answer the bell.

Every servant is responsible for getting his or her own meals at the allotted meal times. The cook will not make up for missed meals for any reason.

No servant is to take any knives or forks
   or other article, nor on any account to
   remove any provisions from the Great
   Hall.
The female staff is forbidden from smoking.
No servant is to receive any visitor into the
   house.
Any breakages or damage to the house
   will be deducted from wages.

As Prudence read each rule she could almost
hear doors slamming shut on her old life. What did
this horrid list of rules have to do with her? She
looked around the barren room, her eyes welling.
What was she doing here? She longed to be with
Ro and Vic, but she couldn't let them know the
depths of her current misery; they were grief-
stricken enough without worrying about her. She
folded her arms around her body and reminded
herself over and over that she wasn't really alone,
even if this list of rules seemed specifically
crafted to keep her apart from her sisters.

A timid rap sounded at the door. Brushing her
eyes, she opened it only to be almost knocked to
the floor by Victoria's desperate hug. A young
woman dressed in a fine afternoon gown hung
back in the hallway.

"I'm so sorry, Prudence! I know Rowena never
meant this to happen."

Prudence heard the wheezing beneath Victoria's

tears. She laid her cheek against Victoria's shining head. "It's okay. Don't cry so, Vic. And I don't want you to come up here again. Those stairs will be the death of you!"

Victoria pulled out of Prudence's arms crossly, then looked around the room. "Is this where they put you? This isn't even as large as our bathroom at home!"

Prudence's habit of placating Victoria stiffened her resolve not to complain. "Well, how much room do you think I need? I might be larger than you, but I still fit perfectly fine in here." She looked at the girl standing in the doorway. "You must be Elaine," she said, then bit her lip. She'd been here but a short time, but had already broken one of Mrs. Harper's rules.

Do not speak unless spoken to.

Elaine looked at Victoria, training and good manners warring on her pretty face. The moment spun out awkwardly while Victoria, the patience of Job expressed in the stubborn set of her mouth, waited for her cousin to join her in her modern sensitivities. Elaine hesitated for another second and then, with the same brilliant smile that showed years of superior Buxton breeding, held out her hand.

The moment contact had been made, Victoria jumped in smoothly, "Elaine, this is my dearest second sister, Prudence. Prudence, this is my cousin, Elaine."

Though Prudence had heard about Elaine from the girls for many years, their opinions were always mixed. It seemed that, away from her mother, Elaine was a darling girl. With her mother, though, she was an unbearable ninny.

Nevertheless, Prudence smiled in greeting. It wasn't her place to judge. Especially now.

Victoria turned back to Prudence. "This is unacceptable. You can't stay here. This isn't fit for a farm animal, let alone my sister."

Over Victoria's shoulder, Prudence saw Elaine cringe. She couldn't agree without insulting the daughter of the house, and besides, what could Victoria do about it?

She patted Victoria's shoulder. "It's perfectly fine for now. It's not like this is forever. And I won't be spending much time up here anyway."

"That's right," Elaine agreed. "She will mostly be with you and Rowena. Mother's maid is so busy she is hardly up here at all."

Victoria narrowed her eyes and gave her cousin a black look. Elaine ignored her and walked about the room as if she'd never seen it before. Which, Prudence thought wryly, she probably hadn't. She stopped in front of Prudence's dressing table. "Is this your mother?" she asked, picking up the photograph and looking at it with a puzzled frown. "She's very pretty."

"Yes it is, thank you. She died several years ago."

"Oh, I'm sorry," Elaine said, putting down the picture.

Something about the way she said it made Prudence think she'd already known exactly who the woman in the photo was.

Elaine turned back to Victoria. "We should go. It's almost time to dress for dinner and Mother will be livid if she finds out we've been up here."

Victoria's lip trembled, but Prudence gave her a little push. "Now go on. Let me change and wash and I'll be downstairs shortly."

"Promise?" Victoria asked.

"Promise. Now tell me how to get to your room."

After the girls had left, Prudence quickly changed and redid her hair. Anything to keep from thinking about how isolated she felt. To her there could be nothing worse than being alone in the world. She didn't feel alone after her mother had died because her family had been there; even if they weren't blood, she knew she could always count on them. Now that Sir Philip was gone, she only had Rowena and Victoria. Victoria was little more than a child and delicate to boot and Rowena had always been so fickle and irresolute. Anxiety crawled over her skin as the reality settled in—only a fool would rely on Rowena.

But what choice did she have now?

Shoving the thought out of her mind, she looked at the photograph of her mother and then back at herself in the mirror. There was little resemblance to the sweet-faced, diminutive woman she remembered. Her mother's hair had been a sunny brown and her eyes sky blue, while her own hair was as dark as mahogany and her eyes almost the color of grass. Her jawline, nose, and cheekbones were delicately etched, while her mother's face had been round and sweet.

Prudence looked around and suddenly realized that her mother may have stayed in this sparse, cold chamber. She may have worked for Mrs. Harper, run up and down the servants' stairs, and dreamed of the day when she might leave Summerset.

Certainly, she had known the Earl and Sir Philip when they were all younger. Prudence frowned, wondering once again why Sir Philip had given her mother, a common housemaid, a position as governess. While her mother was well read and clever, she was hardly as educated as most governesses.

Prudence felt a stirring of longing for her mother. If nothing else, perhaps she could find out more about her, a woman she loved dearly but whose past was shrouded in mystery. There was even the possibility she could find her real family.

Because if she ever needed a family, that time was now.

CHAPTER
FIVE

Rowena paced across the floor of her bedroom in her wrap, barely noticing the new green and gold Morris carpet that had been recently installed. The entire room had been redone since she'd last been here: green ivy wallpaper had replaced the old cabbage roses and the new furniture was all polished white pine, rather than the fussy dark antique pieces that had been here before.

But not even an elegant new room could hide the fact that she was as trapped as a fox in a hole—trapped by her responsibilities, trapped by her social status, trapped by being a woman. Her uncle possessed all of the power and she possessed none. She, Prudence, and Victoria were as helpless as Punch and Judy, completely at the whim of the puppeteer.

Victoria had stopped by on her way back to her room while Rowena was bathing and, with eyes full of reproach, told Rowena exactly what Prudence's sleeping quarters were like. As if she could do anything about it.

As if she could do anything about anything.

Frustrated, Rowena savagely pulled her trunk open to look for something suitable for dinner. Why wasn't it unpacked already? Where was the maid?

She stilled, a lump forming in her throat. Prudence was her maid.

"Bloody hell," she muttered, pulling out a black silk charmeuse dress with a matching lace overskirt.

A tentative knock sounded at the door. She tossed the dress on the bed and strode to the door in her dressing gown. She wasn't in the mood for visitors. Prudence stood on the other side, wearing a plain striped shirt that stretched across her breasts and a black skirt that hung on her slender hips. Both girls stood still for a moment. So much had changed since they'd parted from each other just that afternoon.

"May I come in?" Prudence asked. She stood erect and dignified, but her eyes were red, as if she'd been crying.

Rowena's heart constricted and her uncertainty broke. "You goose. Get in here." She pulled Prudence in and shut the door behind her. She wrapped her arms around Prudence. "I'm so sorry. I didn't know it would be like this."

Prudence returned her hug for a moment, then pulled away. "It won't be forever," she said.

Rowena nodded, even though Prudence's voice rang false. "I'll figure out something, I promise." Even as she said the words, the trap tightened. "It's just, right now, I don't know what to do," Rowena whispered, her arms wrapped over her chest.

Prudence moved away and nodded and Rowena heard her take a deep breath. When she turned back around, a careful smile lit Prudence's face. "Your things are a mess. I'd definitely have a serious discussion with your maid. Good help is so hard to find." She took a stack of Rowena's clothes out of the trunk and began hanging them up.

Rowena smiled back, though the lump in her throat grew. "I don't have a maid, I have a sister."

Prudence's fingers fumbled with the sash she was tying, but when she smiled again it seemed more genuine. "Then why don't you let your sister put away some of your things while you dress for dinner?"

Prudence threw her a simple white cotton chemise from the trunk and Rowena let her dressing gown drop to the floor. She pulled the shift over her head and then deftly caught the silk stockings Prudence tossed.

"I've met your cousin," Prudence said as she unpacked.

"What did you think of her?" Rowena drew the silk stockings deftly up her legs, first one and then the other. Then she stood while Prudence fit the stays of the lightweight corset around her. All three girls had long given up the heavier, more confining corsets, preferring the simple riding corset, as it was much easier to move in. Because most clothing would not fit without the proper corset, the Buxton girls had most of the waists on their clothing altered. They decided long ago as a group that breathing a bit easier was preferable. The corset was only lightly boned and had a long, straight busk; Prudence buttoned up the front, adjusted it a second time, and then laced it up the back.

"She didn't say much, though she did ask about the picture of my mother." She pulled on the laces while Rowena held her breath.

"What did she say?" Rowena asked, clipping the suspender tags to the stockings.

"She just asked if it was my mother." Prudence rummaged around in a small trunk before coming up with a pair of black French-heeled shoes. "It was strange, though. It's almost as if she already knew who my mother was."

Prudence arranged a light petticoat on the floor in a circle, while Rowena slipped the shoes on. Then she stepped into the petticoat and Prudence pulled it up around her. The girls had been helping each other dress for years and knew the routine.

"Why is that strange? Your mother worked here before she married, didn't she? Perhaps Elaine has heard of her?" Rowena held up her arms and Prudence slipped the dress over her head. Then she did the same with the sheer lace overdress.

"That's what is so strange," Prudence said. "Why should Elaine have heard of a mere housemaid who worked here before she was even born?"

Rowena frowned. "I'd never thought of that, but you're right. It's not like at home, where we know our staff so well. Most of the time, I don't think they'd recognize the faces of half the people who work for them."

"That's what I thought." Prudence cocked her head and eyed her critically. "Do you want me to do your hair up?"

Rowena shook her head and sat at the little vanity table. "I'm just going to pull it back and put it in a low knot." She looked at Prudence's reflection and hesitated. "It's so strange for you to help me get dressed and me not doing the same for you."

Prudence gave her a half smile. "What, you don't think they'd appreciate my dinner gown?"

She whirled around and Rowena gave a halfhearted laugh. Even a half smile lit up the planes of Prudence's pretty features and Rowena once again wondered how someone as attractive as Prudence could be unaware of how lovely she actually was. "I think you're beautiful no matter what you wear."

Prudence's smile dimmed, then disappeared from her face entirely. "But it isn't my clothes they would object to, is it? It wouldn't matter if I were dressed from head to toe in an original Poiret, they still wouldn't want me sitting at their dining room table."

table. "Would you like to try an American cocktail before my parents come down?"

Rowena raised a brow. "What are you drinking?"

"Have you tried a gin sling?"

Rowena shook her head.

"Colin taught me how to make one last time he came up from Oxford. They're quite good and will make you silly in a very pleasant kind of way."

"Oh, why not?" Rowena thought she could use a little silly right now. She watched as Elaine expertly mixed the contents of several cut-glass decanters together. Obviously, she'd done this before. "How is Colin, anyway?"

Elaine grinned at her, and once again Rowena was struck by how much her cousin had changed in the last year. Her skin glowed alabaster against the black silk of her gown and the added inches from her French heels made her look voluptuous rather than pudgy. "Do you want the parental version or do you want the truth?" Elaine asked.

Rowena took the glass Elaine handed her. "I always prefer the truth."

"He hates university almost as much as he hates being here. Oh, don't get me wrong. He loves Summerset, we all do, but he doesn't want his whole life to be the price of wheat, wool, and rents. He'd much rather just fiddle with his motors, but who ever heard of the Earl of Engines?"

Rowena took a careful sip of the drink and then

shuddered as it burned its way down her throat. "So what is he going to do?"

Elaine shrugged. "What else can he do? What can any of us do? Exactly what's expected of us, of course."

Warmth spread through Rowena's chest and the tension in her neck and shoulders eased. She took another appreciative sip. "So he gives up being a mechanic to be an earl?"

"Who's giving up being a mechanic?" Victoria came into the room behind them.

"King George," Elaine answered quickly, giving Rowena a look.

Victoria threw herself onto the chaise. "Now you're being silly, but go ahead, keep your little secrets. I have some of my own."

"And what would those be?" Rowena finished her drink and handed Elaine her glass. Elaine finished as well and then secreted the glasses behind a marble statue of Artemis.

Victoria waved her hand. "Oh, you'll find out soon enough."

"Girls! My poor darling nieces. How are you bearing up under the tragic loss of your dear father?"

Rowena shivered at the sound of her aunt's cool, cultured voice. "I can't speak for Victoria, of course, but I am doing as well as can be expected," she said.

"I'm perfectly wretched, Auntie." Victoria rose

from the chaise and clasped her hands in front of her. "I feel just like that poem by Elizabeth Barrett Browning.

"I tell you, hopeless grief is passionless,
That only men incredulous of despair,
Half-taught in anguish, through the midnight air
Beat upward to God's throne in loud access
Of shrieking and reproach. . . ."

"I can just imagine, poor dear," Aunt Charlotte interrupted. Victoria took the hint and went and kissed her cheek without treating them to the final lines.

Rowena took a deep breath and followed her.

Aunt Charlotte had been the most beautiful debutante of her season, perhaps during the entire eighties. Dowagers still spoke of her beauty and the exceptional ease with which she comported herself at such a young age, even among the Prince of Wales's smart set. She'd capped off her stunningly successful season with a brilliant match and was soon giving glittering parties attended by the cream of English society. For years she had been applauded for both her beauty and wit, and even now it was only up close that one could see the slight melting of her lovely features, as if she were one of last season's leftover apples. The renowned wit seemed perennially missing.

Aunt Charlotte suffered through Victoria's kiss, then turned to Rowena. "I'm sorry for your loss, my dear. I know poor Conrad is desolate. Your father was a wonderful man."

Rowena knew that her aunt and her father had a mutual avoidance pact. But then, if the roles were reversed, he would be offering the same polite, empty words. "Thank you, Aunt Charlotte. How are you feeling? I'm sorry you couldn't make it to the service." She leaned in close to kiss her aunt's cheek and then realized her mistake when her aunt started sniffing. She must reek of gin.

Her aunt's blue eyes flickered over her, but Rowena knew she wouldn't say anything. Yet. "I'm feeling much better, thank you for asking, and we will have our own little service here tomorrow. Oh, Conrad, here you are now. Shall we go in to dinner?"

Dismissed, Rowena stepped away as her uncle led Aunt Charlotte to dinner.

Summerset had two dining rooms, a large formal one for parties and a smaller one for when they dined en famille. It was the smaller one they went into now, which was one of Rowena's favorite rooms. With its low crossbeams and built-in china cabinets, it looked like the kind of place built for happy families to break bread.

Of course, the Buxtons did not "break bread," they dined. Even when they were eating informally as a family, there were never fewer than seven courses.

The table, a long, dark, highly polished rectangle, could comfortably seat twelve. Aunt Charlotte sat on one end and Uncle Conrad sat on the other. The girls clustered in the middle. Rowena wondered whether they sat this way when only the three of them were present and decided they probably did. Elaine sat next to her, Victoria across from her.

Rowena eyed her sister with concern. The attack this afternoon had left her pale; only her eyes showed her agitation, darting from Aunt Charlotte to Uncle Conrad. Rowena frowned. What was she up to?

She found out a few minutes later over the poached salmon when Victoria said, "I have to tell you, I am not at all happy about the way you treat guests in your home."

Next to her Elaine dropped her fork into her plate, spraying the table with little droplets of cream. Rowena's breath hitched as she looked from Uncle Conrad, who had frozen in shock, to Aunt Charlotte, who hadn't even flickered an eyelash.

For a moment no one spoke, then Aunt Charlotte smiled gently. "And in what way do you find our hospitality lacking? Was your room not ready? I can speak to the housekeeper if you like."

"Oh, no. The room is wonderful as always, Auntie." Having dropped her pronouncement, Victoria seemed disinclined to hurry, and she buttered a roll with studied nonchalance. After taking a bite and then a sip from her water, she turned to Aunt Charlotte, evidently thinking she would get further with her than with Uncle Conrad.

"As you know, we brought our friend to stay with us. I expected her to be welcomed just as any of my guests would be, but instead I find that she has been given a much smaller room upstairs."

"You've brought a guest?" Aunt Charlotte shook her head, causing the teardrop-shaped diamonds in her ears to sparkle. "I heard of no guest. Just you and Rowena and your maid."

Aunt Charlotte's voice was solicitous, and uncertainty flickered across Victoria's face, but her little sister was nothing if not stubborn.

"Prudence. Prudence is my friend and I would like her room to be changed, please. Or if that isn't possible, she can sleep with me. She often did at home, you know. It's no trouble at all."

Next to her, Elaine actually gasped and Rowena's heart pounded in her chest. She glanced at Aunt Charlotte to see her reaction but there was none.

"Oh, you sweet girl. I can understand your confusion, but the girl is a maid, not your friend. You can be friendly with your maid, and you

89

should be, but they can get uppish if you treat them like equals. Even my own Hortense, whom I adore, will take certain liberties if I show too much familiarity."

Victoria looked stunned.

"But things are changing, Auntie," Victoria tried again, but she was cut off.

"And not for the better. We all have responsibilities—our servants have theirs and we have ours, and one of my responsibilities is to make sure my poor orphan nieces are brought up properly and make good marriages, though why God saw fit to give me three girls to marry off, I will never know."

Rowena couldn't keep still any longer. "But that's just it, Aunt Charlotte. Though Victoria and I are grateful to you and Uncle Conrad, I would say that we're brought up already."

"I won't rest until both of you are safely and properly married. Only then will I feel I have done my duty. Isn't that right, Conrad?"

Uncle Conrad nodded. "I would have to agree."

Victoria looked from one to the other, bewildered. Rowena gave her a fierce frown, but Victoria ignored it.

"I'm sorry. I don't see what any of that has to do with Prudence staying with me," Victoria said.

Aunt Charlotte gave a stiff smile. "That's just it, my dear. As a young girl, you are naturally idealistic. As your elders, your uncle and I have a responsibility to protect you from those who might take advantage of your kind nature. Now let's speak no more about it."

Victoria threw down her napkin, exasperated. "Protect me from Prudence? What are you talking about?"

"That is enough!" their uncle thundered.

Everyone froze in various states of surprise. Even Cairns, their butler of twenty years, fumbled as he served the roast hare. Rowena had never heard her uncle raise his voice. He didn't have to—he got exactly what he wanted without doing so.

She lowered her head but observed him out of the corner of her eye. His chest rose and fell quickly and two splashes of red marked his cheekbones, but instead of looking angry he just seemed . . . pained.

From across the table, Victoria's eyes pleaded with her, but it wouldn't do any good. Rowena dropped her gaze and remained silent.

And hated herself for it.

CHAPTER
SIX

*T*his is all wrong.

The family crypt lay about a mile from the main house, right behind the old chapel. The chapel itself had been allowed to fall into disrepair after Victoria's great-grandfather had built a new one adjacent to the house. The crypt, built into the side of a small berm, had not been relocated. On top of the berm sat a large marble wall that proclaimed the names of the fallen male Buxtons. The female Buxtons had burial plots surrounding the berm.

The entire family stood on the berm where the name Philip Alexander Buxton had been freshly carved at the bottom of the list.

Well, not the entire family, Victoria thought. Prudence wasn't here.

Victoria had whispered that fact to Rowena before they left the house, but had received a black look in return. Rowena hadn't wanted to rock the boat; she was scared of falling over and drowning.

But Victoria was *not* afraid.

Restlessly, she twitched her shoulders and stamped her feet quietly to warm them. She, Elaine, and Rowena had walked to the crypt, spurning a ride in the trap. They had dressed for the chilly weather in tweeds, knitted scarves, and walking shoes, but the cold seemed all-pervasive and she wished the vicar would stop pontificating and get on with it. But he kept talking, talking, talking and not saying a bloody thing. And as she had learned last night at supper, talking did no good at all.

It wouldn't bring her father back.

Someone had set up a spray of white stargazer lilies against the wall and Victoria leaned close to Rowena. "You know, he far preferred *Scilla nutans* over *Lilium orientalis*." She'd meant to whisper it, but evidently wasn't discreet enough because Aunt Charlotte shushed her and the vicar paused for a moment before continuing. "Well, he did," she muttered stubbornly.

To distract herself, she stared at the old stone chapel, almost completely overrun now with English ivy, or *Hedera helix*, she told herself. The overgrown chestnut trees in the back completely shaded the old garden, and she could see that many of the diamond-pane windows had been broken. The church looked like she felt: lonely, empty, and devoid of warmth.

With a sigh, she turned back to the vicar. As she turned her head, she thought she saw something move in one of the windows of the chapel. Turning back, she stared hard but saw nothing. Was it a face? An animal? A chill went down her spine. Could it have been a ghost?

She chided herself for her imagination and turned back to the service. The vicar had finally stopped speaking and a flurry of activity commenced as the pallbearers picked up the coffin. They carried it, slow and dignified, down the little path leading from the memorial on top of the berm to the entrance to the crypt on the other side.

Victoria's heart sped up as the finality of it all hit her.

Papa!

Suddenly she couldn't bear to hear the sound of the iron door shutting her father away from the light. She turned toward the woods on the other side of the chapel.

"I'll meet you back at the house," she said over her shoulder.

"Victoria, wait!" Rowena called, but Victoria ignored her as she hurried down the hill.

She wanted to run, but knew that if she did she wouldn't get very far before her lungs closed up, so she made herself keep it to a brisk walk and prayed that no one would follow her.

Once she stepped into the woods, she felt safe. Automatically she began ticking off the genus and species of the autumn-colored trees she walked past. Silver birch, *Betula pendula*, downy birch, *Betula pubescens*, crab apple, *Malus sylvestris*, wych elm, *Ulmus glabra*.

The names were familiar to her from years of walking through similar forests with her father, listening to him practice his lectures. His passion as he talked botany had been infectious and she loved nothing better than studying plants, growing them, and cataloging them. Watching seeds burst into a plant that would flower and reseed was to watch a never-ending cycle that both reassured and delighted her. She wondered whether there were any woman botanists. She should have asked her father.

Her dream seemed very far away today.

She found a large moss-covered rock near a small creek and sat, wishing Prudence were with her. Prudence's comforting presence always made her feel better, more so than having Rowena by her side, especially now. Since they'd arrived at Summerset, her sister had barely spoken to her. She just looked at her, sadness buried in the depth of her great green eyes. Why wasn't she fighting for Prudence? The whole situation was appalling.

She wrapped her arms around herself, wishing she had thought to wear more than a tweed jacket. Suddenly, she heard a crackle of movement to her left. Her head jerked around and she stared into the dim forest, looking for an animal. Nothing. The sound came again and she thought she saw movement behind an old elm tree. "Who's there?" she called, wishing she didn't sound so young and unsure.

An old woman stepped around the side of the tree. She wore a long, old-fashioned black dress and had a shawl wrapped around her head and shoulders. Her face was wrinkled like a crone's, straight from fairy tales.

"Are you a witch?" Victoria asked. "Because I warn you, I don't think I would taste very good."

The woman laughed. "I've been called a witch and worse by my young charges, but I have yet to eat any of them."

Her voice was strangely girlish for one so old, which didn't comfort Victoria at all.

"Then who are you?"

"Who are you?"

"Do you always answer a question with a question?"

The woman smiled, her face breaking into wrinkles. "Do you always avoid telling people who you are?"

Victoria laughed at that and settled herself more comfortably on the rock. "I could have you charged with trespassing, you know. This is my uncle's land."

"You don't say? Then you must be one of Philip's girls. I'm so sorry for your loss, child."

Victoria nodded, unable to speak for the lump that had suddenly risen in her throat.

The woman stepped closer and held out a burlap bag. "I'm gathering some mallow. My niece has a bit of a cough and I'm making her some tea."

"So you are a witch, but a nice one." Victoria scooted off the rock. "*Althaea officinalis* from the Malvaceae family. I saw some on my way here. Come, I'll show you."

"Oh, you are your father's daughter," chortled the old woman.

They walked back the way Victoria had come. "How do you know my father?"

"I changed his nappy, paddled his bottom, and taught him his letters."

Victoria stopped. "You're Nanny Iris!"

The old woman nodded solemnly. "I am."

"But you can't be Nanny Iris! Nanny Iris was beaut—" She clapped her hand over her mouth, but the woman just laughed.

"Beautiful? Your dad always did have a silver tongue. But believe it or not, I was quite lovely in my day."

They continued walking while Victoria's mind whirled. "But what are you doing here? Father said you disappeared after his parents hired their tutor."

"I hardly disappeared. I took my pension and traveled. I'd always wanted to see the pyramids and the Greek islands and so for twenty years I lived the life of a nomad. I married a number of times and had a great many adventures."

"That must have been some pension."

Nanny Iris snorted. "I was frugal and when the money ran low I taught English to all who could pay. Whenever I felt the urge, I moved on."

It was a most fascinating tale. "So how did you end up back here?"

"I decided I needed to finish out my years in a place where loved ones could take care of me."

Victoria looked ahead and pointed. "I give you *Althaea officinalis*."

"Perfect. Could you gather the seed pods so I can put some in my garden?"

Victoria nodded and dropped to her knees next to the old woman, in spite of her new tweed walking suit. "How do you know that mallow is good for colds? What does it do?"

"It helps coat the throat and clear the nostrils. And I learned from my mother, just like she learned from her mother. Plus, I learned a great deal more about herbs during my travels. I'd like to believe that I'm the reason your father fell in love with plants. I taught him to garden long before I taught him his letters and numbers."

Victoria was fascinated. "And did you teach my uncle, too?"

Nanny Iris scoffed. "I couldn't teach that one anything. He was born too posh for the likes of me. Didn't think I could teach him anything and his mother just indulged him. But your father was a veritable sponge."

Victoria's throat tightened and the old woman patted her hand. She didn't say a word, though, which made Victoria like her even more.

They picked in silence for some time before the old woman stretched her back. "That'll be enough now. We don't want to clean out the patch."

Victoria stood up and helped Nanny Iris to her feet. "Would you like me to walk you home?"

"Lord, no, child. I know the way. And if I'm not mistaken, you'll have the whole house worried if you don't get back soon."

Victoria sighed, knowing it was true. "Rowena will be worried. Prudence, too."

"Are they the girls you were standing with?"

"Rowena is my sister. She was the pretty dark-haired girl in the bucket hat. The other girl is my cousin, Elaine."

"And where was Prudence?"

Victoria frowned, resentment running through her all over again. "Prudence wasn't allowed to come."

"Ah." Nanny Iris didn't ask and Victoria didn't elaborate.

"Well, you're a nice girl and I would love to have you come visit me some time. I was very fond of your father."

"I would love that. Where do you live?"

"A little cottage just this side of Buxton. You can ask anyone and they will tell you where I live."

On impulse, Victoria gave the old woman a hug. "Thank you. I'll come as soon as I can."

"That would be grand, and Victoria?"

Victoria looked up at the serious note in her voice. "Yes?"

"Don't wander around these woods by yourself. They're not very friendly for young girls such as yourself."

Before she could ask why, the old woman turned and nimbly trotted away.

"Everyone works here." The cook tossed Prudence a rag. "Go help Susie scour the copper pots."

Prudence blinked at the rag in her hand. All she had wanted was a cup of tea. The morning had been a nightmare. Mrs. Harper had awakened her at the crack of dawn even though Prudence knew full well it would be hours before Rowena or Victoria would need her for anything. She'd been ordered to help Susie peel carrots and onions for the soup stock that would sit on the back of the stove all day for this evening's consommé. She'd barely had time for a cup of tea before the housekeeper had sent her upstairs to start the fires in Victoria's and Rowena's rooms. Then she ran back downstairs to snatch something to eat in the servants' hall.

The servants' hall was nothing like the fancy Great Hall upstairs. In fact, it must have been someone's idea of a joke that they had the same name at all. The floor of the servants' hall was covered in old brown linoleum, with old rickety chairs sitting at an equally rickety table. It looked small and tacky, an afterthought in a home where the kitchen, on the other hand, was thoroughly modern and well planned. The Indian flagstones on the floor were scrubbed clean and huge earthenware sinks and an enormous cooker took up one entire wall. On top of the cooker sat a huge copper vat with a tap that supplied constant hot water.

Her only relief of the day had been helping Rowena and Victoria into their walking suits, but even that had a pall on it because they were going to say good-bye to their father and she wasn't allowed to go, despite her own immeasurable grief and longing to bid him a final farewell alongside her sisters.

Now Prudence stared at the rag, unsure of what she was being asked to do. She'd never had to clean the pots and pans. Katie had always done that. Susie grabbed her arm and pulled her back to the scrub room, a dingy, windowless room with two more giant sinks. "Here, I'll show you. The work will go so much faster with two of us."

Susie wore her mousy brown hair pulled back into a tight bun. The sleeves on her blue-and-white-striped shirt were rolled up, showing strong arms in spite of her small size. She stood smaller than Victoria, and Prudence thought she couldn't be more than fifteen, but her motions were quick and competent.

Susie grabbed a small bowl and mixed together silver sand, salt, vinegar, and a little flour. Once she'd stirred it into a paste, she took a pot with one hand and a scoop of cleanser with the other.

"Then you scrub like this." She worked the paste into the pan with a quick rubbing motion.

Screwing up her face, Prudence scooped up a small handful of paste. Susie nodded encouragingly. "That's it. Now scrub."

The vinegar and salt stung Prudence's hands, but she scrubbed, tentatively, until Susie reached out and pushed her hand hard against the pan.

"No, you have to press harder. That's why you can't do it with rags, see?"

So Prudence scrubbed.

The pots were so tarnished, she thought it would never come clean, but when it finally did, she found a certain satisfaction in taking a dull pan and making it look shiny and bright.

"Do you have to do this every day?" she asked.

"Every bleedin' day," Susie said grimly. "Look at my hands." She held out a hand for Prudence's inspection. They were small and capable, but the skin was chapped red and the knuckles swollen.

"Language!" Cook yelled from the kitchen.

Susie rolled her eyes and continued scrubbing.

"Do you like your job?" Prudence asked.

Susie snorted, "I'm the scullery maid. What do you think? I'm the lowest of the low." She leaned closer and whispercd, "But I'm hoping to be a cook someday."

Prudence couldn't imagine a life where being a cook was the highest of one's aspirations. But then were hers any better? She just wanted to take care of those she loved. Maybe have a family someday. What she wanted in life didn't seem nearly as important as what she didn't want: to be facing everything alone. But Susie didn't seem intimidated by the thought of a solitary life, because cooks never married. "What's so great about being a cook?" Prudence asked.

"Much better pay. And you get to order other people around all day!" Susie yelled this last part over her shoulder.

"I heard that!" Cook yelled back from the kitchen, and Prudence and Susie giggled.

"I've worked here for about eight months. It's not a bad job. The food is good. I have a roof over my head and I'm working for an earl, which lets me lord it over my sisters on my days off. They just have day jobs in town."

"Do you like the Earl?" she asked.

"Oh, I've never met him. I met the Countess once, when she hired me. She said I looked a likely gal and I got the job. I was so nervous!"

Prudence frowned and scrubbed with renewed vigor. How odd to take such pride in working for an earl when he hadn't even bothered to meet someone in his own employ.

Though Susie said the work would go faster with the two of them, it seemed to take forever. Then the bells started ringing on the bell board and everyone snapped to attention.

"They're back from the service." Cook grabbed

some silver salvers from the china closet. "They'll be wanting their tea."

Hortense came hurrying down the narrow stairs. Prudence had seen her only once, in passing. She noticed *she* didn't have to wear an ugly uniform. Instead, the statuesque black-haired Frenchwoman wore a smart black-and-white-checked twill suit that couldn't be anything but couture.

"Miss Rowena was asking for you. She is in her room." Hortense clapped her hands. "*Rapidement*!"

Prudence wiped her hands on the apron Susie had lent her and started up the stairs.

"*Non*! Take her some tea. Idiot!"

Prudence turned back and Cook handed her a tray with a teapot and cups. Then she hurried up the steps while Hortense muttered in French below.

The servants' stairway had inconspicuous doors that opened up on each floor, so they could move about the house without their presence being known. It seemed odd to Prudence to have a small army of silent, invisible workers keeping the house running in tip-top shape and not even be aware of them. Did Elaine ever wonder about the fire that warmed her room in the morning when she awoke, the never-ending supply of biscuits in the jar next to her bed, or how her slippers and dressing gown were heated and waiting for her to crawl into after she bathed? Prudence wasn't sure she would like that kind of luxury at all.

Even if the rules hadn't stressed being quiet at all times, Prudence would have tiptoed. The inside of the house, with its exquisite art, plush carpets, and the wide, gleaming staircase that seemed to stretch on forever, required a certain decorum. Besides, the last thing she wanted to do was rouse the ire of Mrs. Harper, who already seemed to have taken an instant dislike to her.

She found Rowena in her room, looking out the mullioned window. Ivy had been allowed to grow up the walls on this side of the house and it surrounded the window, making it look as if Rowena were peering out into a secret garden. "I brought you some tea," Prudence said stiffly. Even though she loved Rowena, a part of her smarted at being maneuvered into this situation by her own sister.

"Thank you, Pru." Rowena turned her face away from the window and Prudence's heart melted at the sadness on her face.

She set the tray down on a small table near the window, then put her arms around Rowena.

"It was so sad. He loved Summerset, but I kept thinking that he wouldn't want to spend the rest of eternity here. He loved our home as much, if not more, and he loved to travel so."

Prudence's arms tightened. "Just don't think of him stuck here. He's in a better place, you know."

"I know." Rowena sighed. "Has Victoria come home yet?"

Prudence frowned. "What do you mean? I thought she was with you."

"She was, but then she couldn't bear it anymore and went for a walk. I tried to call her back, but you know how she gets. I felt it would be disrespectful to shout or follow her. One of us needed to be there."

Alarm kicked Prudence's pulse up a notch. "But it's so cold outside. Do you think she'll get lost?"

Rowena shook her head. "Remember, Vic has been here every summer since she was born. She should be fine as long as she gets in before dark."

"We should go look for her." Prudence turned away from the window, but Rowena grabbed her arm. "No, look. There she is now."

Prudence spotted Victoria's slight figure coming up the walkway through the formal rose garden. The roses had been cut back for the winter and looked shorn and disgraced.

A light knock on the door startled both girls.

"Come in," Rowena called.

Prudence swallowed as Lady Summerset gracefully glided in. Her ladyship hesitated for a fraction of a second when she saw Prudence, but then continued her elegant approach toward Rowena. Lady Summerset wore an ivory lace and tulle tea gown with a simple tunic top and softly gathered sleeves that ended at the elbow. Silver threads wound their way haphazardly through her abundant brown hair and one would have to be cruel to call them gray. As she came closer, Prudence detected the pink scent of talcum powder and flowers, as if her ladyship were concealing a hidden bouquet of dusty roses.

Prudence wasn't sure if she should curtsy or disappear behind the draperies, so she stood perfectly still and tried not to stare.

"I wanted to make sure you were doing all right, my dear. Has Victoria returned?"

"She's coming in now, Aunt Charlotte."

"Oh, good. I was hoping to speak to you alone." She paused and both girls caught her meaning at the same time.

Prudence edged away, but Rowena caught her arm. "Aunt Charlotte, I don't think you have met my dear friend, Prudence. She has lived with us since we were both young. Prudence, this is my aunt Charlotte."

For a moment it looked as if the grace and superb manners Lady Summerset wore around her like a cloak would fail, but at the last moment she tilted her head slightly and acknowledged Prudence's presence.

Not to be outdone, Prudence curled her lips into a semblance of a smile and curtsied. "Pleased to meet you, my lady."

She turned and touched Rowena's shoulder. "I am going to go see to Victoria. She's sure to be chilled and in need of a hot cup of tea."

As Prudence left the room, she caught a look that the Countess directed at her before her lashes were quickly lowered. Unlike her husband, who looked at Prudence as if she were a worm, in a purely impersonal way, Lady Summerset looked at her with a malevolent expression in her blue eyes, and, it seemed to Prudence, it was very, very personal.

CHAPTER
SEVEN

It's only been a week and Uncle Conrad just left for London. What was I supposed to have accomplished in a week?" Rowena consciously kept her tone light, but she could feel herself losing patience. Victoria kept hounding her about Prudence, about going home, about the house, *about everything,* and she didn't know what she expected her to do about any of it.

"But you haven't done anything!" Victoria stood in the middle of her bedroom with her hands on her hips. "It is *intolerable* that Prudence sleep in the attic, that she has to wear that horrid uniform, and that she isn't allowed to read in the library! I have to *sneak* her books!"

Victoria's eyes flashed and a feverish color

stained her cheeks. Rowena was afraid she was going to work herself into another episode.

"I don't know what to do about it right now. Remember, we just buried our father! Now is not the time to throw fits! Would you please calm down?"

"I know we just buried our father! I also know *he* would have never stood for this. And I will not calm down until you tell me what you are planning to do about it."

The fact that she had no plan only made Victoria angrier. Rowena knew Prudence was miserable. She knew it was her fault. But she couldn't just defy her uncle. Every time she tried to bring it up, he would become taciturn and grim and she would back down.

And hate herself for it.

Victoria kept on, rubbing salt in the wound. "You don't have an answer for that, do you? You're doing the same thing you always do—wait for someone else to make your decisions for you." She sat abruptly on the bed and crossed her arms.

For the first time in her life, Rowena wanted to slap her little sister. She kept her voice controlled with great effort. "I'm not even going to dignify that with an answer. I'm going to go riding so I can think without someone haranguing me."

Prudence came into the room, her green eyes

wide. "What is going on? I could hear you out in the hall."

Seeing Prudence just made her feel guiltier. "Fetch my riding habit. I'm going out."

The hurt in Prudence's eyes made her cringe. She hadn't meant . . . Oh, forget it. Shamefaced, but unable to back down, Rowena marched into the bathroom, her eyes smarting with unshed tears.

The wind coming over the hills whipped through the netting covering Rowena's face, but she didn't care. Her lips were becoming chapped and her cheeks stung, but those discomforts didn't even come close to the tangled emotions inside.

Why did all this have to fall into her lap? When did she become responsible for everything?

When her father died.

Rowena turned her horse toward the Buxton family cemetery. Carefully keeping her mount to the perfectly groomed walkways, she read the names of the Buxton women who had either lived at or resided over Summerset. She paused at her mother's grave and tears filled her eyes. She only had hazy memories of the small, golden-haired woman who had been confined to a bed for a good portion of Rowena's life, but she would never forget the love shining from her eyes or the sweet smile that lit up her face whenever Prudence's mother set baby Rowena on the bed.

Next to her mother's grave was a statue of a cherub. Halpernia's grave. Halpernia, the change-of-life baby who died at three years old the year Rowena was born. Whose death so affected everyone in her family that they refused to speak of her at all, as if she'd never existed.

Rowena looked past the gravestones and toward the berm where her father was interred. The pain hit her low in her center and she turned away. What had she been thinking to expose herself to such pain? She urged her mount into a cantor, taking a dirt track up over Briar Hill. Keeping her horse to a leisurely pace, she skirted hedges, outcroppings of rock, and dense thickets of flaming red thimbleberries. She loved riding. She rode in London, of course, but riding sedately in Hyde Park could not come close to riding through the forest and fields of Suffolk's countryside.

Once she reached the top of the hill, she slowed to a walk and followed the ridge overlooking the valley below. The town of Summerset lay nestled between the hills and the River Lark. The town had grown quite a bit since she was a child. Back then, it had been an agricultural town providing goods and services to the estates surrounding it. Now it boasted its own glove factory, which provided much-needed employment, a leather processing plant, several blocks of shops, and even a mechanic's garage.

Suddenly she became aware of a low buzzing

noise behind her. The noise grew louder and she turned in her saddle to see what it was. It sounded much like a motorcar but louder and coming from somewhere above her. Her horse spooked and she turned her attention to controlling her mount. Out of nowhere, an aeroplane flew above her so close, the wind of it tugged at her hat and flattened the dried grasses. Her horse leapt in terror and ran about a hundred yards before she was able to stop it.

She'd seen aeroplanes before, of course, but none so perilously close to the ground. The engine spit and sputtered. Rowena watched in horror as the wing hit a tree and the body careened sideways before landing in a mangled heap of canvas, wood, and metal halfway down the side of the peak.

She stared at the wreck in a state of shock for a moment before urging her still trembling horse carefully down the hill. She was only halfway there when her horse stopped and refused to go any farther. He blew and snorted in protest as she dismounted and wrapped his reins around a tree branch.

The brush and rocks tore at her skirt, making it difficult to walk. She gathered her riding skirt more tightly in her hand and made her way downward. She could hear her own heart beating in her ears as she drew closer, afraid of what she was going to find.

As she neared the main part of the aeroplane she could see part of a man's arm poking out from underneath the wing.

"Oh, God, please let it be attached to the rest of him," she prayed out loud.

She grabbed the edge of the wing and pushed it up enough so that she could see the rest of the body the arm belonged to. It was a young man, that much she knew, but his features were obscured by a leather hood and goggles.

He wasn't moving.

By pulling and tugging, she managed to drag him out from under the wing. She pushed his goggles up on his head and then leaned down to see whether he was still breathing. Once she ascertained that he was, she checked the rest of his body to see whether he was bleeding, but apart from a small gash on the side of his head, he seemed to be intact. More worrisome was the red and blue knot swelling above his right eye.

She took off her riding jacket and rolled it up, placing it underneath his head. Then she sat back on her heels, cursing herself for not knowing how to help more.

He moaned and she looked anxiously for signs that he was waking up. Though his eyelids fluttered, they didn't open and she wondered what she should do next. Obviously he needed help, but she didn't want to leave him. Perhaps someone else had seen the crash and would come looking for him. Or maybe someone was waiting for him to come back and would sound an alarm.

He moaned again and she took his hand. "Hush, now. Everything will be all right," she told him softly. She took care not to disturb him as she settled herself beside him and searched desperately for some indication of what do to next.

The pilot looked no older than herself. Red-gold strands of hair escaped from under his leather hood, which meant he wore it as long as aesthetes do. Though none of the aesthetes she knew would be interested in piloting a plane. They were more interested in writing poetry and contemplating art. His lips were thin but well formed, and his jawline square and strong. She wondered what kind of a daredevil he would have to be to fly one of these newfangled aeroplanes into the wide blue sky. She wondered what it would feel like to be untethered from the earth.

A groan came from his lips and his eyes fluttered open. They were a clear blue against his windburned face. He looked around, confused, before his eyes focused on her.

He blinked, but his eyes never left hers. "You're not Douglas."

His voice was thready and weak. She shook her head. "No. I'm not."

His eyes searched her face. "You must be my guardian angel. You have no idea how much I need a guardian angel right now. Please don't leave me, all right?"

Rowena's breath caught as his hand searched for hers. She slipped her hand into his and he gripped it as if he would never let it go. Their palms melded and their fingers curled together so naturally, as if this was the hand hers had been waiting for.

He broke eye contact with her and she felt a sudden emptiness in her chest, as if she had just lost something of great value. He glanced around without moving his head, and Rowena had a feeling he had taken in everything, the trees, the bits of broken plane, and the waning light, in the seconds before his eyes swept back to her. She wondered how his head felt. He seemed very careful not to move it.

"Where am I?" he asked.

"Near Briar Hill."

He nodded and then winced.

She bent closer in panic. "Oh, no. Please. I don't think you should move."

His lips twitched. "Then you expect to spend the night out here?"

She looked around. Unless someone knew where to look for them, they wouldn't be found. "Surely someone will come looking for you."

He nodded and then grimaced at the movement. "Yes. How about you?"

She thought a moment. Yes. They would start to

115

look for her, but not until dark. She wondered whether Victoria would feel bad about their quarrel if she didn't come home. "Eventually."

His eyes glanced over her and she felt her skin grow warm. "Eventually," he murmured.

Then his eyes fluttered shut. Rowena leaned closer, wondering what she should do. "Are you going to be all right?"

His eyes opened again, and the blue of the heavens was a mere inches from her face. "I'll be fine." They drifted shut and then he murmured, "Just don't leave me."

She gave the hand she still held a squeeze to reassure him and then on impulse leaned forward and laid a soft kiss just above the bruise on his temple.

His eyes widened and seemed to glow as he looked at her for just a moment before he drifted off again. She wondered what she would do if no one came after them. Surely it wouldn't do him any good to freeze here with him all night? If it started to rain, they would be in very real danger from the cold. She sat with him, feeling utterly helpless, for perhaps an hour or so—long enough that the thin autumn sun had dipped down over the horizon. She was just making up her mind to break her promise and go for help when she heard someone above them.

"Hello?" a voice called. "Are you all right?"

She stood, staggering a little from having been

in one position for so long. "We're down here! The pilot is unconscious."

A crashing of brambles, along with muttered curses, told her that someone was coming down the hill and none too gracefully. In a moment, one of the largest men she'd ever seen came crashing out of the woods. He wore a leather flight jacket and matching boots with laces. Under his cap, his hair shone a brilliant shade of red. The man's eyes widened when he saw her, then he came and knelt beside her with effort. "Is the lad still alive?"

His accent told her that he came from up north, maybe even Scotland. "Yes, but he's been in and out of consciousness. I had no way of getting him up the hill, so I just stayed with him."

He put his hand on the pilot's face and then on his forehead. "We shouldn't move him. We have no way of knowing if his insides are hurt, but it won't do him any good to leave him like this."

He frowned. "Was that your animal tied to the tree?"

She nodded.

"Do you think you can get him down here?"

"I can try. He's sure-footed, but the crash spooked him."

"If you can, we can toss him over the animal's back and get him up to my motorcar."

She nodded and headed up the hill. The woods were darker now that the sun had almost set and it was rough going. Her horse was exactly as she

117

left it, the sweat from their run dried along his neck and withers. He nickered when he saw her and she patted his nose. "There'll be an extra ration for you tonight, boy."

She led him down carefully, but the horse was more sure-footed than she was and they made better time on their way back.

The pilot still hadn't awakened when she returned, and the big man stood over him, worry written on his face. "I don't like this. I don't like this at all. He should have come to by now . . ."

He was awake before, she thought, worry shooting through her. He musn't die. She had no idea why it was so important that he live, but she wanted him to be all right with every fiber of her being. She held the horse still while the man picked the pilot up as if he were a boy. The pilot moaned.

"Damn it, Douglas, you're going to be the death of me," the young man muttered, and the big man grinned, relief evident on his face.

"That'll teach you to crash my aeroplanes." Douglas carefully arranged him on the side-saddle. "I don't know how you ladies ride like that."

"We're born to it," she answered. "Is he a friend of yours?"

"Aye. I've known him since he was a boy. Now he works for me."

"What do you do?" she asked to be polite,

though she was more concerned with the injured pilot.

"I own a motorcar manufacturing plant in Kent, but I am experimenting with manufacturing aeroplanes. Jon was raised here so we brought some planes down to test them. The fields are so flat, you see."

So his name was Jon. She tried it out in her mind. *Jon.* It felt as right as his hand reaching for hers.

Douglas stopped talking to conserve his breath for climbing back up the hill. They arrived at the top just as the sun set.

The pilot must have passed out from the ride, because he remained unconscious as the big man settled him into the back of his long, sleek Silver Ghost.

"Are you going to be able to make it home safely?" Douglas asked.

She nodded. "Summerset isn't that far and the horse knows the way."

"You live at Summerset?"

"Yes. My name is Rowena Buxton. Could you send word on how he is?"

The man nodded and cranked the engine to life. "I'm Douglas Dirkes. And of course. And thank you, miss, for your help."

She watched the motorcar lurch down the rock-strewn road and wished she had been able to do more for him. Part of her yearned to follow them into town to make sure he was going to be okay. Deep in her bones, she felt she shouldn't let this man disappear from her life. But she had a family of her own that was no doubt worried sick right now. Sighing, she mounted her horse and reined him toward home. Then she thought of Victoria and Prudence and the myriad problems she faced at Summerset and wished she could just ride on forever.

"The scones are ready to take out now, love, if you don't mind. The towel is right over there." Nanny Iris jerked her head in the general direction of the towel and Victoria hurried to comply.

This was the second visit she'd made to Nanny Iris's cottage and she loved the home almost as much as she did Nanny Iris. The cottage stood by itself in the center of a small meadow, which was brown and barren now, but no doubt thick with wildflowers in the spring and summer. The thatching of the roof was the color of warm honey, contrasting with the red ivy winding up one wall. Two deep windows stood guard on either side of the door. A rail fence protected a small kitchen garden on one side, where Nanny Iris grew an abundance of herbs and vegetables. It looked like a fairy house, or perhaps the home of a banished princess waiting for her prince. She'd ignored Nanny Iris's raucous laugh when she told her that the first time she'd come to visit.

Victoria sniffed the rich, buttery scent of the scones before setting the pan to cool on the stone countertop. Then she went to stand next to Nanny Iris, who was making an infusion out of oregano.

"What kind of oil do you use?" Victoria asked, watching with interest as Nanny Iris repeatedly dipped a small net bag of freshly cut oregano into a jar of warm oil.

"You can use olive oil or grape-seed oil. I'm using olive oil because it's easier to come by." After squeezing the oil out a few times, she pushed the bag down into the jar, added more oil, and screwed on the lid.

"And what is this used for again?"

Nanny Iris smiled. "I use it to bring in money from the pharmacist in town. But it's commonly used to ease sore throats and can be helpful in settling digestive problems. Some people also use it to relieve aching muscles." She wiped the jar off with a clean cloth and set it in a cupboard alongside several other jars. "This one will be ready to sell in a couple of weeks."

Victoria laid the table for tea while Nanny Iris put away the herbs and concoctions they had been working on. Working with Nanny Iris in her warm, homey kitchen filled Victoria with the kind of simple satisfaction she hadn't felt since she'd helped her father in his office. From her father she'd learned the genus and species and chemical properties of each plant. From Nanny Iris she learned the myths, legends, and the plants' medicinal uses. Sometimes when infusing or mixing herbs together, she could almost feel her father by her side watching their progress.

Nanny Iris put the kettle on for tea. "How has your breathing been lately? Has the infusion I made you done any good?"

Victoria nodded. "I think so. Climbing stairs is easier and I run out of air less often. But it's hard to tell because my episodes often decrease when I come to Summerset."

"I wouldn't doubt it. The air is much better here than in the city. Does it ever worsen in June or July?"

Victoria nodded. "Yes, and then it's worse out here than in the city."

"Did your fancy doctors ever mention hay fever?"

"A German doctor did when we were vacationing in Davos once. But he also said the increase in episodes could be the thin air, too."

"You are a special case, that's for sure. I'm working on another infusion for you that may help even more. Now tell me, how is your sister doing?"

Victoria poured the tea while Nanny Iris set out the clotted cream and jam. They finally sat and Victoria closed her eyes while Nanny Iris said a quick grace.

Victoria spread her scone thickly with jam and cream and took a big bite. Not even Cook at Summerset could compete with Nanny Iris's scones. "Rowena acts as if she were sleepwalking half the time. Prudence is being treated abominably and Rowena doesn't do anything about it."

"Remember, child, she's grieving as much as you are. Grief does funny things to a person."

Victoria nodded, her throat tightening. "I understand that, but we can't just sit by and let this happen. And they won't listen to me, that's for sure."

"Who won't?"

"My aunt and uncle."

"What makes you think they will listen to Rowena any more than they listen to you?"

Victoria took a sip of her tea and then shrugged. "I don't know that they will, but it irks me that Rowena won't even try. Prudence is family, for heaven's sake!"

Nanny Iris refilled their teacups. "Why don't you all just go back home to London?"

"Because Uncle wants us to stay with him. He doesn't like the idea of us being in London alone. I think he's afraid we'll embarrass him somehow."

"That boy always did worry about what other people thought too much," Nanny Iris observed.

Victoria's lips twitched at the thought of her

uncle as a spoiled boy. "It's not like I hate it at Summerset," she said. "I love it there. If Prudence were being treated like a member of the family, I wouldn't mind staying. But she's treated like a servant just because her mother was our governess. She isn't a servant, she's like our sister. And the worst part is that there's nothing I can do to help her . . . I feel completely powerless. It's appalling."

"It seems so. Why would the family even care? Well, I can see why your aunt would care. Acts like a queen, that one. And you say the girl's mother is dead?"

"She died several years ago. Pru just stayed with us. My father loved her. We all do. Now she has to wear a uniform and act like she's our lady's maid and goodness only knows what they make her do when we're not around.

"You actually might have known Pru's mother," Victoria continued. "She worked at the big house as a young girl."

"Oh, really?" Nanny Iris set her teacup down. "Was she a local girl? What's her name?"

"Alice Tate."

Nanny Iris froze, shock flickering across the wrinkled planes of her face. Then the look swiftly vanished as if it were never there at all.

Victoria stiffened. "What? Do you know her?"

The old woman shook her head. "No. I've never heard of her."

"But even if you didn't know her personally, surely the name rings a bell—" Victoria persisted.

"Many people have worked at Summerset whom I've never met," Nanny Iris cut in. "It's not that unusual that I wouldn't know her. Are you finished with that?"

Victoria nodded and the old woman leapt up and started putting their tea things away. Victoria knew without being told that she was being dismissed. She helped clear up the tea things and left after a warm hug and a promise to visit again soon.

Victoria wrapped a scarf more tightly around her neck. The frozen grass crunched under her feet as she crisscrossed a field over to the main road running back to Summerset.

What was that look all about? Victoria picked up her pace a bit as the sun sunk even further behind the hills. Nanny Iris *had* to know who Prudence's mother was. She had left the family right after Victoria's aunt Halpernia had died in an accident as a child. Victoria sensed that Nanny Iris didn't want to talk about Halpernia. But then again, her own father hadn't spoken about his baby sister either. No one did.

Victoria wondered about Prudence's mother. Why had Elaine seemed to know about Prudence's mother when she saw the photographs? Why did Nanny Iris lie about knowing her? Had there been some kind of scandal? Victoria's blood

125

quickened. Another secret? As a governess, Miss Tate had been warm and knowledgeable and almost like a mother to Victoria and Rowena. But unlike her own father, who treated Prudence as his own, Miss Tate always showed restraint in her affections.

The sun dipped lower and Victoria wanted to hurry, but was worried about having an episode if she did. When would she learn that she needed to take that detestable black box with her everywhere? She'd grown up with Rowena and Prudence worrying over her like a pair of banty hens, not wanting her to do this or that. Bugger that. If she didn't get out of the house on occasion, she was going to go mad like the women in those old French novels. Prudence was off doing whatever it was that Mrs. Harper kept her busy doing, and Rowena was moping in her room, as always. Her sister now spent most of her time woolgathering or out riding.

Victoria spent her days reading until her eyes were blurry or gossiping with Elaine about people she barely knew. Miss Fister had sent her a refund of her money with a note apologizing, but she couldn't teach how to be a good secretary by mail. So now she didn't even have that, though she did have an idea that might work . . . and be an amusing secret, as well.

The truth was, she missed her father. She missed her life. No one did *anything* here. At home, Victoria helped with her father's work, studied her secretarial lessons, or worked on her sketching. She and Rowena and Pru would attend plays and go out to dinner, and every Monday and Wednesday she walked down to Mrs. Humphry Ward's settlement house and helped take care of the little ones while their mothers worked.

Prudence's and Rowena's days seemed equally busy. Prudence was always occupied with her writing, practicing her piano, volunteering at the hospital, or going to museums. Rowena attended suffrage meetings, read, or took long walks or rides in Hyde Park or Kensington Gardens, or played whatever sport she was currently taken with.

Here, the days were spent changing clothes, from morning dresses to afternoon dresses to dinner dresses. One needed a completely new ensemble if she wanted to walk or ride, and the rest of the time, Elaine told her with a derisive giggle, was filled with planning your next change.

Climbing over the stone fence, she reached the main road and resumed her walk.

She knew she could cut through the woods, but Nanny Iris had made her promise she wouldn't go near them at night and to take a friend if she was going during the day. Victoria thought she was being a bit overcareful, but Nanny Iris had an old woman's fear of ghosts.

Lights flashed behind her and the horn of a motorcar bellowed. She jumped out of the way as a car passed and then slowed. There were several laughing young men in the car and, alarmed, Victoria froze, ready to run if need be.

"Cousin Victoria! What are you doing out all by yourself? Mother will be having a fit, I'm sure."

Victoria peered through the gloom. "Colin? Is that you?"

"The one and only. Scoot over, Sebastian, and make room, you big oaf. Get in, Vic. I'll give you a ride."

Unperturbed, a tall man climbed into the back with the other fellow. Victoria recognized Lord Billingsly. She hadn't seen the other man before.

She opened the door to the sedate touring car and climbed in next to her cousin. "I didn't even know you were coming. Do your parents know?"

"No, I'm surprising them for a long weekend. Sebastian and Kit in the back there are along for the ride. I actually came out for Elaine."

"Elaine?"

"Yes. My poor little sis says it's dreadfully dull out here in the sticks, so I try to come liven her up whenever I can take time off from school. Aren't you bored?"

She paused, not wanting to offend. Guessing the reason for her hesitation, he laughed.

"Oh, you can tell me the truth. I know what it's like."

"Well, there does seem to be an inordinate amount of free time."

He threw his head back and laughed. She'd always thought her cousin attractive, but that was when he'd been a boy. In the two years since she'd seen him, he had somehow turned into a man. Like Elaine's, his hair was a warm brown and his eyes were blue, but his nicest feature was the smile that softened the firm jaw that was a male Buxton trademark. He reminded her of a man in a fairy tale—not the hero who won the princess, but the sidekick who made it all possible.

"Very judiciously put, cousin. Didn't you turn eighteen last year? Why didn't you have a coming-out ball?"

She shrugged. "Rowena and I didn't want one and our father never pushed us."

"Smart man. All that stuff is on its way out anyway." He glanced over at her and his mouth tightened. "I'm really sorry about your father, Vic. He was truly one of a kind."

She nodded, fighting that ever-present lump again.

Lord Billingsly leaned forward and stuck his head between the two of them. "You'd better stop talking and hurry. The sun is almost gone and we'll have to stop and light the headlamps. And you know how much fun that always is." His voice held a humorous edge and Victoria knew there was a story there.

"Righto!"

Victoria clung to the door handle as her cousin picked up speed and careened around corners. Once, he almost hit an unsuspecting herd of sheep. She heard the sheepherder yelling at them and began laughing in a breathless way that warned her of a possible episode. She closed her eyes and concentrated on breathing until he pulled up in front of the house.

"You can open your eyes now, cousin. I got you here in one piece."

"Barely," Sebastian said from the back. "And I think you may have given the shepherd a heart attack."

The wide front doors were flung open, spilling light out onto the drive. Prudence rushed out, a shawl wrapped around her shoulders.

"Where have you been? Do you know how worried we've been about you?"

Victoria climbed out of the motorcar, waiting for her lecture.

But Prudence stood frozen with a look on her face that Victoria had never seen before as her gaze focused on something behind Victoria. Victoria's head swiveled to find that young Lord Billingsly was staring back at Prudence. For a moment Victoria thought they were going to run to each other, so strong was the current between them. When that didn't happen she began to squirm.

"Well, I might as well make the introduction, since you both have been struck dumb. Prudence, this is Lord Billingsly, I believe you met him at Papa's funeral. Lord Billingsly, this is my dearest friend, Prudence Tate." She looked at both of them still staring at each other, transfixed. "Now speak for heaven's sake!"

CHAPTER
EIGHT

Prudence blushed and looked away. From the look on his face, it seemed he had recognized her as immediately as she had recognized him. She looked at the ground, realizing how she must look, but still grateful Vic had introduced her as her friend instead of as her lady's maid. Her eyes went back to him, and even in the darkness she could see the color staining his cheeks.

So he was as affected by her as she was by him.

Another young man climbed out of the car and joined them. "Now I know you're not cousin Rowena, even if your coloring is the same." He turned to Victoria. "You didn't tell me you had friends visiting."

Victoria looked from one to the other. "Oh, my apologies. Cousin Colin, this is my dear friend and companion, Prudence Tate. Prudence, this is my cousin, Lord Cliveon, and his friend, whom you've just met, and . . ." Victoria faltered as the other young man joined them from the back of the car. "I'm afraid I don't know—"

He stuck his hand out. "My name is Charles, but you can call me Kit."

Colin and Lord Billingsly laughed as if it were the funniest name ever. Everyone began bowing and shaking hands all around. The men even began shaking hands with one another, which made Victoria laugh. Prudence took the opportunity to draw her aside as the men called for the footmen to unload the motorcar.

"Where have you been? You must be freezing. You gave me quite a scare."

"I went to visit an old friend. I didn't mean to worry you."

Prudence looked at her thoughtfully. While Victoria's voice sounded contrite, there was something about her that seemed a bit brighter than when Prudence had dressed her earlier. As if a burden had lightened, perhaps.

Maybe she needed the company of others? Laughing young men were certainly better company than either she or Rowena had been these last couple of weeks. Prudence shot another glance at Lord Billingsly. When she saw he was looking back at her, she blushed and turned away. Hurrying Victoria into the house, she pressed the call bell for the front door, which would bring Mr. Cairns running. He could sort out the young men and their things. She just wanted to get Victoria inside, for in spite of the brightness in the girl's eyes, Prudence sensed her weariness.

They met Elaine in the hall. She was already dressed for dinner in a Chinese pink charmeuse dress with a matching pleated tunic. The neckline and the edge of the tunic were both trimmed with ermine, and Prudence wondered whether she'd ever seen anything so lovely before. "Where have you been, Victoria? Mother's very put out, I'm afraid, and she's been taking it out on the rest of us, thank you very much. Hurry and dress for dinner before she blows her top completely."

The voices coming from the front door made her pause, and then she began to run with a cry. "Colin! I was so hoping you would come home this weekend!"

"We'd better go and get you dressed for dinner, before you're in any more trouble." Prudence took Victoria by the arm.

"Do you ever get the feeling that we spend most of the day changing?" Victoria asked as they climbed the stairs.

Prudence fell silent and Victoria turned to her, a stricken look on her face. "Oh, I am so sorry, Pru. I didn't think."

"It's okay. I'd almost rather wear this ugly old uniform than have to change three or four times a day."

But in her heart Prudence knew this wasn't true.

She had some lovely dresses still packed away in her trunks. Almost all of them were new, because they'd had so many mourning dresses made up before the funeral. Though most of them were black, she'd had a few made up of dark colors such as plum, maroon, and one a lovely midnight blue. She'd never even gotten a chance to wear them. She often opened her trunk and ran her hands over the lovely silks, laces, and tulle. Her hands had become so chapped from helping Susie with the pans in the morning that they caught on the fine fabrics.

Suppressing a sigh, she quickly helped Victoria out of her walking suit as soon as they reached the Rose Room. Once she had her down to her chemise and petticoat, she shooed her into the bathroom to wash up.

Instead of choosing a completely black dress, she selected a dark blue silk pleated dress with a dotted lace tunic and a blue sash at the waist. Victoria was only eighteen; there was no reason for her to wear black all the time, even if it had only been a few weeks since her father had died. If being around handsome young men could lighten her grief a little bit, Prudence was going to help all she could.

Her cheeks flushed as she remembered staring at Lord Billingsly in her shapeless skirt and shirtwaist. What must he think of her?

Not for the first time did she fervently wish

they could all go back in time. But would it have made any difference? Even in her fine clothes, with her hair done up in a pile of curls, she was still the daughter of a governess. Nothing was going to change that, and Lord Billingsly was heir to a way of life that had nothing to do with her. Rowena and Victoria spurned that way of life, but they could pick it up again at any moment. They belonged, as proven by how well they fit into life here at Summerset. She, ordinary Prudence Tate, did not belong.

Prudence helped Victoria into her dinner dress. At first she was worried about what Vic would say to the color of her dress, as deep mourning forbade it, but all Vic did was smile.

"Father loved that color."

Prudence smiled back and deftly pulled out the pins in Victoria's shining golden hair and brushed it. Loosened, it reached her waist. After brushing it out, she parted it down the middle and then coiled both sides, until they twisted up by themselves. Pinning them securely, she added a double row of blue beads to form a kind of loose headband and then pinned a dark blue feather hairpiece on one side. The little ivory seagulls at her ears had been her mother's.

Victoria tilted her head to one side, a sweet, birdlike movement that never failed to make Prudence smile. "I look quite pretty, Pru. Thank you."

A slight tap on the door alerted her that it was time to send Victoria down.

Rowena poked her head around the corner of the door. "Are you ready?"

Victoria turned around and Ro's eyes softened. "You look lovely, Vic."

Victoria smiled tremulously and then Prudence watched as it faded. The three girls were motionless, feeling their separation as they never had before, Victoria and Rowena dressed in their finery, going down to dinner with friends and family, while Prudence, shabby in her uniform, was heading down to the servants' hall. It was Prudence who broke the silence. "Go on with you both. You don't want to keep Aunt Charlotte waiting."

Victoria squeezed her hand as she walked past, but Rowena avoided Prudence's eyes as she waited for her sister.

Prudence looked around the room after the girls had gone, feeling more alone than she had ever felt. Loath to stay by herself, she quickly straightened up Victoria's room and headed down the hall to the servants' staircase. She paused outside Rowena's room and then shrugged. Rowena could jolly well clean up after herself. She knew it wasn't fair, but part of her couldn't help but feel that Ro was responsible for this whole mess.

She tried to open the door to the servants' stairs

only to find it stuck. She tried again, but it wouldn't budge. Could someone have locked it? Why? Frowning, she looked down the big sweeping staircase. The servants were only supposed to use the main staircase if they were cleaning it, but Prudence couldn't see any way out of it. Not if she wanted to eat, and she did. Well, the family would all be in the sitting room or the dining room anyway and Mr. Cairns and Mrs. Harper would be busy. Looking around, she hurried down the staircase, her hand trailing along the satiny smoothness of the handrail.

"Oh, excuse me."

Startled, she stumbled on the bottom step. Firm hands shot out to steady her.

Lord Billingsly smiled and her heart ricocheted around her chest. His hands, one lightly resting against her shoulder and the other at her elbow, sent a shot of fluid warmth through her entire body.

"It's Prudence, isn't it? Are you coming in to dinner? May I escort you?"

His dark eyes were so compelling that it took a moment for the words to sink in. When they did it felt as if a bucket of ice water had been dumped over her head.

She leapt away from him as if she'd been burned, anger and humiliation heating her cheeks. "Are you making fun, Lord Billingsly? Because I am not amused."

He jerked back as if she'd hit him. "Pardon?"

Hot, angry tears burned at her eyes. "Does it look as if I'm ready to go in to dinner?"

His eyes widened as he took in her clothing at a glance. Her hands clenched by her sides. Good. He understood now. She whirled away and stalked to the servants' door behind the staircase, which mercifully wasn't stuck. Miserably, she noticed he didn't call for her to wait this time, wanting to know who she was.

He knew who she was now.

Susie was scurrying around the kitchen when Prudence arrived downstairs. The kitchen staff, the footmen, and the butler would eat their meals after the family had been fed. The housemaids, the valets, and the lady's maids got their dinner as the family ate. This order of dining ensured that there would always be someone to answer a call should a bell on the bell board ring, and it was practical: not all of the house staff could fit at the table at once anyway.

Susie waggled her fingers as Prudence walked over to the large kettle filled with cock-a-leekie soup for the staff. Upstairs, the family was having a nine-course meal starting with a thin vegetable consommé with a splash of cream added into the bowl as it was being served, oyster patties, roast goose, kidney pie, braised fennel and celery served with game chips, cherry tart, raspberry ice, and fruit and cheese.

She filled herself a bowl of the soup and watched as Cook took the roast goose, golden from bacon drippings, out of the oven. She placed it on a silver platter and added a few roast potato florets as a garnish. The goose was still sizzling as Cook hurried it past Prudence to the dumbwaiter, leaving the rich, crackling scent of meat in its wake.

She turned away and cut herself a piece of bread from the common loaf. Balancing it on top of her stew, she made her way to the servants' hall. When she got there, they all stopped eating and looked at her. Usually, she bolted her food in the kitchen or took it to a quiet corner, but she was tired of being alone. Hesitating, she took a free chair next to Hortense and gave everyone a tentative smile.

"Well, guess who finally decided to join us for dinner?" one of the housemaids said with a snort.

"Look at the likes of her, mixing with the likes of us," another one sniggered.

Prudence looked down at her bowl, her throat tightening. Maybe this had been a mistake.

"That's enough, girls," Mrs. Harper said as Prudence sat down with her food. "I'll not have dissension among us." She cast Prudence a pursed-lips look, making it clear that she considered the trouble Prudence's fault even though she hadn't said a word. "I trust you read the rules that forbade you from using the staircase and this evening was an aberration, correct?"

Prudence swallowed. She wanted to tell the housekeeper that the servants' door wouldn't open, but the bold stares of the housemaids stirred up suspicions in her mind. She bit her lip and looked down. "Yes, ma'am."

Mrs. Harper nodded and moved on.

"You're nothing but a flock of chatty birds," Hortense scolded the maids. She turned to Prudence. "Pay them no mind, my dear girl. They're just jealous of your fine position."

Prudence stared at the Frenchwoman, laughter bubbling up inside. Her fine position? Then the laughter died. Well, compared to scrubbing pots and pans all day long as Susie did, taking care of someone's lovely clothes, drawing her baths, and doing her hair must seem like a very fine position indeed. Instead of laughing, she gave Hortense a hesitant smile.

Out of the corner of her eye, she caught the two maids who had spoken to her rolling their eyes. Prudence wanted to crawl under a rock and stay there. But she couldn't do that. They obviously thought her a snob already.

She addressed Hortense. "How long have you been Lady Summerset's lady's maid?"

The woman raised an eyebrow. "About seven years. Before that I was the Marquise du Henault's lady's maid until her death."

Another roll of the eyes from the housemaids.

Prudence hid a smile. Hortense's description was right, they did resemble nothing more than flighty magpies in their black-and-white uniforms.

Hortense took off her reading glasses and put down her newspaper. "And what did you do before you became the lady's maid for the Honorable Rowena and Victoria?"

Conversation at the table had ceased and though no one looked directly at her, Prudence knew they were all waiting for her answer. Instinctively, she knew better than to reveal her exact circumstances, though part of her desperately wanted to tell them that she wasn't like them, she wasn't in service at all. "I've always lived with them," she said in a small voice. "My mother was their governess."

Hortense's eyebrows almost shot off her forehead. "Indeed."

Prudence could tell that everyone wanted more, but she concentrated on her stew. Eventually, the talk went on to other things and Prudence finished her meal and washed her dishes so Susie wouldn't have to. Susie, still busy with the dinner dishes, gave her a grateful smile.

"Don't go yet. Why don't you sit with us a while? It will be hours before your girls need you. You might as well make yourself comfortable."

Prudence hesitated for a moment, then relented. The only way to combat her own loneliness was by getting to know other people, right? She settled herself next to Hortense and Susie brought her another cup of tea.

As soon as she sat, two of the maids exchanged glances and excused themselves. Prudence watched them go with a frown, but soon Hortense captured her attention again.

"Let me tell you about my first assignment and see if you don't feel better, *oui*?" Hortense took one of Prudence's hands as she spoke, a friendly gesture no doubt, but as the older woman told her story, Prudence began to feel more and more like Hortense's hand were a manacle holding her down. She listened as Hortense told her about her former employer back in France, who thought so little of the help that she never even bothered to learn Hortense's name.

As miserable as Prudence was, she realized she could have it worse. When Prudence rose to leave, Hortense stood as well.

"You're not going to bed already, are you?" Hortense asked sharply.

Prudence shook her head. "No. I have to go straighten up Rowena's room first." Her forehead wrinkled. "Why?"

"Oh, no reason." Hortense waved her hand. "I just thought it was rather early, that's all. But if you have work to do . . ."

Prudence was lost in thought as she tidied Rowena's room. Why did it please her so much that the other servants believed she was better than them? In spite of everything Sir Philip had taught them about the equity of all men and women, she still didn't want to be thought of as a mere servant. But in reality, they were more her sort of people than Rowena and Victoria were. Or Lord Billingsly. Her mother had begun as a maid. She had no idea what her father had done for work, as her mother never spoke of him, but she knew she had family who lived in the village. No doubt many of them had worked for the Buxtons or one of the other titled families in the area.

Was there really a fundamental difference between those of the lower class and those of the upper class, aside from the circumstances of one's birth, something over which a person has no control? Why did those of the lower classes put up with being made to feel as if they were second-class humans? Prudence could see the need for lower-tier jobs—no one was going to like cleaning the privies, after all. She rubbed her head. No wonder things changed slowly. There were no easy solutions.

When Rowena didn't appear for her bath, Prudence walked down the hall to Victoria's room. What room would she have if she were a real guest? She hadn't been able to see much of the house beyond the servants' quarters, the girls' rooms, and the Great Hall. She had hardly even been outside since she arrived. Instead, she spent her afternoons off reading one of the books Vic had smuggled her from the library.

More tired than she had ever been, she climbed the never-ending stairs to her room. Rowena and Victoria could jolly well put themselves to bed tonight. She wasn't really a maid, no matter what it currently looked like. The encounter with Lord Billingsly and her experience with the staff in the servants' hall had left her feeling fragile, as if one more incident could break her into a million pieces.

The gas lamps in the long stretch of petticoat hall were spaced far apart and on the lowest setting. "No reason for servants to be able to see," she muttered. She left the door open, so she would have enough light to get her own small gas lamp burning. After locking the door, she peeled off her clothes, not even bothering to hang them up. Her teeth began to chatter as she pulled on a fine lawn nightgown. Even though her skin gloried in the softness of the material, she almost wished for wool bloomers to fend off the chill. Her room was more like an icebox than a bedroom.

Hurrying now, she raced across the room and leapt into bed, but as she shoved her feet down, they were stopped by something about halfway down. Uncomprehending, she pushed her feet down harder and then realized what had happened. Someone had given her an apple pie bed, snuck into her bedroom to pull a prank on her. Sobs erupted from her mouth before she could stop them and she clapped her hands over her face. She wouldn't give anyone the satisfaction of knowing they had gotten to her. For a few minutes she sat on her bed, her knees pulled up to her chest, trying to get control of herself. She had no friends here, she thought. Except for Susie, she was completely alone, and she was better off remembering that.

When your bed is short-sheeted, you have no choice but to get up and remake it all over again. Wearily, she climbed out of her bed. Her feet ached from cold and her muscles throbbed with exhaustion, but she managed to get it done.

Finally under the coverlet, with her tears drying on her cheeks, Prudence made a decision. Her next day off was tomorrow. She would take advantage by going into town and trying to find some of her family. Anything was better than being trapped here in isolation, suspended between the upstairs and downstairs worlds of Summerset, and truly belonging to neither.

The next morning, Prudence took out her new rust-colored serge walking suit and brushed it out, being especially careful of the black braid trim and cloth buttons. Slipping on the skirt, which came to just above her ankles, she tucked in a creamy white blouse and pulled on the matching jacket. She loved how the ruffles on the sleeves of her blouse peeked out from under the cuffs of the coat. Then she did her hair the best she could in the cracked mirror and topped it with an oversized black velvet beret. Her feet were clad with a pair of two-toned black and brown leather walking boots that laced up the front. In no manner could she be mistaken for a maid today.

She swept into the servants' quarters and poured herself a cup of tea, ignoring the stares she was getting.

Hortense's eyes widened. *"Belle fille"* was all she said.

Prudence knew that her actions wouldn't make her any friends among the servants, but she didn't care. She now saw that they judged her every bit as much as Lord Summerset did.

She saw Susie peer around the corner, her eyes wide. Prudence's stomach was bouncing so much, she decided against porridge and opted for just tea.

"Today is your half day, *oui*? Do you have any plans?" Hortense wanted to know.

"I thought I would go into town," Prudence answered.

"Why on earth would you want to do that?" Hortense sniffed. "It's not even a town. More like a village."

"How long has it been since you've been there?" one of the footmen asked. "It's grown a lot in the last couple of years. Industry is coming in a big way." He smiled at Prudence, showing a wide grin and strong white teeth. "My name is Andrew, by the way. Andrew Wilkes."

She smiled back, recognizing him as the kind-faced young man from her first day at Summerset. She'd seen him about since of course, but as they rarely ate at the same time, she hadn't met him formally yet. She guessed this was as formal as the servants got. "Prudence Tate," she said, and then felt stupid. Everyone already knew who she was.

One of the maids snorted and snatched her cup and bowl from the table. "I don't have time for this. Some of us have work to do."

Andrew kept smiling. "Don't mind her. She's just jealous. It's evident to everyone here that you're a real lady."

"That will be all, Andrew. I'm sure you have work to attend to, as well," Mr. Cairns said from the doorway.

"But—" Andrew started to say.

"Now," Mr. Cairns interrupted.

Andrew gave her a cheeky wink and, gathering up his breakfast dishes, also left the table.

Mr. Cairns gave her a withering look and Prudence turned away, her cheeks heating.

"You had better be off before Mrs. Harper gets a look at you, my young friend. Or there will be all kinds of hell to pay," Hortense said.

"But the clothes are my own and it's my day off. Surely she can't object to my wearing my own clothes on my day off, can she?"

"Oh, she'll find a way. Now off. Enjoy your day, even though I don't know how you're going to find any amusement in a muddy hamlet like Summerset."

Prudence took her cup back to the utility room to wash it.

"I'll get it," Susie said gruffly, not looking at Prudence. "You'll spot your dress if you do it."

"Thank you, Susie. I'll get you a surprise while I'm in town."

Prudence thought she saw a half smile on Susie's face, but she couldn't be sure. Contrariness had made her avoid Victoria and Rowena this morning, even to ask whether they would like anything from town or needed anything before she left. Both of them had disappeared several times since they had come to Summerset and didn't tell her where they went.

It was hard to keep up with your friends if spending time together was frowned upon. Even though there were occasions when they would spend time reading together in their bedrooms in front of the fire, Ro and Vic couldn't be expected to spend all their time in their rooms. They weren't the prisoners.

She was.

Shaking off her thoughts, Prudence made sure

to leave by the servants' door and avoided the front of the house. The last thing she needed was to be rebuked for being uppish, and after her behavior this morning, she knew she would be a target. Shame heated her cheeks. What had ever possessed her to go to breakfast dressed up in an outfit that would cost any one of them more than a year's wages?

But still, now that she was finally outside the house, she felt as if she could breathe. The clouds hung low and gray in the sky but didn't seem threatening. Her sturdy walking boots were comfortable. The trees along the drive had been emptied of all their autumn leaves and now stood like stark and naked sentries above her.

When she reached the end of the drive, she paused, feeling foolish. Why hadn't she thought to get directions to town? She heard the rattle of a motorcar behind her and stepped to the side as it slowed.

Lord Billingsly tipped his hat to her. "Good morning, Miss Tate."

"Good morning, Lord Billingsly." She felt her cheeks flush, then glanced back at the house.

"No one can see us from here if that's what you're worried about."

She swallowed. "Of course not."

There was a long pause. "Are you going to town? May I give you a lift?"

She squirmed inside as she remembered how

149

she'd scurried away into the servants' door the last time she'd seen him. At the same time she was annoyed by her reaction to him. She was finally getting out of the house and here he was, his very handsome presence making her feel self-conscious. "Yes, I am going to town, but I am perfectly capable of walking there. In fact, I'll enjoy the exercise. Good day, sir."

She turned left and resolutely walked down the road.

"Miss Tate?"

She stopped and closed her eyes for a moment. Somehow she had known that wouldn't be the end of it. "Yes, Lord Billingsly?" she asked without turning.

"Are you planning on walking all the way to London? Because Summerset is the other direction."

Of course it was. The absurdity of the situation hit her and laughter bubbled out of her before she could stop it. It was the first time she'd laughed so freely since Sir Philip died. The thought pained her, but it didn't stop the laughter. When his laugh, warm and rich, joined hers, she finally turned. Oh, what would be the harm in joining him? Her sensible side knew the answer to that. In her position, there could be quite a bit of harm, but recklessly she ignored the risk. "Lord Billingsly, I would very much like a ride to town."

He leapt out of the touring motorcar and opened her door for her. Once he had climbed back inside, he rooted around in the backseat and then handed her a dust blanket.

"No reason to get your fine dress muddy or dusty."

She tucked the blanket around her dress and they took off, heading the right direction into town.

"So Miss Tate. You're rather the mystery girl, aren't you?" His tone was light and Prudence snuck a glance at him.

His bowler hat tilted slightly to one side and his dark hair curled over the collar of his suit in the back. In profile, she could see that his mouth curled slightly at the corners, as if he could find the humorous side of anything. "Trust me, Lord Billingsly, there is nothing mysterious about me whatsoever."

"I beg to differ. The first time I met you, I couldn't get two words from you, though that was understandable considering the circumstances. I met you again last night and you were wearing a uniform and were a bit, how shall I say it, aggressive? Now this morning, you're a different girl altogether. See? Mystery."

His eyes squinted in a smile and Prudence relaxed. Something kind in his expression put her at ease. "All of those things can be explained, Lord Billingsly."

"I would be pleased if you could enlighten me, Miss Tate."

A smile played about her lips. It was so nice to be riding along in a motorcar with a handsome young man teasing her. As if she were a normal young woman. Prudence knew that all hell would break loose if Mrs. Harper or, heaven forbid, Lady Summerset found out, but at the moment she didn't care.

"I think I'll keep the mystery alive a bit longer. I've never been considered mysterious before, and I must say I rather like it."

"Fair enough. But do me the honor of answering me one question. I did give you a ride to town, after all."

The town was just ahead of them. Prudence gave him a sidelong look. "I guess that depends on the question, Lord Billingsly."

"Wherever did you get that hat?"

Her mouth dropped open for a moment and then she laughed. "I didn't take you for the velvet beret type, but if you must know, I bought it from Caroline Reboux's new shop on Bond Street."

"My *little sister* thanks you," he said pointedly. "Now, do you think this town has a teahouse where we could get a cup of tea? That is if you would care to join me in a cup of tea." He pulled the motorcar over and regarded her steadily, his dark eyes asking a question she dare not answer.

Her pulse kicked up a notch before she reined it

in. Despite her sudden desire to spend more time in his company, Prudence knew that tea with Lord Billingsly would *not* be a good idea. "I'm not sure if there is a teahouse or not, Lord Billingsly, but we cannot have tea. Not only because I have many errands before returning to the house, but because I'm not sure having tea together would accomplish anything except to cause trouble."

She took the dust blanket off her knees and folded it.

"But why would a simple cup of tea cause trouble, Miss Tate?"

She gave him a half smile. "I think you know the answer to that. Thank you for the ride into town. I do hope your sister enjoys her beret."

"I don't really have a sister," he said quickly as she opened the door.

She stepped down out of the motorcar and looked up at him. His dark eyes were suddenly serious. "Then why did you want to know where I got my hat?" she asked.

He smiled and she noticed he had very straight white teeth. "Because I knew you wouldn't answer anything else." Prudence couldn't help but smile back, though she quickly tried to hide her expression.

"Very astute. Thank you again for the ride," she said matter-of-factly.

She turned away and hurried down the side-walk, trying to look as if she knew where she was going, which she most emphatically did not. She half wished she'd taken him up on having tea with him in any one of the tea shops that lined the street. But no. What was that old saying about borrowing trouble? Resolutely, she turned her attention to her surroundings.

The footman, Andrew, had it right. Even though she'd never been there before, she could see that Summerset was burgeoning with a sense of its own dawning importance. Unfortunately, it wasn't the tiny two-street village she'd hoped for—it would have been so much easier to find news of her family if that were the case. She supposed she could have asked one of the other servants, but she felt embarrassed to admit that she had no idea who her family was.

She looked around for a dry goods store, or perhaps a clothing store where she wouldn't feel too out of place asking whether anyone knew any Tates.

A far as she could tell, the old side of town lay to the north and the new part stretched out south and west toward the hills. She headed toward the older side, figuring that if there were any Tates, they would probably have been there for quite some time. Of course, knowing only one of her family names was just another obstacle in a whole line of them.

She glanced at the people bustling past her. Women in shapeless, old-fashioned gowns and shawls walked side by side with young women in trimmer, modern dresses that barely skimmed their ankles. There were few motorcars on this side of town and more horse-drawn carts.

She rounded a corner and spotted a shabby old library across the street, flanked by a boarding-house and a laundry. The acrid scent of strong washing powder mixed with that of the horse dung in the street, but she didn't care. No doubt this was the only library in Summerset, and considering how much her mother enjoyed reading, chances were she came here for her books.

Prudence hurried across the street. The wooden door creaked as she opened it and she wondered how many people actually came here every day. The inside was dim, depending on several gas lamps and the dingy front window for light. The shelves were surprisingly tidy, with the books stacked across them in neat rows. A door set on several wooden boxes served as a desk in the back of the room, and an old man sat behind it, looking at her expectantly.

He wore no hat, and his head shone baldly pink in the dim light. White, bushy eyebrows sat over his eyes like a conjoined pair of fuzzy caterpillars. He probably had more hair in his eyebrows than on his entire head. He put his finger on the big book he had propped in front of him and smiled. "May I help you?"

"Yes, actually." Now that she was really here looking for her family, nerves bounced in her stomach.

He beamed. "And exactly what kind of book were you looking for?"

"I'm not actually looking for a book. I'm looking for some information."

His face fell. "Well, if you need directions you can ask anyone on the street."

"Actually, I'm looking for information on a person."

"Oh." He looked slightly mollified by this unusual request. "I'm not sure how I can help."

She smiled apologetically. "You see, I've always thought that librarians have their fingers on the pulse of everything that happens in a town."

He brightened at this for a moment and then looked at her glumly. "Well, that used to be so, miss, but not anymore. Seems like the young people aren't interested in books. It's all motorcars, aeroplanes, and telephones now. I've been in this library since it began thirty-five years ago and I've never had so few patrons." His face fell into sorrowful lines.

Prudence felt a stirring of excitement. If he'd been here that long, he'd have to have known her mother. "I love books," she assured him. "Next time I will see what you have, but today, I am looking to find someone."

He sighed. "I'll see what I can do."

"I am looking for information about a family called Tate." It shamed her that she didn't know her mother's maiden name or her father's first name. How could she find out anything without those two simple names? Her stomach sank. "Or perhaps a girl who grew up around here about twenty-five, thirty years ago. Her name was Alice?"

The change that came over the man was astonishing. His face shuttered like bay windows awaiting a storm. "I'm sorry. I know no one by that name." He cast his eyes downward.

"Are you sure?" she pressed. "I know—"

"I'm very sure. Now if you will excuse me, miss. I am closing up now for lunch. A man has to eat." He arose from his chair and, with a firm hand on her elbow, ushered her out the door.

Moments later she stood on the sidewalk as the man pulled the curtains across the front window.

CHAPTER NINE

Rowena lounged back on the chaise, waiting for tea to be served and thanking God that her cousin Colin and his friends had come to visit when they did. Her aunt kept making little comments about her disappearance the other day and Rowena didn't want to talk about her experience with anyone other than Victoria. Somehow very nearly being hit by an aeroplane and saving a pilot's life didn't seem like polite dinner conversation. Plus, it went deeper than that. The time she sat with the injured pilot on the side of the hill seemed more real than anything else since her father died. Her time at Summerset seemed fuzzy and tinged with gray, while every moment from the aeroplane crash to carting the pilot up the hillside seemed infused with color. She didn't want to share that with anyone because no one could understand.

Across the sitting room, her aunt held court, flanked by her daughter and her son. Uncle Conrad was nowhere in evidence, having gone to inspect some properties earlier in the morning.

Remembering how taken Lord Billingsly had seemed with Prudence, she observed him discreetly. There was no doubt he was exceedingly handsome with his dark curls and dark eyes, but Rowena had never trusted handsome men, especially those among the peerage. They always seemed to be too full of their own sense of self-importance. *No doubt brought on by doting mothers,* she thought, as her aunt stared adoringly at her son. But there was little in Lord Billingsly's mannerisms to suggest conceit. On the contrary, his mouth seemed to indicate a sense of humor and he behaved very politely to everyone he met, including the servants.

Unlike the other friend Colin had brought home. Kip? Kit? Whatever it was. Another handsome young man, tall and well built, with dark, ginger-colored hair and blue eyes. His nose was crooked and he seemed older than the other two young men, but that wasn't what Rowena objected to, it was his barely concealed amusement at everyone and everything around him. It was disconcerting to meet someone and get the sneaking suspicion that he was laughing at you.

Victoria sat close to Elaine, looking more rested in spite of her outing last night. Where had she gone? Victoria had refused to tell her and Rowena hadn't pressed her. It was enough that Victoria acted as though she felt better.

At least someone was feeling better. Rowena found herself avoiding Prudence, because she just felt so helpless about the situation, about everything, it made her hurt just to think about it. She was by turns frustrated by her apathy and resigned to it. She had the knowledge of her own cowardice, but couldn't seem to overcome it. She hated conflict, and the thought of confronting her uncle made her skin crawl with apprehension. She envied Victoria her unassailable confidence that she could change things by the force of her own will. Where did that come from?

The footmen rolled in the tea carts loaded with delicate treats, from an ornate platter filled with the customary watercress and cucumber sandwiches to a Herculean platter of savory ham and beef sandwiches, no doubt in concession to the young men in attendance. Scones with jam and clotted cream were plentiful, of course, along with sponge cakes, biscuits, and chocolate-covered strawberries, pickled kippers, and hard-boiled eggs. After everyone had been seated at a round table near a bay window, Aunt Charlotte turned to Elaine.

"Elaine, darling, would you please do us the honor of pouring tea?"

"Of course, Mother."

Rowena intercepted an amused glance between Elaine and Colin and wondered what it meant.

"Sebastian, my dear boy, tell me, how is your mother?"

"She is doing well. Thank you, Lady Summerset."

"And I trust you will both be coming for the holidays?"

"We wouldn't miss it for the world."

Rowena caught another volley of amused glances, this time involving Lord Billingsly. Victoria's forehead furrowed and Rowena knew her little sister had caught some odd under-currents as well.

"I do hope you young people won't be bored out here in the country. Elaine and I are planning some small gatherings, and of course our servants' ball is always amusing. We will also be having a New Year's Eve ball and I'm sure that will be delightful. Elaine is so good at that sort of thing, Lord Billingsly."

"Oh, Mother, you flatter me."

Rowena hid a smile at the tone of Elaine's voice, so demure and grateful and altogether false.

Aunt Charlotte tilted her head as if she'd caught something, too, but wasn't quite sure what to make of it. "Nonsense," she said sharply. Then she smiled as if to soften her brusque tone. "You are a very accomplished young woman." She stared hard at both Lord Billingsly and Kit. They avoided her gaze.

"So where did you disappear to this morning, Billingsly?" Colin asked.

"I had an errand to attend to." Lord Billingsly spread jam on a scone so nonchalantly that Rowena was instantly suspicious.

"An errand in that little town?" Kit's voice held amusement. "Whatever could there be to do in Summerset?"

"Oh, you'd be surprised." He glanced toward Rowena and then reddened as if she might know something of it.

Again with the double meanings. Unless . . . it couldn't have anything to do with Prudence, could it? She viewed Lord Billingsly with renewed interest.

The rest of the tea passed without incident and the group seemed to exhale as the footmen wheeled away the carts and Aunt Charlotte returned to her boudoir.

"Good grief, I thought she'd never leave," Colin said, lounging back on the settee.

"Watch your tone, young man," Elaine said. "I'll have you know you're talking about my sainted mother."

Colin laughed. "True. Our sainted mother could flirt with our dearly departed King, outwit Confucius, and make the pope cry, all before breakfast. A most formidable woman." He gave a mock shudder. "Do me a favor, little sister, and bring us a drink, will you?"

"Cocktails for everyone," said Kit. "Since you're so accomplished at these sorts of things, Elaine."

Elaine curtsied and turned to Rowena. "Would you like one, Ro? Vic?"

It was on the tip of her tongue to tell Victoria no, but she looked so interested that Rowena didn't have the heart to disappoint her. "Yes, please. Thank you."

Kit stood up to help her and they soon had glasses all around. "What shall we drink to?"

"How about the Cunning Coterie?" Colin said, raising an eyebrow.

"How about a reunion of the Cunning Coterie Christmas?" Elaine countered.

"I do love me a clever alliteration," Colin approved.

"What's the Cunning Coterie?" Victoria asked.

Rowena let the warmth of the spirits lull her into even deeper listlessness, allowing her to watch the activity around her without actually participating in it. No wonder people took to drink, she thought. It was a wonderful way to dull unwanted feelings.

"Ah, we have novices," observed Kit.

"Greenhorns." Sebastian smiled.

"Perhaps they would like to join us?" asked Elaine.

"Would that make us Cunning Coterie Cousins?" Victoria asked with a smile.

Colin clapped his hands. "Clever!"

"Crafty," added Sebastian.

"Confusing," Rowena roused herself to answer, and the others laughed.

"The Cunning Coterie, as it's most commonly known—" Kit began, sotto voce.

"But also can be called the Corrupt Coterie or the Cosmopolitan Coterie," Elaine interrupted.

Kit continued as if Elaine hadn't spoken. "Started at Kings College and has grown to include the fairer sex, because any club without women is not worth belonging to. Because there are so many of us who are pressured by well-meaning—"

"Or not-so-well-meaning," Colin added.

"—relatives to attend all the same parties, balls, and sporting events, we started our own society to ward off death by boredom."

"But what do you do?" Rowena asked, interested but perplexed.

Kit shrugged a shoulder. "Play pranks."

"Make merry," said Elaine quickly.

"Cut capers," Sebastian added.

"Authorize antics," Victoria murmured, and they laughed.

"In other words, not very much," Kit said. He took a long drink.

"But we talk about it a lot. Which is what clubs usually do, isn't it?" Colin asked.

Kit nodded. "Talk about how wonderful they are." He held his glass up, signaling to Elaine that he was out.

She got up and made him another drink while he lounged indolently on the settee.

"It's fine by me if they want to join, but we should wait until the holidays to make it official. The others will be here by then and we can do a real old-fashioned initiation."

Victoria leaned forward, animation lighting her face. "It's a secret society, isn't it? What kind of initiation? Would you make me walk the plank? Bring you back green cheese from the moon? Fight dragons?"

Kit regarded her with an almost predatory smile and Rowena shifted uneasily.

"You are the perfect candidate," he said. "Imaginative and beautiful. And I would never have someone as lovely as you fighting dragons." He reached for her hand and kissed it.

Victoria tilted her head and flashed him an audacious smile.

"Perhaps since we're keeping it all in the family, we should find out what kind of society the old granddaddy earl belonged to and see what their initiations were like," Kit said with a sidelong glance at Colin.

Colin shrugged but Rowena could tell that a nerve of some kind had been touched. "If he did belong to any kind of club, it was no doubt the club of one. No one else could stand to be around him for any length of time. My sister and I certainly couldn't."

"Neither could Vic or I." For some reason Rowena was compelled to shake off her lethargy and rise from her seat. Though her father and his brother had often butted heads, family loyalty was important to him. She stood behind Elaine and in a casual show of fidelity, as if they'd been best friends for years, she laid her hand on her younger cousin's shoulder. "Amongst ourselves, we used to call him grandpapa with the icky nose." The Buxtons broke up laughing.

"What was that thing growing on the side of his nose?" Colin asked, the tension forgotten.

But Rowena saw that Kit's sharp eyes had caught her movement and discerned its meaning. "On second thought, perhaps adding more Buxtons to the fray would cause us to be lopsided. Family loyalty and all that." His voice was light, teasing, but Rowena detected the warning underneath.

Elaine's eyes narrowed, but Victoria beat her to it. She leapt up onto a highly tufted Turkish ottoman and came to a halt in front of Kit. She waved her drink under his nose. How many drinks had Victoria had? Of course, Vic was so petite; one drink for her was more like two for a larger person. "No, you don't, Mr. Kit," Victoria said. "You promised me a bona-fide club and I intend to have one, unless you want me to tell your mother that you don't keep promises to a lady?"

"The horror," he cried, waving his arms about. "Someone save me!"

"You got yourself into this mess, now get yourself out," Colin said, laughing.

From her high perch, Victoria shook her fist at him, giggling. Her black-and-white-striped tea dress was topped with a short black bolero jacket, and her golden hair was coming undone under the black rose–covered bucket hat she wore. Victoria was as charming and adorable as Rowena had ever seen her, and she swiftly stepped in between Kit and her sister. Elaine, bolstered by newfound family loyalty, joined her.

"Too late now, Mr. Kit. The club now includes three Buxton women." Elaine helped Victoria down off the hassock.

The three girls stood shoulder to shoulder and Kit grinned. "If this is what losing is like in the Coterie, I'll have to aspire to lose more often."

Sebastian looked at them and smiled. "You may have a point. I would love to stay and banter with you people all day, but I have to get back to town," Sebastian said, rising.

"More errands?" Colin asked.

"I have a package that may need picking up." A smile played about his mouth. "May I borrow the motor again?"

"Of course," Colin said.

In a swiftness that almost made her dizzy, Rowena made a decision. "May I trouble you for a ride?"

"What are you doing in town?" Victoria asked.

"I would like to check on that friend I told you about." Rowena was sick to death of sitting around doing nothing except becoming even more tired and sad and blue. Maybe actually doing something would snap her out of it.

Victoria's eyes widened in comprehension. "Have fun. Will you be home in time for dinner?"

A wistfulness in Victoria's voice caught at her heart. "In plenty of time, and I'm sure Elaine will keep you company."

Elaine nodded. "Come, poppet. I grow weary of the company of men. Let's go listen to the gramophone, shall we? I'll teach you that new dance step I was telling you about."

Kit stood and stretched. "We're being abandoned, Billingsly. Sounds like it's time to utilize the billiards room Summerset is famous for."

"Meet you out front in twenty minutes?" Sebastian asked Rowena.

Rowena looked down at her tea gown. "Twenty-five," she promised.

She hurried upstairs, cursing her aunt's unspoken mandate that everyone change her clothes for every occasion. The thin black lace and tulle tea gown she wore was completely inappropriate for visiting a hospital. Or for doing anything else in for that matter, except sitting at the tea table looking decorative. The only good thing about tea gowns was that one didn't have to wear a corset.

Oh, where is Prudence? she thought as her fingers fumbled with the dainty silk-covered buttons running down the side of the gown. Finally free, she tossed it onto her bed and grabbed a black tweed walking skirt, not bothering to put on a corset. It wasn't as though she could get into it herself anyway.

She'd been wanting to inquire about the injured pilot for the past couple of days but wasn't quite sure how to go about it. She kept hoping that Mr. Dirkes would send word, but she hadn't heard anything. She could send a note to the hospital, of course, but she didn't know his full name, and it would sound rather strange asking about the health of someone she didn't know. Besides, she was rather afraid her aunt and uncle would find out and she knew they wouldn't approve. Not that there was anything wrong with her concern, but her aunt and uncle were just such sticklers for etiquette.

She tucked her blouse into the skirt and reached for her jacket. Kicking off her useless slippers, she shoved her feet into her boots and discovered the bootlaces were easier to do without a corset. She sucked in a deep breath and let it out slowly, reveling in her freedom. Everything was easier without a corset.

She tried to pull a knitted stocking hat over her head, but her hair, still piled up into a complicated mass of rolls and curls, wouldn't allow it. Frustrated, she pulled out the pins, brushed it loose, and tied it with a ribbon. Tucking the ends down the back of her jacket, she was now able to put her cap on. She snatched up a woolen wraparound coat to put over her jacket in case she got chilly.

She ran down the stairs, pausing as she passed the servants' door, wondering again where Prudence was. This was the first morning she hadn't seen her. Granted it was her day off, but she usually just stayed in Victoria's room, reading, or up in that frigid garret they called a bedroom.

Then she had another thought. Dashing down

the servants' stairs, she burst into the kitchen. "Has anyone seen Prudence?" she asked, her eyes darting this way and that. The entire staff had frozen in their places, staring at her as if she were a stylish ghost come to wreak havoc in their domain. Rowena looked around the kitchen. In all her years of coming to Summerset, she had never been down here. In spite of being large and modern, the kitchen felt dark, steamy, and crowded with people.

A small, wiry, brown-haired girl edged forward. "It's Prudence's day off, Lady Rowena. She went into town. May I help you with something?"

A plump, motherly looking woman flicked the girl in the back of the head with a towel. "Mind your manners and get back to your pots. My apologies, Lady Rowena. I'm the cook here. Is there anything I can do for you?"

Rowena wanted nothing more than to run back up the stairs the way she had come. This is where Prudence spent her time? "I was hoping Prudence could help me make up a basket of baked goods for a sick friend, but . . ."

The room burst into activity as maids and Cook scurried to do her bidding.

"Don't worry, miss, we'll have you fixed right up. Would you like a cup of tea while you wait?"

"Um, no," she said, taken aback. "Thank you."

One woman dressed as a parlor maid snatched a

basket down from a shelf. "Is this too big, miss?"

It was the size of a small boat, used for family picnics. "Um."

"Of course it is, you ninny," Cook said. "Go on with you. Susie, get some of those leftover tea scones and wrap them in a clean cloth. Regina, bring two small jars from the cupboard and fill one up with plum preserves and the other up with the clotted cream. Don't get any on the outside."

Rowena watched in amazement as the basket was filled with scones, lemon tarts, ham sandwiches, and biscuits. Moments later, the basket was in her arms and they all stood at attention awaiting her next order.

"Thank you," she told them weakly. She spotted Susie peering around the door again. Had Prudence mentioned Susie? She hadn't heard her say anything about the other servants, but then, Rowena hadn't been a very good listener lately. Just being around Prudence made her feel like a failure. Rowena wondered whether Prudence had taken pains to make friends with the scullery maid. No doubt she had. Prudence was just like that.

"Thank you for the information, Susie," she said before leaving the kitchen. The girl blushed with the pleasure of being singled out.

Sebastian was waiting for her when she finally made it down the front steps.

"I thought you might have gotten lost." He

smiled and took the basket from her hands. "Are you going on a picnic?"

"No, actually, it's for a friend."

"Lucky friend."

He helped her into the car and then went around to the front to start it up. They were silent as they motored down the long drive and it wasn't until they turned onto the road into Summerset that he spoke to her.

"You know, I could tiptoe around with a lot of small talk, but I have a feeling you're not a small-talk kind of girl."

She looked over at him, surprised. "I don't mind small talk, it's the pointlessness of most society talk that I can't abide."

He nodded. "I agree. You must find tea with your aunt most vexing."

She sighed. "Very perceptive of you."

"So I'll get right to the point, Lady Rowena."

"Please call me Ro." She liked this young man. Even though he was no doubt the same age as her cousin Colin and his friend, he seemed steadier, more mature.

"All right, Ro. Who is Prudence?"

The question caught her unawares. "Prudence? My sister. Well, not really my sister." She turned to him, her eyes narrowing. "How do you know Prudence?"

"I ran into her at your father's funeral," he said. "And then again last night. Literally."

Her eyes widened. "Literally?"

He smiled. "Yes. And then I gave her a ride into town this morning. She said she was going to meet someone."

Rowena frowned. Who could she have been going to meet? She didn't know anyone in Summerset. Or did she? *How would I know?* she thought, regret tightening her stomach. The days of whispered confidences and telling each other everything were long gone. Rowena slumped down in the fine leather seat and pressed her hand to her forehead. She felt as if she was losing everything. She sat silent for several moments, listening to the purr of the motor. "What do you want to know about Prudence?"

"How is she your sister but not your sister?"

How much would Prudence want this strange young man to know? He was obviously interested. She could tell by the light in his eyes and the way he leaned slightly toward her, awaiting answers. "She grew up with Victoria and me in our home from the time we were all just toddlers. It's always been just the three of us." Her heart caught in her throat. Until recently, that is, but she wasn't going to tell him that. Would Prudence care if she told him her mother was their governess? Rowena decided against it. Interest or no, it was no one else's business. And Ro was learning that having a governess for a mother made Prudence a person who wouldn't *do,* or who, in other words, wouldn't fit in or be accepted into polite society. She was learning there were many people who wouldn't *do* according to the dictates set down by the likes of Aunt Charlotte and her circle. If you wouldn't *do,* you weren't invited to any of the important social events.

"She was my father's ward," she said. It was the best she could do. Well, not the best she could do. "Prudence is right in the middle of Victoria and me in age, and she has always taken care of us. I'm the eldest, but Prudence is a natural-born caretaker, so she just played that role. Victoria is delicate and no one can care for her as Pru can. We both adore her."

Sebastian's brow furrowed thoughtfully. "She's never been to Summerset before? I would have remembered if I had seen her here."

"No. She and her mother went to the seaside every summer when Victoria and I came here."

"I thought you said she was your father's ward? But she was with her mother?"

Usually wards were orphans, and Rowena could have bitten her tongue off. They were motoring into town and she took the opportunity to change the subject. "I think the hospital is in the older part of town," she said, pointing.

He nodded and turned the car. Within minutes they were sitting in front of an old brick building that had been the town hospital for over two hundred years. The Buxtons had recently donated money for it to be renovated and the new addition hugged the back of the building like a fancy new bustle on the back of a rag dress.

"Are you sure you don't want me to wait? I can give you a ride back."

"No. I'll walk. I'm not sure how long I'll be. Thank you for the ride." She waved as he drove away and she wondered whether he was going to look for Prudence.

She turned to the hospital and took a deep breath. Now that she was here, nerves bounced around in her stomach. *You're being silly,* she chastised herself. *He might not even be here and probably won't remember much about me anyway.*

Gathering her courage and her coat tighter around her, Rowena entered through the wide wooden door. The old part of the building had been poorly converted into an administration area, desks and medicine cabinets lining the walls where beds had once stood. A woman about Rowena's age sat behind one of the desks. Her hair was pulled back into a tight bun and she wore a modish brown and black suit with whorls of black braid.

"May I help you?"

"Yes. I've come to check on a patient."

"The name?"

Rowena cleared her throat, feeling more and

more ridiculous in front of this smart young woman. "His name is Jon."

The woman raised an eyebrow until Rowena was forced to admit that she didn't know his last name.

The woman smiled. "Well, lucky for you we only have one Jon in the hospital today, and you're certainly not the first visitor he's had."

Rowena's cheeks burned. The girl made it sound as if she was just one in a long line of admiring females. "I actually don't want to visit him; I just thought I would leave this . . ."

"Rowena! Er, Miss Buxton, rather."

She turned to find Mr. Douglas Dirkes lumbering toward her from a door in the back. "I'm so glad you came to visit. Our boy has been feeling a bit blue."

Our boy? She didn't think her cheeks could become any hotter, but evidently, she was wrong. "I didn't actually come to visit. I was just going to drop this off . . ." she tried again weakly, but he would have none of it.

"Of course you're going to go back and visit! After you've gone to all this trouble."

He offered her his arm and, giving him a resigned smile, she took it. The modern part of the hospital was quite nice. The windows reached almost floor to ceiling, bringing in light and air, and the tiles on the floor were clean and shining. Each patient had ample space, and she saw that several had screens around the beds to give them more privacy.

"How is he?" she asked, her throat suddenly dry. What if he was still unconscious? What was she even doing here?

"You can see for yourself," Mr. Dirkes said, waving his hand with a flourish.

The young man in question was sitting up in bed as a pretty, dark-haired nurse fussed over him. His golden red hair had been brushed and the nurse was cleaning up some shaving supplies.

Rowena's pulse quickened at her first look at the man lying in the bed. She'd known on the hillside that he was handsome, but she could not have known that he was simply the most beautiful man she'd ever seen. No, he wasn't classically beautiful, like Michelangelo's David, nor even conventionally good looking like her cousin Colin or Lord Billingsly. His appeal had to do with the way the sunlight lit up the mixture of gold and cinnamon in his too-long hair, or how glints of light seemed to come from the blue, blue shade of his eyes. His lips were too thin and the planes of his face sharp and well defined, but his entire being seemed to be lit from within and once again, Rowena's drab world was drenched in color. Rowena flushed when she realized she was staring. Thankfully, Mr. Dirkes filled the gap.

"I suppose introductions are in order, though that seems rather foolish, considering the circumstances. Lady Rowena Buxton? May I present Jonathon Wells. Jonathon Wells, this is Miss Rowena Buxton, the young woman who saved you from a fiery death."

"Oh, no. It was nothing like that." Ro felt her cheeks flush again.

"Save your breath, Miss Buxton. Douglas's version of the truth is the only one he cares about. In his story, you are the plucky heroine who saved the unworthy hero from a fate worse than death, though I have yet to figure out what's worse than death." He grinned at the nurse. "Thanks, Nora. You have a smooth touch."

The interaction made Rowena squirm inside, though the nurse just winked at him. She gave Rowena a sulky look as she took away the shaving bowl.

"So tell me, Miss Buxton, what would a *lady* like yourself be doing visiting the likes of me?" He stared at her frankly, his blue eyes cool.

Rowena gave him an uncertain smile, not sure whether she liked the way he said "lady." But before she could answer he continued.

"I'm sure you won't mind if I don't get up and bow, miss." He touched his leg, which she just now noticed was in a cast. "But this makes it a bit difficult."

"Of course not." She bit her lip, feeling ridiculous. "Not that I would expect you to bow anyway," she added quickly.

He raised a brow. "No?"

"No."

"I told Jon here what a brave woman you were to pull him out of the wreckage and wait with him for help," Mr. Dirkes put in.

Rowena squirmed. "I just did what anyone would have done."

"I doubt that, miss. He was a total stranger to you, and you are a well-born young lady. Not many in your position would have helped at all."

She wanted the floor to swallow her up. "But you knew where the plane went down. I'm sure you would have found him sooner or later."

"Not in that light." He turned to Jon, who looked as uncomfortable as Rowena felt. "Did I tell you dark was coming on and still she sat there with you?"

What was Mr. Dirkes trying to do?

"You owe her quite a debt of gratitude, young man," he continued.

"I'm sure you would have found me at some point," Jon ground out. His face was now the same shade as his hair.

Rowena's mouth dropped. Even though she'd said very nearly the same thing, he could at least have thanked her. Common courtesy alone should have prompted that.

She shoved the basket at him. "I brought you some goodies." Her face flamed. "In case you were hungry."

He gave her a patronizing smile. "Because they don't feed people sufficiently at the hospital?"

She gasped, half tempted to throw the basket in his face. Of all the rude . . . "No, because it was the nice thing to do."

"Ah yes. And the Buxtons are nothing if not *nice,* right, Lady Summerset?"

Rowena stared for a moment before drawing herself up to her full height. Evidently, this man had something against her family. Or thought he had something. At any rate, it had nothing to do with her. So, if she thought as they sat together on that hillside that he looked as if he might be someone she'd like to know, she'd been mistaken, that was all. It wouldn't be the first time.

She wrapped her breeding and manners around her like a cloak and gave both men a condescending smile. "Thank you so much for seeing me. I am so very glad to see you feeling so, *feisty* today." She handed Mr. Dirkes the basket. "I hope you enjoy these leftovers from our tea. I thought of sending a servant around, but then thought that perhaps it was my duty to see to it myself. Now having done it . . ." She twitched a shoulder delicately.

Jonathon crossed his arms and glared at her, blue sparks emanating from his eyes.

"Now, if you will excuse me, gentlemen. Good day."

She nodded to both of them, trying not to see the look of reproach in Mr. Dirkes's eyes. It certainly wasn't his fault that his young friend had turned out to be a disrespectful boor.

Head held high, she swept past the eavesdropping nurse, and the smart modern woman sitting at the desk, and out the door.

A range of emotions tugged at her, the first being disappointment. When she'd sat there on the hillside tending to the pilot, she'd gotten the feeling that he was somehow going to be important to her life.

But clearly she'd been wrong.

"You got a good price for the house, then, darling?" Lady Summerset sat in front of her dressing room table, trying to choose which jewels to wear for dinner that night. It always felt like a festive occasion when Colin brought his friends home. Especially Lord Billingsly or Kit Kittredge. Both were perfectly acceptable for Elaine, if the girl would stop acting like everyone's little sister and more like the coquette.

Lady Summerset riffled through the boxes that Hortense held with a judicious eye. She preferred to choose her jewelry before her dress instead of the other way around. The dress, after all, was mere silk and lace, while the jewels had taken thousands of years to attain perfection.

"I did. I do feel bad for the girls, though. They did seem so attached to their home."

She watched in the mirror as he paced the room behind her, looking over a sheaf of papers. She often told her friends that the secret to her successful marriage was her boudoir, and they laughed as if she were sharing a blue secret with them. Lady Summerset laughed as well, not letting them know that she was in deadly earnest. Most women decorated their boudoirs with lavish femininity, showing none of the restraint they presented in the rest of the house. Lady Summerset studied her husband for a year before redecorating hers and by the time she was done, it was one of the Earl's most favored rooms in the house, though he couldn't really say why. The room lacked any of the fussy accoutrements that other women's boudoirs seemed to collect, instead relying on plaid wool throws that looked as if they could be used without being ruined, and comfortable pillows covered with tweed and completely devoid of lace. Perhaps it was the perfectly comfortable buttery leather club chairs in front of the fire, or the silver ashtrays set about the room, that made the Earl feel as though he had permission to smoke in here, though he rarely did. It wasn't really a masculine room, but a room in which masculinity and femininity existed in such comfort and harmony that it lulled members of either sex to a peaceful sense of well-being. At any rate, it loosened the tongues of both her friends and her husband. In this room, and this room only, were she and the Earl able to let down their guard and become the partnership that ruled what was basically a small kingdom.

Lady Summerset pointed to her topaz and diamond gold collar and matching earrings. She had an ivory brocade skirt and tunic trimmed in ermine that would set off the jewels perfectly. That order of business done, she waved Hortense away and turned toward her husband.

"But don't you think those young women are better off here at Summerset? Your brother loved his girls dearly, but if it hadn't been for his unorthodox methods of child rearing, Rowena would have already made a brilliant match by now and you know it."

"He did bring them here for part of the season," Conrad told her defensively. "They spent most of their summers here."

"But not one holiday! I think he lost all sense of decorum after Christine died. Look how he moved that maid in to serve as the girls' governess." Her tone was leading and she watched him carefully.

Years ago, when she had originally gone to him with her knowledge, he had only wanted to know who had told her, not acknowledging that she could be helpful in keeping the whole sordid mess under wraps. But her mother had warned her that men would never understand just how helpful and necessary a wife could be—it was her job to be her husband's helpmeet, whether he desired one or not. It took years for the Earl to see what an asset she truly was. By the time he had, she'd already maneuvered herself into becoming one of his most valued advisors on all things both social and political. Only to herself did she admit that manipulation was not the same as power. If she had to manipulate Conrad to get what she wanted, instead of just demanding it outright, then she wasn't truly his partner.

The Earl took out a cigar and looked around for a cutter. Hortense handed him one and then melted back into the shadows. "I honestly thought the girl would have left by now. She wasn't brought up to be in service, no matter who her mother was," he said.

He sounded perplexed and Lady Summerset handed him a lighter. "Evidently, she is far more loyal than we first assumed, which is commendable, of course, but the longer she is here . . ."

"The more liable she is to discover our secret." The Earl puffed his cigar to life and stared into the fireplace. "If it gets out, it will follow our children and our children's children."

Lady Summerset gave her husband a grim smile, one that few people had ever seen. "Then we will just have to make sure it does not come out. When should we tell the girls about letting the London house?"

"I'm going to discuss it with Rowena and leave it up to her to tell Victoria."

The corners of Lady Summerset's mouth twitched and her husband gave her a rueful smile. "You're right, I'm being a coward. But I hate seeing the child sick and she always gets herself so worked up."

"I feel sorry for whoever marries that one," she agreed.

"Perhaps she will be the one who takes care of us in our dotage. She's an interesting little thing."

Lady Summerset didn't tell her husband that Victoria always made her feel uneasy with her bold remarks and birdlike mannerisms. She was a sweet child but so . . . different. "Would you like me to be there when you tell Rowena?"

Her husband shook his head. "I should do it myself. It was, after all, a business decision."

Her husband stood. "I'm going down to the stables to inspect the new polo pony before dinner." She held out her cheek and he kissed it.

"Don't be late for dinner, darling. And don't fret so over the girls. They will be fine. The young always spring back. And one way or another, we'll take care of that other little matter."

He patted her arm and left the room, worry still evident on his face.

"Hortense."

Hortense reappeared from the shadows. "Yes, my lady."

"Are you sure it was Prudence your friend saw Lord Billingsly with yesterday morning? I know that Rowena went to town with him after tea yesterday and the girls both have that dark-haired, white-skinned look."

Hortense gave her a decisive nod. "She was positive it was Prudence, my lady. She knows both girls."

Lady Summerset was dying to know who the friend was, but it was better not to ask. It gave Hortense too much power to know things her boss did not. And if this was true, and she had no reason to believe it was not, she had more worrying things to consider. Such as Lord Billingsly motoring about town with a lady's maid? Perhaps he didn't know she was a lady's maid? But how could he not, considering her clothing?

Hortense helped her dress and Lady Summerset noted that the jewels did indeed look lovely with the ivory brocade, but as she sat to have her hair done, her mind went back to the issue at hand. It was time to do more than make Prudence uncomfortable. "I think it's time for you to befriend the girl. Earn her trust. Keep your friends close, but your enemies closer, yes?" Lady Summerset glanced up in the mirror and Hortense smiled her assent. "Before we can figure out a successful way to make her leave, we have to find out who she is and what she wants. The staff, they dislike her?"

Hortense deftly wound a small section of hair around her finger and curled it. She pinned it in and then began on another one. "Yes, my lady. Her mannerisms are too fine for her to have been born to service and they sense the difference in her."

Of course there would be a difference. Blood doesn't lie. But then again, her mother was a nobody. There was no way of knowing when that side of her would come out. "Tell her she can wear her own clothes now. Make up something. The staff will hate her even more. And start some rumors, but do it in a way that can't be traced back to you. We don't want Mrs. Harper snooping about."

"What should I say?" Hortense asked, raising an eyebrow.

"How should I know?" Lady Summerset twitched a shoulder, suddenly irritated. "I'm sure you can make something up as well as I can. Use your imagination."

Hortense's features stilled as she put the finishing touches on her hair. Lady Summerset wanted to roll her eyes. Honestly, the woman was so touchy. She sighed. "I'm expecting a new shipment of kid gloves this week from Perrin. If you like, you may take your pick of last season's gloves." She watched her maid carefully. Pleasure lit up her dark eyes and the sharp angles of her face.

"Thank you, my lady!"

Lady Summerset knew that Hortense would save the gloves along with the other gifts she'd given her and sell them at a secondhand shop the next time they went to London. With the money she made from such sales, she would be fitted for several severely chic outfits from an expatriate French designer. Hortense would never be seen in Lady Summerset's castoffs. Oh, no. Lady Summerset had to admit she begrudgingly respected the woman for it.

"Thank you, Hortense. That will be all. Keep me apprised of how our little project is coming along."

CHAPTER
TEN

The dim hallway stood silent and dark like a tunnel, stretching out in front of her. Most of the gas lamps lining the walls had been extinguished, leaving the shadows long and ghostly. Victoria waited, hardly daring to breathe, listening with every fiber of her being. A delicious shiver ran through her. This was the most fun she'd had since coming to Summerset.

Once she had ascertained that all was quiet, she slipped back inside her room and picked up her typewriter box by the handle. She shifted her weight to the other side, trying to balance. Why did these things have to be so heavy? With her free hand, she settled a large leather pack over her shoulder. It held her shorthand book, her old course work from Miss Fister, several copies of *Botanist Quarterly Review*, paper, and extra candles. She wished she had something warmer to wear than her nightgown and dressing gown, but she hadn't wanted Prudence to get suspicious when she came to help her get ready for bed. She would start a fire when she got there.

Victoria tiptoed down the hallway, past all the family staterooms. If she could get past them without detection, she was free unless she ran into a night watchman. She wasn't even sure whether her uncle had them, but it stood to reason.

It had taken her a week of poking about Summerset's southern wing before she found the room she was looking for. The south wing of the home had been unused for several generations. Summerset had over one hundred rooms, but only thirty or so were in regular use. Another twenty were kept clean for large house parties, and the rest were barely maintained and only inspected on occasion for dry rot, leaks, or broken windows. Not even the servants went back there to clean, which made it perfect for her needs. When they were children, they had played hide-and-seek in the dusty rooms until Colin had fallen on a loose step and broke his arm, but Victoria still knew her way around.

She silently opened the servants' stairwell and paused. The faint sounds of voices, punctuated by quiet laughter, reached her from the bottom. Did they ever sleep? Her heart gave a pang and she wondered whether Prudence was down there, laughing with that young Susie she was always talking about. Maybe Susie had replaced her in Prudence's heart, she thought jealously.

Instead of going down, Victoria went up a flight and then exited at the next landing on the other side. This was the floor the young men were relegated to. Far from the girls on the other side. The lights were few in this hallway, but where she was going there were no lights at all. She'd brought a box of matches, but the fear of being alone in the dark on that side of the house coiled in her stomach. She now wished she'd never listened to Colin's ghost stories when she was in pigtails and pinafores. It didn't help that she was now walking through the hallway known as the statue gallery. Every few feet on either side of her, a niche, curving into the wall, held some new and terrifying statue. Even gentle St. Francis of Assisi glowed ghostly and pale in the moonlight.

At the end of the hall she took a right turn, leaving the spectral statuary behind. She came to a pair of ornately carved mahogany doors that curved sixteen feet toward the ceiling. They were so heavy she had to put down her things just to open them. Setting her candle in a niche in the wall that had been made for that very purpose, she unloaded the rest of her things. Then she would have to pack everything through to the other side and do the same. Or she could just leave the door open. When she'd first come back here, she'd been half afraid that it would be locked, sealing off the treasures in that part of the house. Fortunately, the owners had always been too arrogant to think that anyone would steal from them.

A blast of dank, freezing air rushed out at her as she pulled the doors slowly open. A loud creaking noise shattered the silence and her head jerked back stiffly. Beads of cold sweat formed on her upper lip as she waited for Colin, Sebastian, or that rather rude, handsome young man, Kit, to come out and demand to know what she was doing.

When that didn't happen she eased the door open inch by inch, her pulse spiking at every creak of the door. She would leave it open for her return trip, she decided. Her nerves couldn't take trying to open and close it again.

She gathered up her things and stepped into a part of the house that hadn't been heated in generations. It was the oldest part of the estate and she remembered that even as a child, it'd had a chill that the sun never warmed. The scent of the centuries pervaded the wing in the form of mold, damp, and dust.

It seemed as if the walk took forever, but she finally reached the room she'd decided on. Over the past week, she had brought in everything she had thought she'd need, from newspaper and wood for the fire to clean blankets and office supplies such as ink and pencils and blotters. It was easier to move around the house without arousing suspicion during the day, though the armload of wood had been nerve-racking.

She lit the lantern she had brought and the light relieved her with its glow—as long as she didn't focus on the ghostly shadows it cast along the walls.

The room had no doubt been the study of some austere kinsman from long past. It had been done in blues, long faded, with stern portraits of antecedents. She wondered which one had worked in the study and if he would disapprove of her presence. For surely it was a man who used the large, round desk in the center of the room and the inlaid filing cabinets on either side of the stone fireplace. The cold of the marble flooring seeped through her slippers and she hurriedly set her things on the desk and lit the fire she had already laid out, praying that the flume still worked.

She'd cleaned the room a little yesterday, hoping the scent of beeswax would overcome the scent of dust and damp that hung over the room, but her efforts hadn't even made a dent in it. On second thought, she rather liked it. She wondered what Nanny Iris would think of her room. She would probably say there weren't enough books, but she would like the knickknacks from all over the world.

The fire brought more light into the room, killing the last of the gloom and crackling cheerfully. After lighting a few more candles and placing them about the room, she looked about satisfied with her handiwork. Happier than she'd been in weeks, she took out her typewriter and set out her things on the desk. Now she had another secret—a secret place. Her own place where she could work and study in peace away from Prudence's and Rowena's prying eyes. Tonight, she wanted to organize her things and study her quarterlies. Perhaps if she worked really hard she could pass the entrance exams and go to college. Or something.

Suddenly there was a loud creak from the hallway and Victoria froze. Seconds spun on forever as she strained to hear over the sound of her own racing heart. It was the fire. Or a timber settling. The house was over three hundred years old. All houses make noises.

She glanced at the doorknob but couldn't see a lock on it. It was fine. This was her home. Well, her family home anyway. Ghostly ancestors wouldn't hurt her, she was blood.

Don't think about blood.

Her breath started coming faster and she closed her eyes. If she didn't calm down, she would have an episode and die here. How long would it take for them to find her body? No. Instead of concentrating on who or what was outside the door, she would concentrate on breathing. One, two, three. Tiny breath. One, two, three. Tiny breaths.

"Victoria?"

The scream ripped out of her chest shattered the still air. She opened her eyes to find Kit staring at her, horror written all over his face.

"Good God, woman. Do you want them to find you? Do you know what kind of scandal that would cause?"

She shut her mouth and sunk into the chair behind the desk. Closing her eyes, she began her careful breathing again.

"Victoria?" His voice came closer and had a worried edge to it. "Are you quite all right?"

She shook her head and kept breathing until she felt her body calming, her lungs opening. Then her eyes popped open and she stared at him accusingly.

"You followed me!"

He stared back at her, his eyes wide. Then he smiled. "I thought you might be sneaking off to do something fun." He looked around the room. "What are you doing, anyway?"

She tilted her nose. No matter what she said, he

was going to tease. He was just that sort and she was not going to let him poke fun at her secret. "I'm looking for the rabbit hole."

He blinked. "And have you found it?" he asked, his voice amused.

"Not yet. But I remain ever hopeful."

"And what would you do if you found it?"

"Fill it up, of course. Wonderland seems a nasty sort of place."

He laughed at that and began wandering around the room, looking at this and that. He didn't mention the typewriter or her office supplies and she liked him the better for it.

"What are you doing here, really?" he asked.

Something wistful in his voice stopped her from saying she was building a time machine. "Haven't you ever wanted a place where you could truly escape from everything? Where you could just read and think and be silent?"

He didn't answer for the longest time. Instead, he busied himself putting another log on the fire and poking at it with the poker.

"Most people don't want to be alone with their thoughts," he finally said.

"Maybe they have boring thoughts."

He stared at the flames and Victoria arose from the desk to join him. The heat felt good. She supposed she should probably feel uncomfortable standing in her nightclothes, unchaperoned, talking to a young man who was practically a stranger, but she didn't. She would be ruined if anyone discovered them here this way, but she didn't care about that either.

"Don't you think everyone thinks their thoughts are interesting?" he said, his brow furrowing. "That was confusing."

"I understood."

"And, to continue along those lines, I really don't care if people's thoughts are boring, except when people with boring thoughts are compelled to share those thoughts with others, namely me."

Victoria looked at him. His voice had taken on a world-weary tone that she disliked, as though he'd searched the world over for something of interest and had been sorely disappointed. "So what do you care about, Mr. Kit?"

"I suppose this is where I should say my mother, or Britain or the poor, shouldn't I? Or whatever else is in fashion. But my mother is a fright, patriotism is deadly dull, and I can't do anything about the poor."

She frowned. "Don't say anything that isn't true. There's no one here to impress."

"Are you saying I couldn't impress you if I tried?" He glanced over at her, a smile playing about his lips.

She stared back at him. "You don't know me well enough to know what would impress me. I think you're smart enough not to bother."

He laughed at that. "Well, I know what would

impress most debs, but you aren't like most debs. Most debs wouldn't be in an abandoned part of an old castle teaching themselves to type."

She said nothing.

"So back to your original question. What do I care about? I suppose I care about my friends. I care about being amused. I care about finishing my exams well enough so I don't disgrace my mother and because once I do, I shall get a sizable annual trust and will be able to travel at will. What do you care about, Miss Victoria? Most young ladies only care about dresses, balls, and making good marriages."

She picked up the extra blanket and wrapped it about her shoulders. Then she sank down to the worn, dusty rug in front of the fireplace. "Oh, I like dresses well enough, but balls are boring and I'm never getting married."

He laughed in disbelief and sat down next to her.

"Oh, you don't believe me, do you? Well, no matter. I know what's what, and there is no marriage in my future. I discovered early on that the most interesting women who lead the most interesting lives either don't marry at all, or marry quite late in their lives. I'm going to travel and read and have all sorts of adventures." She thought of Nanny Iris as she said this. That was exactly what she wanted to do. She wondered what Nanny Iris would think of a man like Kit.

"And what does typing have to do with that?"

"A girl should be able to make a living, don't you think? What if I get robbed by marauders in Istanbul? I could work in an office until I make enough money to go on to Cairo." She didn't tell him that she wanted to work as a botanist. That secret was just too close to her heart to share freely.

His eyes widened. "You do have it all figured out, don't you?"

He sounded amused and she shifted. "You don't believe me, do you?" she asked again.

"I believe you believe that. You maybe even mean it. I just know how insistent family can be, and your aunt and uncle are going to marry you off posthaste. Not before Elaine or your sister, so you may have a few years of freedom yet. Poor Sebastian."

"Poor Sebastian? What do you mean?"

"Your aunt has already chosen him for Elaine and his mother concurs that they would make a lovely match. Elaine and Sebastian are jolly friends and have been for years, but neither of them are the least bit interested in the other in that way. But I predict it will only be a matter of months before their engagement is announced. The combined wills of Lady Summerset and Lady Billingsly is a force unto its own."

She snorted. "Poor Lainey. But my aunt and uncle can't make me do anything I don't want to do," she said, though she was less convinced than she sounded. Wasn't Prudence in the servants' hall against her will?

"I don't think you even believe that." His voice was kind and she gave him a sideways glance.

"Well, not about marriage anyway. Arranged marriages are against the law, and I am very well aware of my rights. My father made sure of that."

"Don't tell me you're a suffragist?" he said in mock horror. "God save me from a well-meaning suffragist."

"Of course I'm a suffragist," she snapped. "All thinking women are."

He laughed, but it no longer sounded kind. "I find them as boring as the simpering deb. They may pretend to want suffrage, but if a well-born man asked for their hand in marriage, they would give up their political views in a heartbeat."

She stood. "Which just shows me with what little regard you actually hold women. At least suffragists care about something. I've always found those who are bored of everything to be the most boring. Now if you will excuse me, Mr. Kit. I think I should be going back to my room."

He looked surprised at her reaction and she didn't blame him. She was surprised herself. She remembered how passionate her father was about everything—politics, art, science, music—and it saddened and angered her that he had died, while a young man, with everything ahead of him, sat here insisting that there was little in the world of interest.

He put a placating hand on her arm, the warmth of his fingers transmitting itself through the thin cotton of her nightdress. "I didn't mean that. I don't mean half the things I say, really."

He sounded surprised and Victoria stopped. "Then why do you say them? You say things as if you believe them."

"Probably because it's easier than trying to figure out what it is I really believe." His voice sounded rather shocked and she laughed.

"It's much easier to pretend you're bitter and don't care than to admit you're just lazy."

The corners of his lips twitched. "You have a point. But you are right, we should be going."

They banked the fire and put the screen up. She was almost sorry their tête-à-tête had ended. She'd rather enjoyed herself. After lighting their candles and putting out the lantern, they walked quickly down the dark hall. It wasn't nearly as frightening as it had been before.

They reached the main door. "You can find your way from here, can't you?" he whispered.

"Of course. I was practically raised here."

He nodded as she slipped out the door. "And you are wrong, Miss Victoria."

She paused. "How's that?"

"There is something I find very interesting and intriguing."

She waited for a moment, her heart speeding up.

"You."

Victoria awoke the next morning to the sound of Susie lighting a fire in the fireplace. Last night's nocturnal wanderings seemed like almost a dream in the morning's light and she wondered whether she hadn't imagined her conversation with Kit. Did he really think her intriguing?

She raised up on one elbow, watching Susie. The girl seemed to be having a tough time of it this morning and Victoria could see her hands shaking. "Are you feeling all right?"

The girl startled, dropping the kindling on the floor. "Oh blast," she said, looking at the mess on the sheepskin rug. "Oh, I'm sorry, miss."

Her cheeks went so ashen that Victoria thought she was going to faint. "I'm sorry. I didn't mean to startle you." She kicked her covers off and went to the girl, shrugging into her icy dressing gown. "Here, let me help."

"Oh no, miss. I'll get in trouble . . ."

"Oh, nonsense. No one is going to find out. Why isn't Prudence here this morning?"

"Hortense, Lady Summerset's lady's maid, told her that she wasn't supposed to be starting your fires in the morning, that it was my job."

Victoria deftly wadded up some paper and lay it in the fireplace, then added kindling. Then she reached for a match and lit the paper. "There, that should do it."

"How did you know how to do that?"

"My father taught me when we went camping in Switzerland once. Is it your job to start the fires in the morning?"

Susie nodded. "Yes, miss. I start all the ladies' fires and the hall boy starts the men's fires. But then Hortense told me not to, that Prudence would be doing it for you and Miss Rowena."

Victoria leaned back on her heels. "Then she told Prudence that you were supposed to be doing it? That doesn't make any sense at all."

She helped Susie pick up the rest of the kindling on the floor, her mind puzzling. Why would someone do that? As a cruel joke? "Tell me, how does Prudence get along with the rest of the servants?"

Susie's face puckered up as if she were unsure of what to say.

"It's all right, Susie. I need to know."

"Well, I like her just fine. And Cook does, too, as much as Cook likes anyone. But everyone else thinks her sort of uppity because of her fine manners and such. She acts like she's never been in service before, so all the maids want to know how she managed to get a good position. So they play little tricks on her and such."

Victoria stood and wrapped her dressing gown tighter, and she shivered in spite of the fire crackling in front of her. Susie turned away and added more wood.

"What is this Hortense like?"

Susie's mouth turned downward, hiding her slightly bucked teeth. "Oh, no one likes her at all, but the mistress dotes on her so no one dares cross her."

"Do she and Prudence get on?"

"They didn't at first, but now Hortense is acting more friendly like. But Prudence doesn't know her like the rest of us do."

Victoria tilted her head, wondering. Perhaps Susie could be useful in figuring out the mystery behind Mrs. Tate. "Susie? Can I ask you a few more questions before you go? I promise you won't get into trouble."

The girl nodded, but her pinched face told Victoria that she wasn't comfortable about this turn of events. Before the girl could change her mind, Victoria ran and snatched the quilt off her bed, then wrapped it about their shoulders. When she sank to the ground in front of the fire Susie had no choice but to follow. "Have you lived in Summerset your whole life?"

"Yes, miss."

"What kind of strange stories did you hear about Summerset when you were growing up? There had to have been a few. Every old castle has them."

The girl's face grew slightly pale. "Oh, I don't

listen to anything bad about a place, otherwise I'd never be able to go in. Then what good would I be?" she demanded. "I crawl all over the house in the early dark morning, lighting the fires and such. But there are some good scary stories about the outside of the place."

Susie's thin face contained the excitement of one with a good story to tell, and it took little encouragement from Victoria for the tales to spill out of her.

"You know of the kissing well, right? Well, let me tell you, that does not work . . ."

"Susie!"

"Not from experience! My mum. She found a young girl strung up there on the rafters above the wheel when she was just a girl herself."

"That's horrible! But that isn't a story, it truly occurred. What else?"

"Of course it happened!" Susie spit indignantly. "Did you think I'd lie to you?"

After being assured that Victoria didn't, Susie continued, while Victoria realized that this girl sitting so close to her—and smelling of body sweat, washing powder, and soot—was probably just a few years younger than she was. Why hadn't she ever noticed before? She'd seen girls younger than Susie in poverty before, girls with two, sometimes three children, and they had always broken her heart. But it never occurred to her that her aunt and uncle could be perpetuating the problem. She had completely lost the thread of the conversation, but then something Susie said caught her attention again.

"Wait . . . did you say that they found another young woman?"

Susie nodded, her eyes wide.

"At the same place?" Why hadn't she heard about this? Victoria wondered. A real-life mystery right here at Summerset and no one had told her!

"No. You weren't listening! She was found in that old chapel by the bend in the creek where they found Lady Halpernia." Susie clapped her hands over her mouth.

"Oh, no. It's all right. You won't get into trouble here between us."

Susie looked unconvinced as she climbed to her feet. "I've got to get to Miss Rowena's room or she's going to freeze. But thanks for letting me get warm. I feel much better now."

"You're welcome, Susie. And we don't have to tell anyone we talked about this, right?"

Susie shook her head and was gone.

But talked about what, really? Victoria started out trying to learn some rumors about her grandfather and ended up getting treated to a good old-fashioned horror story instead. Where could she find more information? Cairns might know something, but he would rather die than repeat something negative about the Buxtons, even to a Buxton. She would go to Colin or Elaine and then perhaps to the only person she could think of who could give her some answers.

Nanny Iris.

Morning came early in the servants' quarters. Early and cold, to the cruel sound of Mrs. Harper's short, jarring knocks on the door. And if that didn't roust one quickly enough, the housekeeper would open the door on her way back down the hall, letting in a draft that seemed to sweep in from Siberia itself. Prudence quickly learned that another five minutes of sleep wasn't worth it.

"I'm up!" Prudence called rather crossly to Mrs. Harper's knock. And she was, too, up and already in her chemise, staring at the clothes in front of her. As she fingered the soft, warm wool of the dress she'd laid out, yesterday's conversation with Hortense played through her mind.

After lunchtime, Hortense had told Prudence that she needed to speak with her. Prudence waited until she was done with lunch and they walked up to the family rooms together. Taking her arm in an uncomfortably intimate way, Hortense had whispered to her, "That work you do in the mornings? The scrubbing of the pans? The rest of the labor they give you? As a lady's maid, it is not your job."

"What?" Prudence hadn't understood her meaning.

"They resent you, you see."

When Prudence asked why they resented her, Hortense had laughed. "We are different from the rest of them, yes? We are more or less friends with our employers. Educated. This is our choice. It is not as though we do not have other choices."

Prudence found the older woman fascinating and strangely threatening. Her hair, her severe yet rich clothing, even her very Frenchness, seemed exotic. "Other choices?"

Hortense had tilted a shoulder. "I could have married. Opened a dress shop. Many things. But what do I want of that? Here I am paid well, my efforts are valued, and I do not have to answer to a man. Lady Summerset and I get on very well, even when she is vexed. And trust me, I have ways of reminding her how much she depends on me when she does treat me badly. I do not always follow her instructions to a T. Sometimes I even do just the opposite of what she asks and then pretend ignorance. Other mistresses have made it clear they would love to have my services and have offered generous sums of money for me. I am . . . how do you say? A union of one." She'd smirked.

Prudence had hesitated over her next question, but she needed to know the answer. "Aren't you afraid or, you know, scared of being alone?"

The other woman looked at her in amazement. "*Non*! I *dream* of being alone! But then you are young and you must be careful now. The others will try to make trouble for you. If you have any problems, just come to me, yes?"

Prudence had nodded. "Thank you," she'd said carefully, for she trusted Hortense only one shade more than she trusted Lady Summerset herself.

"And Prudence? Wear a different dress. You see what I am wearing? It is up to you girls to decide what you wear, not Mrs. Harper. Surely you have other clothing? The things you are wearing now?" The older woman made a spitting noise with her mouth and moved away.

So now Prudence stood, a big decision in the form of a dress lying in front of her. Was Hortense right? What would Mrs. Harper or Mr. Cairns say? But on the other hand, if Hortense was correct, what right had they to say anything? Her pulse raced as the truth dawned on her. She was Rowena's and Victoria's servant, *not* a Summerset servant. Why hadn't she realized that before? When guests had stayed overnight in their London home, they'd occasionally brought servants, and no one had any authority over the servants except their employers. Relief came over her as she finished dressing, in her pretty black mourning dress. She would comply with Summerset rules, of course, but they were not in authority over her. Only Ro and Vic were!

She went downstairs, her new knowledge lightening her step. So the servants didn't like her, poor devils had to stay here under the combined iron fist of Cairns and Mrs. Harper. She, thankfully, did not.

The young men had left late yesterday afternoon, and even though they'd stayed for only a few days and she'd barely seen them, the house now felt as if all the air had been sucked out of it. Victoria had told her, in a rather animated way, that they were all returning for the holidays. Prudence wondered whether that meant Lord Billingsly, as well. Her heart skittered at just the thought of him. She twitched her shoulders, annoyed with herself. What was it about him that made her feel as if she'd melt every time she saw him? Was it his ever-so-slightly crooked smile? The sound of his laughter as it filled a room? Or was it the way he looked into her eyes as if he wanted to know every thought and feeling she had ever had on everything? Her attraction to him grew every time she saw him, which only strengthened her resolve to avoid him should he return. She knew very well what happened to servant girls who had gone wrong. Her mother had been very opinionated on the subject, and Prudence's work with the poor had also imparted grim lessons. Of course, girls went wrong with all sorts of men, but dallying with a man from the upper classes only assured there would *not* be a fairy-tale ending. She knew there was no future for her and Lord Billingsly. The romantically lurid tales of poor maids marrying dukes only happened in the penny dreadfuls. In reality, the scandal of such a marriage usually ruined any chances for happiness such a couple might have.

Prudence hurried down the stairs and into the coffee-scented warmth of Cook's domain. Cook grunted and shoved a cup of tea at her. This must mean she liked her, as everyone else had to get her own tea. Prudence wasn't sure why this crotchety old woman had taken to her, but figured it had something to do with Prudence's habit of helping Susie whenever she could. Cook sniped at the scullery maid constantly, but always held back a bit of extra pudding from the employer's meals and slipped it to Susie on the sly.

Prudence smiled in gratitude and was putting her apron on to help Susie when the bell board rang.

"Someone's up early," Hortense said with a yawn. Automatically, everyone looked to the board to see who it was. The personal servants, Hortense, Prudence, and Katz, the Earl's valet, were usually the only ones called this early. The footmen also arrived early in case a member of the family wished to go riding before breakfast.

Andrew nodded toward Prudence, his characteristically friendly smile brightening his face. "That would be you, I'm afraid."

Checking the board, she realized it was Rowena. What was she doing up so early? And why was she ringing a bell for her? Her good spirits dissipated at her sister *summoning* her to her side.

Folding the apron back up, she set it to one side and picked up a silver tray. Cook had already readied it with a pot of tea, cups, and the cream Rowena couldn't do without. Then Prudence headed up the stairs she had just come down.

Rowena was still in her nightclothes when Prudence walked in. Her long, dark hair hung down her back in thick waves. She paced the room, agitation evident in the set of her jaw. She pounced the moment Prudence entered the room.

"You must go to town for me."

Without answering, Prudence set the tea tray down on a small gilt table near the bed. Something about Rowena's tone bothered her. She sounded almost demanding. "I brought you your tea" was all Prudence said.

"I'm afraid I was very rude to someone and you need to deliver a note for me right away. It might be too late already."

Prudence raised a brow. Rowena had yet to say please. The girls had begun to fall into an easy routine: Prudence helped them dress as she had always done, and picked up their rooms for them, but she thought she did so mostly to stay as far away from the other servants for as long as

211

possible. But now Rowena was coming perilously close to treating her like a true maid.

Rowena ignored the tea and didn't bother to say thank you. Instead, she held an envelope out to Prudence. "Here. Take this to the hospital and make sure it is delivered to Jonathon Wells. He should still be there. If not, try to find out where he is, and if he's left town, get his address and I can send it by post."

Prudence looked at the envelope. "Do you know what time it is?"

"Yes, yes. It's early. Have one of the footmen drive you."

Prudence frowned. Rowena's lovely complexion was sallow, and dark circles bruised her eyes. While Victoria seemed stronger here at Summerset, Rowena had become more listless and indifferent to what Prudence and her sister were doing. She slept a great deal and rarely looked at Prudence when she spoke. Whatever this was all about, it evidently meant a great deal to her. Prudence hadn't seen her this worked up in weeks. So in spite of her resentment at Rowena treating her like a servant, she took the envelope without argument. "I'll do it after I see to Victoria," she said. "Now drink your tea. Shall I tell Cook you are ill and would prefer to have your breakfast brought up on a tray?"

Rowena gave her a half smile and sank into a chair next to the table that held her tea, as if she couldn't stand any longer. "That would be nice, Prudence, thank you. I am so very tired. I feel as if I could sleep for a week."

Prudence slipped the envelope into her pocket as she left the room. Victoria was already dressed and reading in a chair when Prudence tiptoed into her room. Prudence smiled. "What are you doing up and dressed so early?"

"Susie helped me dress. Any chance you have my tea?"

"I'm having Susie bring up your breakfast. Rowena doesn't feel well and I have to run an errand for her."

Victoria stood. "What's wrong with Ro?"

A note of anxiety undercut her voice. After Sir Philip's sudden death, Prudence didn't blame her.

"I think she's just tired." *And missing her father.* Prudence felt sorry for Rowena and the burdens she carried, but she couldn't help but feel, at the core of her being, that exhaustion and grief shouldn't be enough to explain away how Rowena had begun to treat her. Her stomach twisted. *Or to excuse it.*

Victoria chewed on her lip. "I'll make her feel better."

"I know you will."

Prudence made up the bed quickly after Victoria had left and then hurried to her own quarters to get her coat and hat before heading back down to the kitchen.

Andrew was still drinking his tea and eating his breakfast when she arrived.

"Could you please take me into town? Rowena has an errand she needs me to run," Prudence asked him.

"*Miss* Rowena," corrected Cook from the stove.

"Miss Rowena and Miss Victoria will be eating their breakfast in Miss Rowena's room." She turned to Susie. "Can you please take it up to them while I'm gone? I should be back by the time they need to dress, but if not, could you please draw their baths and ask them if they need anything?"

She heard an intake of disapproval from one of the housemaids, but Susie blushed with pleasure at the responsibility.

Prudence's chest grew tight. How sad it was that something as inconsequential as this small task could give someone so much pleasure.

"Do the girls need anything special?" Cook asked.

Prudence shook her head. "Whatever you're making for the family is fine."

Andrew clapped a chauffeur's cap onto his head and shrugged into an overcoat hanging on a hook. With the change in cap and coat, he had transformed himself from a footman into a driver. "I'll get the motorcar ready and meet you outside the door."

Minutes later she was in the auto, with Andrew

tucking a driving blanket around her legs. "You don't have to do that," she protested.

"That's too nice of a dress to ruin with mud spatters," he said.

She cast a glance at him as he drove. He was young, probably not much older than Rowena, with kind green eyes, a strong chin, and non-descript brown hair. His attractiveness, and he was attractive, lay in his overall kindly nature and sense of humor. He would look more comfortable in farm clothes than in the brilliant red of his livery, she realized.

"Did you grow up around here?" she asked to break the silence.

He nodded. "My parents own their own farm closer to Hollings than Buxton. Mr. Cairns was visiting some family out that way and noticed how tall I was. I wasn't sure if I wanted to go into service, but with three older brothers, there was little room on the farm. This will tide me over for the time being. I hope to own my own land someday. What about you?"

"What about me?" Prudence was evasive.

"The whole staff is talking about you. Your manners are too highborn to be servant class, and since you stopped wearing uniforms, your clothes are too nice as well. You're a real mystery girl."

A sudden image of Lord Billingsly telling her she was a mystery popped into her head. She couldn't tell him who she was, but somehow she felt safe with Andrew. Did that mean she was more comfortable with the servant class than with the Buxtons and their friends? Did it really matter? "My mother was Victoria and Rowena's governess. Before that she was a housemaid at Summerset. But none of that mattered in London. We girls did everything together and Sir Philip raised me as one of his own."

"So why are you their lady's maid now?"

"Because the Earl doesn't want to show hospitality to a girl who is obviously from the lower classes." Bitterness crept into her voice. "Rowena told him I was Victoria's companion and their lady's maid in order to keep me with them."

Andrew snorted. "Not sure I would like that at all."

"I don't," she admitted. "But Rowena and Vic had just lost their father. They didn't want to lose me, too."

"Why didn't you all just stay in London?"

Prudence shrugged. "The Earl insisted. Apparently, Sir Philip didn't own our home, the Earl does."

Andrew whistled. "That's tough on you."

A thought niggled. "You won't gossip about this, will you? I would hate for Ro and Vic to be the topic of the servants' conversation."

He laughed. "Nothing you can do about that. It

seems they don't have much else to do except gossip about their betters."

"They aren't their betters," she said shortly.

"You know that and I know that, but they certainly don't seem to. Nah, you have nothing to worry about from me. I'll keep your secrets."

He smiled at her from across the seat and she smiled, her heart warming. She felt as if she'd found another friend, someone she could relate to. They reached the edge of town. "Where do you need to go?"

"The hospital. Do you know where that is?"

He nodded and turned down a narrow street. She took the envelope out of her pocket, wondering about it. How did Rowena know Jonathon Wells? Was he an old friend? She'd never mentioned him before.

"Do you know a Jonathon Wells?" she asked Andrew suddenly. If she'd been a real servant, perhaps she wouldn't have asked, but she wasn't. She was Rowena's friend, her sister, and she was concerned.

Andrew frowned, trying to think. "I've heard of the Wells family, of course. Everyone has. But I don't know a Jonathon."

"Who are the Wells family?"

"Gentry. Landowners. Their estate abuts the Buxtons'. I guess long ago the Buxtons gave the Wellses a sizable piece of land for service in some war. There's bad blood between them now, but I'm not sure why. I never paid too much attention. I was always more concerned with the price of sheep and cattle." He gave her a sheepish smile and she decided she liked him very much.

"That sounds reasonable to me. I shouldn't like to concern myself with gossip about the highborn when taking care of my own family."

He nodded and pulled up to the front of the hospital. "Here you are. Do you need me to wait for you?"

"No, you can go ahead and go to the post office. I will walk around a bit until you get back."

They agreed to meet in front of the hospital in an hour, which would give Prudence plenty of time to walk over to the library and back after she dropped the message off. She wanted to talk to that old man again.

"May I help you?" asked a young woman sitting behind an enormous desk when she walked in. In the corner a young man sat on a bench, reading a newspaper.

"I have a message for Mr. Jonathon Wells," Prudence told her, holding out the envelope.

The secretary took the envelope. "May I have your name, please?"

"Oh, the message isn't from me. It's from . . . my friend."

The woman smiled. "I need to know who delivered it as well. Policy."

Prudence felt foolish. "Oh, I'm sorry. Prudence Tate."

She heard a rustle of papers behind her.

"Would you like to wait for a reply?" the woman asked as she got up from her seat.

"Oh." Rowena had said nothing about that. "Yes. I suppose so."

"You may take a seat."

Prudence turned and moved to the bench. A young man with dark blond hair was staring at her quizzically and she wondered whether she'd forgot a button or had something on her face.

"Did you say your name was Tate?" he asked.

She nodded. "Yes. Prudence Tate." Then she realized what his question could mean and her heart sped up.

He stood and held out his hand. "Mine is, too. Wesley Tate. I thought I knew all the Tates in this area, but I think I would have remembered you."

She faltered, her manners deserting her for a moment. This young man might actually be her kinsman. "My mother and my father were born here," she said, regaining her voice. "So we might actually be family. My father died when I was a baby. I don't even know his name but my mother's name was Alice. I don't know her maiden name."

His brows shot up over eyes so blue, they looked as if they had been torn from the sky. A

219

lump formed in her throat. Like her mother's eyes. "Wait. Do you mean your mother was Alice Tate?"

"Did you know her?"

He froze, his hand still in hers. "No. I didn't know her."

Prudence's heart fell. The look on his face was very similar to the librarian's expression when she had mentioned her mother. But then Wesley continued.

"She moved away when I was just a baby." He smiled and squeezed her hand. "My father is her older brother. That would make us cousins, cousin."

Prudence had to look away, she was so overcome by emotion. Gratitude and hope mingled with relief. She did have family. She had always thought of Ro and Vic as her family but in the last few weeks, everything had turned upside down and she no longer knew who her family was. With Rowena so remote and treating her more and more like a servant, Prudence felt more alienated than ever. Maybe now she had another chance at a real family.

She took a deep, trembling breath. "It's very nice to meet you, Wesley. I can't even tell you—" She stopped as the emotion caught in her throat. He led her over to a bench.

"Here. Let's sit down. You look as if you're about to faint."

She sat gratefully. "I'm not usually the fainting type."

They sat, their knees pointing toward each other. "The family rarely mentions your mother. All I knew is that she moved to London when she was seventeen. I didn't even know she had a child."

Prudence frowned. "You didn't know she had a baby? That's strange. I was born here. We moved to London after my father died." Her breath suddenly sucked in as the realization hit her. The look on Wesley's face told her it had dawned on him as well. Tate was her mother's maiden name. And it was Prudence's name as well. Her cheeks grew hot.

Her mother had never been married.

She didn't even try to pretend that he didn't understand as well. She looked down at her hands trembling in her lap as her world tilted and then righted itself. She tried to fold her fingers together but they wouldn't quite connect. She swallowed. "I see. That would explain why my mother never took me home for the holidays."

She gave a wobbly smile and he reached over and captured her hands. "You didn't know this?" he asked.

She shook her head. "No. I never even suspected. There was no reason to. She rarely spoke of her family or my father, but I don't know, I just never thought to ask. I had a family and a happy childhood. It never occurred to me that anything was amiss. She died several years ago, so I can't even ask her about it."

Her mind raced, wondering whether Sir Philip knew. Maybe he felt sorry for her mother and that was why a maid was given the job as governess to his children. And who was her real father? She shifted. For that matter, who was her mother? The woman she knew—staid, firm, and careful with her only child, had lied to her for her whole life. Prudence might never know who that woman really was. Anyone who could tell her was gone.

"You had a happy childhood? So your mother married again?"

She looked up at her cousin, whose blue eyes had darkened with concern. Concern for her? Or concern over a family scandal? Her cheeks reddened to have someone she didn't even know, a stranger, know about her shame. "No. We lived with the Buxtons. Sir Philip and his daughters. My mother was their governess."

His eyebrows raised so high, they almost disappeared into his hairline. "Blimey."

She closed her eyes a moment, afraid she was going to faint again. She had no idea what she was supposed to do with this new knowledge. There was just too much to sort out and she didn't want to do it in front of someone she had just met, even if he was her cousin. She swallowed and changed the subject. "What about you? Your father must be my uncle, then?"

He seemed to understand her desire to change the subject. "It would seem so. He runs the livery down the street. He and my mum scrimped and saved for years to start their own business. It wasn't easy but they did it."

Prudence could hear the pride in his voice and she felt a pang of longing. Not too long ago she also had been proud of her family and who she was. Now she knew even less about her family and herself than she did before.

"They wanted something to pass on to us, but even they understand that cars are the way of the future. My older brother had already left to work in a factory outside of town and my little sister works in the office there, so I'll probably be the one who gets the livery. It's a good thing I like it well enough."

"Were there any other siblings besides my mother and your father?" Prudence's hunger for information had increased tenfold.

He grinned. "There were six altogether and tons of cousins. You can't throw a rock in this town without hitting a Tate. Getting together for Christmas was like organizing a fair, though we don't do it like that anymore. Too many of us."

"Sounds wonderful," she said. And it did, though Christmas with the Buxtons had always been wonderful, too. Sir Philip had showered everyone with gifts, and Prudence had received just as many as Rowena and Victoria had. She blinked away the tears. What was wrong with her? How sentimental she had become. "So what are you doing here? Everything is all right, isn't it? Not that it's any of my business, of course. I didn't mean to presume."

"No, of course not. I'm just visiting Gran. She took a little tumble and broke her foot. The nurse is cleaning her up a bit so I'm waiting." He looked at her, his eyes wide. "She's your grandmother, too, you know."

Prudence's heart felt as if it would beat out of her chest. "I've never met her."

The woman came out the door with a note in her hand. "Here is the return message for Miss Rowena Buxton."

Prudence stood and took the note. Slipping it into her pocket, she turned to her cousin. "It was really nice meeting you. I would love to see you again, if it wouldn't be too much trouble. There is still so much I would like to know."

"I can imagine." His blue eyes were sympathetic, then he brightened. "Say, would you like to meet Gran right now?"

Prudence backed up a step and shook her head. "I don't know if that's a good idea. Obviously the parting wasn't a good one, and now we both know why. I don't want to upset her, especially with her being down and all."

"Huh. A little broken ankle couldn't keep her down, could it, Nora?" He addressed this last part to the young woman who had returned to her seat behind the desk.

The woman snorted in answer.

He lowered his voice. "We wouldn't have to tell her who you are. We'll just say you are a friend of mine. You don't much look like the picture I've seen of your mum, except for a bit around the mouth. I think it would work. Wouldn't you like to meet her?"

Prudence took a deep breath. Her mother's mother. "Yes. I think I would."

The young woman looked up from the desk where she obviously had been eavesdropping. "Your Gran is finished with the nurse now, if you want to go in."

Wesley looked at Prudence, who nodded.

They walked through the doors and into the main room of the hospital. The scent of sulfur and lemon hung heavy in the air, and for a moment Prudence wondered which of these screens was hiding Rowena's Jon. But then she forgot everything as they approached an old woman lying in a narrow white bed. Her face had that soft, blurry look that comes when a stout woman grows old and loses all her plumpness. Other than the sharp blue of her eyes, Prudence saw little of her mother in this old woman.

"Thought you'd got tired of waiting and left me

here to suffer all alone, just like the rest of you heathen young ones." The woman's voice was brusque, but the glance she shot Wesley was soft, and Prudence knew that whatever she said, this particular grandchild was a favorite.

"You must be talking about my ungrateful siblings and cousins, because I would never leave my sainted grandmother alone." He paused a moment and then grinned. "Someone needs to protect the nurses."

His grandmother snorted and he winked. Drawing Prudence forward by the arm, he turned again to his grandmother. "And look, I brought a friend to meet you."

"I noticed that, but was ignoring it because I couldn't believe a grandson of mine would bring a special girl to meet his grandmother while she was lying on her back and couldn't be properly intimidating."

"I'm sure you will find a way. Grandmother, this is Prudence. Prudence, this is my grand-mother, Mildred."

The old woman fumbled at the small table until Wesley handed her a pair of small wire spectacles.

"It would be nice to meet you, dear, if I didn't feel like I was at such a disadvantage. What is your last name? My grandson evidently doesn't know how to make proper introductions."

Her eyes took in Prudence's clothing, hairstyle,

and carriage in one shrewd glimpse. Prudence faltered as she tried to come up with a last name. "Buxton," she said quickly, without thinking. "Prudence Buxton."

The still silence coming from the bed spoke louder than any words. For a long moment, no one said anything and Prudence's chest tightened.

"You look like a Buxton," the old woman finally said. "All that dark hair and those green eyes. Been the downfall of many a town girl." Her voice was bitter, but then she shook it off with a distasteful shiver of her gray head. "I heard you girls came home to Summerset after your father died. What are you doing hobnobbing with a boy like my grandson? Isn't he a bit beneath you?"

"Don't worry, Gran. It's not like that. We're just friends." Wesley cast Prudence a frown and she smiled weakly.

She hadn't meant to say Buxton. It just popped out. What a muddle. Her grandmother must think she was Rowena.

"In my day, girls were friends with girls and boys were friends with boys. But your generation thinks they can change the world, so I guess this is no different. But mark my words, no good comes from such friendships." She glared at Prudence.

"I think much good can come of it," Prudence said, stung. "If I weren't friends with your

227

grandson, I never would have been able to meet you."

The old woman's lips twitched. "I see you got the Buxton silver tongue. Some of your class think they deserve to have whatever they want because they're wellborn, but you Buxtons get what you want because you can talk people into it. No matter. You will all do what you please. Now off with both of you. Wesley, please try to remember that you can act like a gentleman even if you weren't born one."

She leaned back and closed her eyes and Wesley leaned forward and kissed her on the cheek before taking Prudence's arm.

He didn't speak until he had escorted her outside into the crisp autumn air.

"What did you do that for? She's going to find out the truth eventually."

"I'm sorry. It just popped out."

Wesley took out his pocket watch and checked the time. "I have to get back to the livery stables. Would you like to come for supper some time? I'm sure my father would like to meet you."

"Are you sure about that? I'm the"—she choked on the word—"bastard daughter of a fallen woman. If the family never mentions my mother, it's obvious they want to forget the shame she caused them."

"Why don't you let me talk to them first? Discreetly, of course. Then I'll send you a message to come for tea or dinner. I would like to give my family the benefit of the doubt. After all, *you* aren't to blame for the circumstances of your birth."

After her cousin had left, Prudence sat on a bench in front of the hospital to wait for Andrew. Her throat ached from holding back the tears. She wondered who her father was and how much of her mother's story was true. Was her father really dead? And did any of it really matter?

She was so engrossed in her thoughts that she hadn't realized that Andrew had pulled up with the motorcar until he honked the horn at her.

She climbed into the seat, blushing.

"You looked as if you were a million miles away."

"I felt like I was a million miles away," she admitted. "I was actually thinking of my family."

Andrew pulled the auto back onto the dirt road. "You said your mother was a servant at Summerset. Does that mean you have family around here?"

Prudence hesitated, wondering how much to tell him, as he smiled at her warmly, encouragingly. What would he think if he knew she was the illegitimate daughter of a maid? "I actually just met a cousin for the first time," she finally said. "He was at the hospital to visit my grandmother, whom I also met."

"How wonderful! What did you think of them? Sometimes I think it would be fine not to know who some members of my family are."

"It was interesting." She smiled. "But my cousin was very kind. I'll be meeting with him again, I hope."

"That's good for you, then."

She looked over on hearing the stiff tone of his voice. He stared straight ahead, his jaw set. Could he be jealous? Because the London Buxtons had avoided most formal society, none of the girls had learned the first thing about attracting a man. Flirtations and coquettishness were completely foreign to them. Prudence's mother had been too straightforward to teach them such things, although, Prudence reflected bitterly, her mother obviously knew something about attracting men, if not keeping them.

She quickly cast thoughts of Andrew out of her mind. Her goal was to stay at Summerset only as long as she had to—she couldn't let herself get attached to the abbey, or the people who resided and worked within its walls. She hoped that she, Vic, and Ro would be returning to their London home, where they could pick up their lives as best they could.

Though what kind of life that would be, she didn't know.

Andrew cleared his throat. "I was wondering if you would like a tour of Buxton on your next afternoon off? If our afternoons fall on the same day, that is."

She glanced at him, torn. She didn't want to risk growing close to Andrew, but, for now, she couldn't deny how much she truly longed for a friend. Then Lord Billingsly popped into her mind. She immediately shook the image of his dark eyes out of her head. He would never, could never, be her friend. Such a friendship would bring only pain to his family. If nothing else, her time at Summerset had taught her that. Amazing, really, that she'd lived all of her life without really knowing what it meant to be the daughter of a maid. Now she had to come to terms with being the illegitimate daughter of a maid. "I would like that very much," she said. "And you don't have to worry about the afternoons off. I can take an afternoon off whenever I want to, so just tell me when yours is."

"You can do that? That must be nice, not having to beg Mrs. Harper for it. How about next Thursday, then? The holidays start the week after that and Summerset will be overflowing with visitors. We'll both be busy."

She smiled at him as they pulled up to the servants' entrance. "That sounds grand."

And it did. Spending an afternoon with a young man sounded like a treat compared to being cooped up in the kitchen or lying on her bed, reading.

Or thinking about where her mother's lies began or ended.

Rowena snatched the message out of Prudence's hands with barely a thank-you. The last few days she had become obsessed with her behavior at the hospital. Whatever had possessed her to act as if Jon and Mr. Dirkes were beneath her? She sounded as snobbish as her aunt or any of the other horrid dowagers who possessively guarded their status. She kept thinking about the look in Mr. Dirkes's eyes.

What would her father think about her behavior?

She waited until Prudence had left the room before opening the envelope.

Dear Miss Buxton,

You have nothing to apologize for. My own behavior left something to be desired and I am sure I deserved much worse than the dressing-down you gave me. Douglas also gave me quite the tongue lashing and I have come to realize that I must make it up to you. I will be leaving the hospital today and would be honored if you could meet me in the dining room for tea tomorrow afternoon at the Freemont Inn, followed up by a short outing with me and Mr. Dirkes. We would be properly

chaperoned, so no need to concern yourself about that. No need to reply. If you
don't show up, I will understand.

Sincerely,

Jonathon Wells

Rowena pressed the note to her breast for a
moment before she realized what she was doing.
Of course she wouldn't go. She would post a
short note telling him that such a gesture was not
necessary and that if they had both forgiven each
other for their rude behavior, nothing more need
be done.

On the other hand, refusing his attempt to
apologize might be seen as rude. Wouldn't it be
much better to accept, be very proper at tea, and
then have nothing further to do with him? After all,
she really should show him that not all Buxtons
were ill-mannered snobs. Yes. That was what she
would do. She didn't need to go anywhere with
him. Just having tea would be enough.

She awoke early the next morning, surprising
Prudence by being awake and digging through
her closet, looking for something to wear. Just
how much black could one girl have? She felt
ashamed, reminding herself exactly why her
wardrobe was filled with black. Her father had
only been gone a month and here she was
complaining because she had to wear black.
Perhaps she shouldn't go at all?

No, her father wouldn't want her to become a hermit. He deplored the mourning customs that kept young people from enjoying their lives. When her grandmother died he had refused to put them in deep mourning at all.

So she would go.

"What are you doing?" Prudence asked from behind her.

"I'm looking for something to wear, but I don't have anything appropriate." She gave Prudence a look of desperation.

"Well, if you told me what you are looking for, I might be able to help," Prudence said, her voice reasonable. Rowena hated when someone was more reasonable than she was.

"Oh, bother! I don't know. If I knew, I could find something."

"What are you doing?"

Rowena gave Prudence a sidelong glance. "I am going into town for tea and then going on a short drive. Maybe."

Prudence didn't ask with whom, and Rowena was grateful. She didn't know whether she could articulate what it was about this young man that made her so nervous and excited all at the same time. Certainly, Lord Billingsly or Kit didn't make her feel this way. Maybe it was because she'd seen Jon looking so helpless and vulnerable. She felt as if she knew him on a level on which she had never known any other man.

Prudence pushed her back into a chair. "You sit. Let's see what we can come up with. Now, where are you meeting him for lunch?"

Rowena frowned suspiciously. "How do you know I'm meeting a man?"

"You don't have to be Sherlock Holmes to figure that out. I took a message to a young man yesterday and today you are going out to tea and a drive, and you're all flushed and excited about it."

Rowena's cheeks burned even hotter. "I'm meeting him at the Freemont Inn. Father would take us there sometimes—we would stop for tea when we were riding. It's nice but not too terribly grand."

Prudence brought out a crisp white cotton blouse with a high lace neck and fitted sleeves. She laid it on the bed next to Rowena and then paired it with a walking skirt of dark maroon wool and black braid. A black riding jacket had ruffles at the cuffs, a double row of ruffles down the front, and a flounce under a deeply nipped waist. Even Rowena couldn't get away with forgoing a corset with this ensemble, and she knew it would flatter her. It would show off her slender figure without looking coquettish and be appropriate for both tea and whatever activity would follow. "It's perfect. Thank you, Pru."

"You can thank me by telling me all about it later. Promise?" Rowena nodded. "Now go have a bath," Prudence told her. "I'll brush out your wool coat. It's far too cold to go out with just a jacket."

Rowena nodded and was soon soaking in the giant white tub, wondering exactly what it was she thought she was doing. Her little sister was practically sick with grief and Prudence was stuck in the kitchen washing pots and pans and God knew what all, while she was running off to tea with a young man she didn't even know. She closed her eyes against the tears that were welling up. She hadn't done anything to keep her uncle from selling their home. For the last month she had sunk under a never-ending grayness that discolored her every thought and mood. She knew she should be up and taking care of things, but had fallen under a spell of inertia that made it difficult for her to get out of bed in the mornings. The only times the lethargy had truly abated were that afternoon she had watched over Jonathon and their visit in the hospital. She just wanted to feel normal again. Was that so terrible?

She allowed Prudence to wrap a giant Turkish towel around her and brush her hair until it was smooth. They didn't speak. Rowena was half afraid that Prudence was angry with her. She had every right to be, after all, but she didn't want to talk about it. Not today. She knew they would have to talk sometime soon, but today she just wanted to live in the moment, escape from her grief and the crippling burden of her responsibilities—and broken promises—to Vic and Pru.

Prudence dressed her, pulling the corset laces until her waist was as small as a child's. Then she did her hair, her fingers deftly curling, pinning, curling, and pinning as if she had been trained in France.

"Where is Victoria?" Rowena asked, frowning. It was already almost time for luncheon and she hadn't seen her little sister at all.

Prudence shrugged. "Susie helped her dress this morning and told me to leave her be for the rest of the day. She didn't look as if she were going out, but she had that mysterious expression that she gets when she has a secret."

Rowena shook her head. The only secrets she could manage right now were her own. "She'll be fine. Still, will you check to see if any of the horses are gone? I will make sure she hasn't gone to town when I have the driver take me in."

Prudence nodded and then cleared her throat. "I won't be here next Thursday. I'm taking the day off."

Rowena looked up. "So now you have secrets, too?"

Prudence smiled ruefully. "No. You just haven't asked. If you must know, I am going to spend the afternoon with Andrew."

"Who's Andrew?" Rowena asked more sharply than she intended.

"One of the footmen, actually."

"Oh, Prudence." Rowena hadn't meant to sound so disappointed, but she was shocked. She never thought of Prudence in relation to a young man, and if she did, it was a young man more like the ones Rowena had met. Rowena's cheeks flushed at her own pretentiousness. "I didn't mean that the way it sounded," she put in quickly. "I was just wondering about Lord Billingsly, Sebastian. He seemed very interested in you."

Prudence put down the brush and comb, her manner stiff. "Your hair is finished, Miss Rowena. Would you like anything else?"

Rowena turned, her stomach wretched. "Don't be like that, Prudence. I didn't mean it like that, at all."

"Lord Billingsly is not a possibility for me, Rowena," Prudence said quietly. "Perhaps your father was optimistic in believing that things were changing between the classes, because it seems to me that in places like Summerset, things are very much the same. Andrew may be a footman, but he is a very nice young man and remember, I am nothing but the daughter of a maid turned governess. And now, as *you* well know, I am a lady's maid."

Prudence spoke these last words matter-of-factly as she left the room and Rowena sat frozen. Then tears came to her eyes. She sat at the dressing room table, unable to look herself in the mirror. After a few moments, she stood up and snatched her coat off the arm of a wing-backed chair where Prudence had set it. She didn't care that she would be early to town. She couldn't stay here one more moment.

Victoria's room was still empty when she passed it. Cairns hurried to have the auto brought around for her as soon as she ordered it. Her father may have detested having an army of servants and spoke often against the sense of entitlement it brought, but it certainly was handy, Rowena thought.

From beneath her lashes she covertly studied the young man driving her. He only said "Yes, miss" and "No, miss" to her, and Rowena wondered what he had said to Prudence to make her want to go on an outing with him. Did they talk and laugh naturally? Prudence loved to read. Did this young man have a hidden passion for books? Did they discuss politics or music? How could she have said "Oh, Prudence," as if seeing a footman was something to be ashamed of? Andrew faced straight ahead, his mouth set. He looked nice enough, with blunt, simple features, but nothing special. But maybe he wasn't showing her the side that Prudence saw.

Restlessly, she asked him, "You know where

the Freemont Inn is, don't you?" She hated the way her voice sounded so peevish and cross.

"Yes, miss."

She turned away and fell silent. Evidently, Prudence possessed some charm that she didn't. Or perhaps he was just being smart. She recalled what Prudence had said earlier that day, about the classes—that nothing was going to change. Perhaps Rowena herself was a part of the problem. Would Jonathon think that way? Who was he, anyway? Nerves bounced around in her stomach and she felt crosser than ever. She hated feeling like this.

"What time would you like me to pick you up, Miss Buxton?"

She blinked, realizing they had stopped in front of the inn.

She waited to answer until he had leapt out of the car and came around to open her door. "I will get my own ride home, Andrew, thank you. And don't worry about your outing with Prudence. She can take the days she needs."

He stared at her, his eyes carefully blank. "Yes, miss. Thank you, miss."

She flounced out of the motorcar, feeling at a disadvantage. She hadn't meant that she would give Prudence the days off, but that Prudence could have whatever days she needed. That they were Prudence's days, for goodness' sake. She had a feeling she'd been misunderstood.

Taking a deep breath, Rowena smoothed her skirt and went into the inn, hoping that she wasn't too early. Mr. Dirkes was sitting alone at one of the tables and Rowena's heart fell with disappointment, but she put on a smile and approached him, her hand outstretched. "Mr. Dirkes, how wonderful to see you again."

"Good afternoon, Miss Buxton. Jon will be down in a moment. Have a seat."

She sat down at the table, her spirits lifting.

"Please, call me Rowena. How is Jon feeling? I was worried that he would be too tired for tea today. He did just get out of the hospital."

"Oh, no. He is a trouper, that one. Can't keep him down for long. That's why I wanted the lad to go into business with me."

"And what kind of business do you do again, Mr. Dirkes?" she asked politely. She didn't really care that much; her eyes kept flicking over to the staircase that led up to the guest accommodations.

"I'm in the motorcar business, but I'm expanding into aeroplanes. Right now, Jonathon does all the testing. He does a fair bit of the planning, too."

She turned her attention to him. She found him infinitely more interesting when he was speaking of Jonathon. "Don't you think they're just a fad? My uncle certainly does, though my father wasn't sure."

"Ah, the peerage hates to see such sweeping changes. Most of them find it too much to cope with. I'm hopeful that you younger lot will adapt better."

Her father had said the very same thing.

"And no, I don't think they are just a fad," he continued. "I think they are going to revolutionize travel, the shipping of freight and warfare. My compatriots think I'm either a genius or a madman."

"Ah, going on about the future of aeronautics again? Are you trying to bore our pretty guest to death?"

Even with a cane, Jonathon Wells had come up behind her so silently that she hadn't heard him. He smiled down on her and her breath caught and held as she stared up into his strikingly blue eyes. The sounds around her—the muted conversation of the other diners, the soft clinking of the dishes and silverware, and the muffled street noises from the front—were drowned out by the deafening beat of her heart in her ears. She smiled back, and for the first time since her father had died, she had an unwarranted urge to giggle at how ridiculously giddy she felt. She lowered her eyes for a moment to gain her composure, then met his gaze.

"I am so glad to see you up and about, Mr. Wells. Thank you so much for inviting me to tea."

He smiled, showing straight, even teeth.

"Thank you." He tapped his leg with his cane. "As you can see, my leg is actually healing quite quickly. And please, call me Jon. Mr. Wells sounds like my father. And I am going to call you Rowena, if I may. After what we've been through, Mr. and Miss sound ridiculously formal."

"Adapt or die! That's what I always say," Mr. Dirkes put in, waving his arms about. His curly black hair was streaked with silver and his moustache was waxed stiffly against his lips. He looked quite mad, but in a nice sort of way.

"You may call me Rowena." She paused for a moment and then added, "Jon."

He smiled and inclined his head. A maid in a crisp black uniform wheeled a tea cart out to them and poured their tea. The men spoke excitedly about this and that, and Rowena forgot her manners, so interested was she in their conversation.

"But don't you think at some point the labor unions will have their day in court? I know the last lawsuit was a devastating loss, but I think it will either be overturned or answered with another lawsuit, which will set precedent."

Mr. Dirkes sat back in his chair and blinked. "I daresay we've been boring you?"

Jon's lips curved, showing dimples just above the corners of his mouth. "I don't think so. She seems very knowledgeable on the subject, maybe more so than you. What do you always say?

243

Adapt or die? I think this is one of those instances. Perhaps Rowena is one of the *New Women* you hear so much about."

Mr. Dirkes held up his teacup in salute. "Touché."

Rowena gave Jon a rueful smile at his teasing use of the derogatory term *New Woman* before answering. "My father was good friends with Ben Tillett, so labor issues were a normal topic of conversation. And if you're asking if I'm a suffragette, I would have to say yes, of course. Women certainly should have the vote, but I also think we should be educated equally in order to use our vote most effectively, don't you agree?"

Jon raised his brows. "I do agree. I just didn't know that anyone of your class did. For instance, it's hard to believe that your uncle would feel that way about independent women."

She lifted a shoulder. "I can hardly speak for my uncle. We've never really touched upon the subject."

"I'll bet not."

Rowena frowned. The tenor of their tea had suddenly changed. Instead of being lighthearted, Jonathon now looked as if hc had bitten into something unpleasant and couldn't quite get the taste out of his mouth.

Mr. Dirkes took up the plate of scones. "Would anyone else like a scone?"

Both Rowena and Jonathon declined and Mr. Dirkes looked disappointed. "Well, if you two are done with your tea, perhaps it is time for the second half of our afternoon. Are you still up to it, my boy?"

Jonathon nodded, but he didn't seem as thrilled about the prospect as he did earlier. There was no doubt that Jonathon's demeanor toward her had changed, but what had done it? Her mention of her family? Wasn't that what had upset him so last time?

They walked out of the inn and got into Mr. Dirkes's green Silver Ghost. She sat up front with Mr. Dirkes, who drove, while Jonathon lounged with his injured leg in the back. She was conscious of his eyes on her and she hoped her hair hadn't come undone and that her hat was on straight. She very much wanted to touch her hat to see, but didn't want to let on that she was concerned with her appearance. Her neck flushed under his gaze. Unable to stand it, she turned in her seat. "So where are we going, Mr. Wells?" she asked above the sound of the motor.

"So we're back to being formal again, are we, Lady Summerset?"

"I'm not Lady Summerset! That's my aunt. I'm not the daughter of an earl. I'm the *Honorable* Rowena Buxton, but we don't really want to carry things to that extent, do we, Mr. Wells?"

He smiled at the little lesson in peerage

etiquette. "Jonathon! And no, Rowena, we do not. It's much easier if we are simply Jonathon and Rowena, isn't it?"

Her cheeks heated at the way he'd spoken, as if they had an intimate relationship. She nodded, unable to answer, but something had lightened between them again and Rowena was able to relax and enjoy the drive.

The wind bit her cheeks and lips, and she wished she had thought to bring netting to protect her face. No doubt she would be all chapped and windblown before they reached their destination. The trees stood stark and bare against an ominously gray sky. "I do think it's going to snow," she said to Mr. Dirkes.

"It feels like it will, but maybe it will hold off until your flight is over."

Rowena's stomach sank. "My what?"

"Now you've gone and spoiled the surprise!" Jonathon said, leaning forward between the two seats.

Just then Mr. Dirkes pulled off the road and into a field. Rowena's eyes widened as she saw several men working on an aeroplane in the middle of the field.

"So what do you say, Lady Rowena?" Jonathon's voice was thick with challenge. "Are you ready to take an aeroplane ride?"

She sat staring at the machine as it got closer and closer. "I'm not a lady," she said, swallowing.

He laughed as Mr. Dirkes helped her out of the motorcar.

"Are you sure you're up to this?" Mr. Dirkes asked.

She opened her mouth to say *No, no, I am NOT,* but then she noticed he'd addressed the question to Jonathon, not to her.

"I guess we'll have to see, won't we?" He laughed and cast a challenging look at Rowena.

She lifted her chin and firmed her shoulders. There was no way she was going to back down now. She felt as if her sex and her class were being tested.

She followed a limping Jonathon over to the aeroplane. "Don't worry," he called over his shoulder, "this one has been tested before. It's usually quite safe."

Rowena tried to not show her alarm as they got closer and closer to the machine. It looked rather small to take two perfectly normal-sized people into the sky. "What kind is it?" she asked, trying not to show her nerves. The men servicing the plane smiled at one another. Evidently, she wasn't successful at hiding her fear.

"It's a Bristol T.B.8H. We built it for the Royal Flying Corps, you see," Mr. Dirkes answered.

"What's this part?" She touched the side of the plane, trying to keep talking. Maybe if she kept talking, she would forget the terror turning in her stomach.

"The fuselage."

One of the men had handed Jonathon a clipboard with a list on it, and he suddenly turned serious as he hobbled around the plane and began checking things off. Rowena realized she hadn't seen that particular look on his handsome face before. She'd seen him flirtatious—with the nurse at the hospital—and angry, with her, but this expression was completely different. Rowena found it thrilling to observe someone so wholly engaged in his work, and she was so busy watching that she forgot her fright.

Suddenly Jonathon nodded. "Load her up!"

One of the men took her arm and Rowena realized that meant her. "Oh, I'm not sure this is a good idea," she said to Mr. Dirkes as they guided her toward the front seat of the aeroplane.

"Oh, don't worry, he's quite good," he assured her.

"But the first time I met him he was crashing!"

"That was an experimental plane!" Mr. Dirkes had to yell to be heard above the propeller of the aeroplane, which had just started up.

Jonathon was suddenly behind her, so close she could feel his breath on the back of her neck. With one hand he took off her hat and then she gasped as he began taking the pins from her hair.

"What are you doing?" She whirled around but couldn't escape, as she was trapped against the fuselage of the aeroplane. He kept picking pins from her hair as if he were grooming an animal. His brow was furrowed in concentration, but she saw the humorous glint in his eye.

Her hair finally tumbled down and she reached up and gathered it up in one hand so she could see. He held up a small leather cap with goggles attached to the top. "You have to wear this for safety. It will protect your eyes and keep your hair from flying about."

"Oh. You could have told me."

"But it was so much more fun my way." He grinned.

What cheek! The man was positively insolent. But she found herself smiling back at him. She took the cap and the hairpins. Then, before she could react, he turned her back toward the plane and put his hands around her waist. She gasped as he lifted her up onto a stepladder that had been brought out for the job. She climbed into the passenger seat of the aeroplane, her legs numb with fright. Dropping the hairpins quickly into the pocket of her coat, she then twisted up her hair and tucked it inside her blouse before settling the leather cap over her head. After she settled down into her seat, he buckled a harness around her. She couldn't look at him. Not with the imprint of his hands on her waist still hot beneath her corset.

One of the men helped him up into his seat behind her. She turned her head to see. The men moved out of the way and her mouth got dry as they made arm movements to Jonathon, who was busy checking instruments. Her heart started beating rapidly as she realized that there was no turning back now. Mr. Dirkes yelled something to her but she couldn't hear it.

"What?" she asked, leaning toward him.

"Adapt or die!"

She smiled and nodded and tried not to show she was on the verge of fainting. Suddenly the machine lurched forward and Rowena gripped the front of her harness. She might have screamed but she had no air left in her lungs. The engine whined as they went faster and faster. She wanted to close her eyes, but she didn't want to go to her death with her eyes closed. Her father had called her his brave one. She wondered what he would think if he could see her now.

Adapt or die.

She was being jarred so badly by the wheels of the aeroplane on the field that by the time they actually lifted off the ground it was almost a relief. The wings dipped this way and that and for a moment she thought they were going to plunge back down to the ground, but they soon leveled off and began climbing steadily into the sky. She looked down and caught her breath at how rapidly the earth beneath was falling away and shrinking. Then they entered the low clouds and everything turned gray and foggy. Her heart pounded and her mind had trouble grasping what was happening, it was so far-fetched, so unreal.

She was flying.

"How can you see?" she yelled above the sound of the motor.

"I can't," Jon yelled back.

That didn't make her feel any better. Suddenly the mist surrounding them turned into a shimmer of silver. The minute particles of light sparkled and danced around her like a microscopic ballet. The pirouetting glittered brighter and brighter until suddenly they were floating above the clouds in a totally different world. A world of infinite sunshine, where vast miles of blue spread out all around them and below, white and gray pillows of clouds drifted.

Rowena's heart soared along with the plane as they dipped and played. Jon didn't try to speak to her and she was glad, for there was absolutely nothing to say about the breathtaking spectacle that surrounded them. Tears gathered in her throat and eyes. She had never really thought of heaven, and her father, with his love of free will, had rarely spoken of his own beliefs, but up here she could feel the presence of God. Who but God could create such a wonderful vista? And who but man, created in his image, could build a way to view it?

Rowena twisted around in her seat to yell something to Jon, but couldn't think of anything that would even come close to how she was feeling. His mouth softened into a gentle smile and he nodded at her, understanding the extent of her awe.

It seemed as if they'd flown on forever before he turned the plane, the wings dipping down low on one side, almost touching the clouds. Her heart beat wildly at the maneuver but she felt excitement stirring in her veins. What it must feel like to be in control of such a machine, to be able to do this whenever one desired!

Slowly he flew the plane downward and they disappeared into the clouds again, the mist chilling her to her bones. When they finally came out underneath the clouds, her heart sank at the grayness of the world below. But now she knew what it was really like, that there was a place where the sun always shone and mist glittered below.

As they flew, Rowena could see the town of Summerset as well as Thetford, a neighboring town off in the distance. Jonathon flew over a ridge of rolling hills. Houses, some big and some small, dotted the fields beyond and Rowena gasped when she spotted Summerset. For a moment, she was frantic to have him turn around, but then she realized that no one could possibly see her. She laughed at the freedom it gave her and twisted around to see Jon. He winked at her from behind his goggles. She grinned and nodded and they swooped down lower. Soon they were flying just above the turrets of Summerset, so close she could see some of the outside servants, staring up at them in wonder. She spotted a lone woman walking down the drive toward the house and she wondered whether it was Prudence or Victoria. She twisted to get Jon's attention and then pointed. In response, he turned the plane and swooped lower, and coming up on the woman, he waggled the wings above her. She looked up, her hand shielding her eyes, and Rowena could see it was Prudence.

All too soon he turned the plane toward the hills and flew back to the field. Rowena closed her eyes, terror once again churning in her stomach. She remembered what happened the last time Jon had flown a plane and she could almost hear the snapping of the trees and the shattering of the wings.

A gentle jarring told her that they had landed safely and she opened her eyes as he navigated the plane back to the gigantic tin building and the men waiting outside.

Her ears were still roaring after the engine cut off and she wondered whether she would ever be able to hear normally again. But she didn't care because it was worth the sacrifice.

Jonathon was helped out of the plane while another man helped her out of her harness. Rowena didn't hesitate when Jonathon lifted his arms to her. He held her against his chest briefly before setting her gently on her feet.

She whipped off her leather cap, laughing. "That was the most wonderful thing I've ever done!"

His hands rested lightly on her shoulders and they stood only inches apart. A smile played about his lips as his blue eyes searched hers. Rowena wanted to launch herself into his arms to thank him for the ride, for helping her to see, for just being here with her. She laughed at her thoughts, embarrassed, but she met his eyes, more carefree and brave than she'd ever felt in her life.

For a long moment she thought he was going to kiss her and something in her hoped that he would, dared him to, almost, but then he pulled away and linked his arm with hers.

He smiled sideways at her as they walked away from the aeroplane. "Weren't you afraid?"

For a moment she felt a twinge of disappointment, but was still too elated from the ride for it to last. "I was terrified! But it was so lovely up there. I wanted it to last forever!"

Mr. Dirkes was walking toward them. "That went off perfectly. I think the RFC is going to be royally pleased."

Rowena looked up at Jonathon. "Is it hard to learn how to fly? How long have you been flying?"

"For the last year. And it isn't too hard. The hardest part is what to do in emergencies. Sometimes all you can do is hold on."

Mr. Dirkes chuckled. "Luckily, you haven't had to do that too often."

"You've crashed other times before?" Rowena pressed, anxious. "Besides the time I found you?"

"The crash you witnessed was my fourth, though two of them were takeoff mistakes. I never even got off the ground. But planes are much safer nowadays."

"What happened with the last crash?"

"It was an experimental plane. Aeronautics is still a young science, and not all our experiments work the way we think they will."

"Are there any women pilots?" she wondered.

Both the men laughed and she tensed. "Not many English ones," Mr. Dirkes said.

"Why ever not?" she asked.

"I don't think there has been any interest as of yet."

"I should like to learn," she said, trying to muster as much dignity as she could.

Both men laughed again. "You made that decision moments after your first flight. Perhaps you should think on it a bit," Mr. Dirkes said, shaking his head.

"But I must say, you did make an excellent copilot," Jonathon said.

Jonathon smiled tiredly and Rowena was

instantly contrite. "I'm sorry. You must be exhausted. You should be resting."

"I am rather knackered," he admitted.

"Let's get you back then, and I will take Miss Rowena home," said Mr. Dirkes.

When they reached the inn, Jonathon took her hand.

"I hope that surprise helped you to forgive my boorishness at the hospital. I would very much like to see you again. Perhaps we can take another flight together."

His eyes were the faraway blue of the sky she had seen above the clouds. "I'd like that very much," she said, her heart giving a little leap.

He squeezed her hand and limped slowly toward the inn. When he disappeared behind the door, Rowena felt as if the world that just moments ago had been bright and full of promise returned to the dingy gray it had been before she'd seen it.

Breathlessly, she skipped into the house, a story at the ready in case anyone asked where she had been and who the strange man was who had driven her home.

She handed her coat to Cairns, who'd entered the Great Hall moments after she had. How he never missed anything that happened within the house was beyond her. No doubt he had a network of spies at his disposal. "Good evening,

Cairns. It's quite bitter outside. Could you have Prudence bring some tea to my room?" She would tell Prudence every blasted thing and beg her forgiveness for her earlier blunders. Life suddenly felt too beautiful for her to have misunderstandings with the people she loved.

"Your uncle has requested that you go straight to his study as soon as you come in, Miss Rowena."

She froze. Had her uncle discovered something? How? "Oh, how long has he been waiting? I lost track of time, you see." She watched his face, hoping to garner a clue as to how dire the situation was.

"I'm not quite sure, miss." His face remained impassive, but she detected a note of disapproval.

"I'll just go to my room and tidy up, I must look a sight. You may have my tea taken directly to Uncle's office."

She unbuttoned her gloves as she hurried up the stairs. What could her uncle possibly want with her? A sense of foreboding filled her. What if he already knew she'd had tea with two strange men in town? And why wouldn't he? Her uncle had many contacts in town.

She burst into her bedroom, trembling with all she had seen and done and yet anxious over her uncle's summons. She needed to clean up before she saw him, but where was Prudence? Then she remembered how they parted that afternoon and reality came crashing down on her. Oh. She sat heavily on the edge of a chair and pressed her hand against her forehead, once again over-whelmed by her own inability to make things right.

She eyed the bell ringer to call Prudence, but hesitated to use it again. Prudence was already angry with her. Calling her like a maid, again, would only further irritate her. On the other hand, she did need help. Her uncle was waiting for her and wasn't that what sisters were supposed to do? Help each other?

She was saved from ringing the bell, however, when Prudence came through the door. Her pretty features were impassive, neutral, and Rowena flushed with a myriad of emotions running through her: anger, guilt, annoyance, and most of all regret, because a couple of months ago, Prudence would have been the first person she would have run to after today's experience. No one could listen as well as Prudence could.

"My uncle wants to talk to me. Could you help me get ready? I don't want to be late."

Prudence nodded but said nothing.

"I'll just change into a fresh blouse and redo my hair, I don't want to keep him waiting."

Her voice must have betrayed her anxiety, because Prudence gave her a worried look.

"Do you think he found out where you went?" she finally asked, brushing out Rowena's hair.

Rowena shrugged, trying not to feel so much relief that Prudence still cared enough to worry about her. "I'm not sure. Maybe." She paused, but then couldn't help herself. She had to tell someone . . . "I went flying in an aeroplane today!" she burst out. "For real!"

Prudence's mouth fell open. "I thought you were just going to tea?"

"We did. He took me after. In his aeroplane."

"You went to tea with someone who has an aeroplane?" Prudence's voice squeaked at the end of the sentence and Rowena laughed. This felt good. Almost like it used to. The thought both gladdened and saddened her. *How things have changed,* she thought.

Then comprehension widened Prudence's green eyes. "That was you who gave me such a fright! I thought the world was coming to an end!" Prudence finished pinning up her hair and handed Rowena a wide belt for her skirt. "And now your uncle wants to see you? That does not bode well."

Rowena shook her head. "No. It doesn't." She stood awkwardly. In the old days she would have given Prudence a hug and apologized for her behavior and all would be well between them. Prudence had one of the biggest hearts of anyone she had ever known. But now . . . now there was so much to apologize for, and what good would an apology do if nothing changed afterward?

Prudence picked up the discarded blouse. "You'd best go see what your uncle wants."

Rowena hesitated, but couldn't think of anything to say that would fix things between them. "Yes, of course. Thank you."

Dejected, she made her way to her uncle's study and took a deep breath before knocking on the door. When a voice bade her enter she did so. She wasn't sure she'd ever been in this particular room. No doubt it had been strictly off-limits when they were all children. The study, however, suited her uncle exactly. Spanish leather paneled the walls, lending the room a rich, serious air. She recognized the French lines of the dark furniture, and several austere Dutch masterpieces graced the walls. The odd object in the room was a small grand piano inlaid with delicate mother-of-pearl tucked away in one corner.

She curtsied before her uncle and sat on the leather sofa he indicated. He sat across from her and crossed his legs.

"Do you play, Uncle?"

He looked startled. She waved a hand toward the pianoforte and a rare smile crossed his face.

"I used to play. I still do on occasion, though I'm seriously out of practice now. Do you girls play? I'm afraid there was much I missed out on when you were growing up so far from Summerset."

A timid knock on the door signaled their tea

and, after pouring some for herself and her uncle, she took a grateful sip, letting the pungent flavor firm her resolve not to let her nerves be overwhelmed this time. She had done nothing wrong, after all, and she was clearly of age.

"I have some news to discuss with you, but first feel it prudent to inquire as to who dropped you off at Summerset this evening and why he wasn't introduced?"

She was ready for that one. "That was one Mr. Dirkes. He owns a motorcar factory in Surrey. He also manufactures aeroplanes for the Royal Flying Corps. I ran into him and a friend in town and had tea. It was getting dark, and I felt it unwise to walk home alone and so persuaded him to offer a ride. I would have introduced him, but he was anxious to get back to Surrey." She took another sip from her tea, hoping she hadn't sounded too rehearsed.

Her uncle nodded. "I've heard of Mr. Dirkes. His company is doing some very interesting work in aeronautics." He actually laughed out loud at the look on her face. "Did you think me incapable of changing my mind? I've come to think that aeroplanes are perhaps here to stay. You must remember that I'm not just a landowner, I'm a businessman, which has held Summerset in good stead. While many old estates are struggling for money, or having to sell out altogether, the Buxtons and Summerset remain solvent, due in

261

part to the hard choices I've had to make.

"Your father . . ." Here her uncle stumbled, and a lump rose in her throat as she realized that he must be missing his younger brother, no matter how little they had in common. "Your father was not a businessman, and was often just as glad to leave the business side of Summerset in my hands, though if he had moral reservations with an investment, he had no compunction about telling me so."

Rowena smiled through the tears in her throat. How like her father. "Did he often win?"

Her uncle gave her a rueful grin. "On occasion he would make his point and I would pull an investment, usually over what he called human rights. But other times, for the good of Summerset, I would have to follow my own instincts and he would either bow to my experience or give me the cold shoulder for several months."

During the last part of her uncle's speech, Rowena had a bad feeling creep over her and she knew he was preparing her for something unpleasant. "You've sold our house," she blurted out.

He stopped, surprised, and then shook his head. "No, actually, I haven't. But I did let it out. It's a long-term lease; the contract is for seven years. By that time, you and Victoria will be settled with husbands and you will know better what you both want to do with the house. It would have been easier to just sell it, mind you, but I won't have you running about thinking I'm an ogre." Rowena disintegrated into tears. Calmly, her uncle handed her a white linen handkerchief monogrammed with the Buxton crest.

"The staff?" She sniffled.

He smiled. "All but one wished to stay on for the new people, Americans with more gold than breeding."

"Who didn't want to stay?" Rowena asked curiously.

"The scullery girl. It seems my brother was paying for her secretarial course and she obtained a job at an office down at the shipyards."

It was so like her father to help Katie, but while a small part of her was pleased for Katie, the truth settled more deeply in Rowena's heart. While they might still have a home, they had no place to go home to.

Because they were already home.

Summerset was their home now, and, in a way, it always had been, Rowena suddenly realized. They'd spent almost every summer here since they were children. They knew its secrets, the best meadows for gymkhanas, the best places for a rope swing into the water, which groomsmen to avoid and which could be persuaded to look the other way. Even Victoria's sickness occurred less frequently here in the countryside than it did in the city. Summerset was their home, their only home now.

But it wasn't Prudence's. Prudence truly had no home.

Rowena only half listened as her uncle went on about how happy he and her aunt were to have them live at Summerset full-time until they were married. He stood, signaling that their meeting was over. He patted her shoulder and Rowena felt more than ever like a child being patronized and comforted at the same time. All she could think of was the words echoing in her own head.

How am I going to tell Prudence?

CHAPTER
ELEVEN

Prudence's garret looked as if a dress shop had been plucked from Bond Street by a mighty wind and tossed into her room. She had emptied the chests of all the dresses she had brought with her. Of course, she hadn't known when she packed them that only three of them were even remotely suitable for the work she was now doing.

She stood in her chemise uncertainly, wishing she could ask Rowena for advice on what to wear, just as Rowena had asked her a few days ago. But Rowena had never returned from her meeting with her uncle and had been avoiding her ever since, and Victoria, too, was nowhere to be found.

So instead of Rowena or Victoria helping her choose a dress for her outing with Andrew, it was Susie, who was so awed by Prudence's finery; she was much less helpful than Prudence had hoped.

"Oh, look at these stockings," Susie moaned, pulling out a pair of silk stockings so sheer, you could almost see through them.

Prudence smiled indulgently. So far all Susie had done was create a mess as she dove through the chests, tossing things here and there in an orgy of delight.

"You can keep them if you like," Prudence told her. "I've got six pairs."

Susie's blue eyes widened as she stuffed them in the pocket of her apron and then pulled out four pairs of soft kid gloves. Each was of a different length and she rubbed one of them reverently against her cheek. "The leather is so soft they feel almost like velvet."

Prudence gave a sharp sigh. She'd been a different girl when she'd packed for Summerset, thinking that she, like Victoria and Rowena, would be required to change her clothes several times a day—that she might go visiting at nearby estates and need tea gowns and dinner dresses and riding clothes.

She'd been a fool, that's what she'd been.

Biting her lip, she turned to Susie. "But what should I wear?"

Susie pointed at a wispy black lace dinner dress

trimmed with lustrous jet beads at the hem and neckline.

"That's hardly appropriate for a tour of Summerset and dinner at the inn." According to Susie, who heard it from one of the housemaids, who heard it from the mechanic, who heard it from Andrew himself, he was taking Prudence to the inn for dinner. With a pang, Prudence realized it would cost him almost a month's salary. She wondered how offended he would be if she offered to pay. Prudence had some money of her own, and her mother had left her eight hundred pounds when she had died. Sir Philip had told her not to touch it and she had taken his advice. And like Rowena and Victoria, she always carried the five pounds for emergencies he had demanded they carry on their person at all times.

She almost asked Susie about offering to help pay for dinner, but thought better of it. Susie's admiration over her things made her uncomfortable, as though she were showing off. But truly she was just starving for female companionship. She missed the easy relationship and intimacy she used to have with Ro and Vic.

She missed having a family.

She'd received a note from Wesley yesterday, telling her that his father had broken down and cried when he'd heard his baby sister had died, and that he was willing to meet his niece. Gran was moving in with them for a bit to recover and

Wesley would contact her as soon as things had settled. A smile crossed her face. So maybe she would get a family after all.

But they wouldn't able to take the place of Vic and Ro.

Turning back to Susie, she held up a dark, plum-colored silk dress with draped panniers on the hips. The skirt was slim enough to move in easily, but the ruffles on the wide collar and sleeves made it elegant enough for dinner at the inn.

Susie just nodded, her eyes wide. She jumped up off the bed to help Prudence finish dressing. "So, what are you doing with all these clothes? Did Miss Rowena and Miss Victoria give them to you?"

Prudence hesitated. She didn't want Susie to think she was further distancing herself from service, but neither did she want to lie. In the end, she decided to tell her the truth. Susie listened, silently buttoning up the double rows of tiny buttons on the back of the dress. After Prudence had finished, Susie turned her around and kissed her soundly on the cheek.

"That's like a fairy story, it is. You're a princess being held captive by the evil Mrs. Harper, and Andrew is your prince come to rescue you."

It sounded so much like something Victoria might have said that Prudence had to laugh. "Andrew is far too nice and honest to be a prince," she said.

Susie snorted. "True. A better prince would be one of those handsome lords who came to visit last weekend."

Prudence thought of Lord Billingsly's dark, expressive eyes and short, black curls. Her breath caught; he would make the perfect prince. She shook her head impatiently, causing Susie, who was now brushing out her hair, to fuss.

"Hold still now or you'll keep him waiting." She stood back a few minutes later to check out her handiwork. "I didn't do too badly. Goodness, but you look like a lady. But you did even when you were wearing that ugly uniform."

Prudence gave her a tremulous smile. Now that it was time to go, nerves fluttered in her stomach. If she had been living at home, she probably would not have gone out without Vic or Ro tagging along. Sir Philip may have been socially liberal, but he was still protective when it came to his girls and the opposite sex.

She picked up some of the clothing that had been strewn about the room, but Susie handed Prudence her little black beaded reticule and gave her a small push. "You go on. I'll tidy up. And don't forget, you have to tell me everything."

By the time Prudence reached Andrew, her nerves were jangling like coins in a collection plate. His jacket was too tight across his back and a bit short in the arms and her throat tightened with tenderness, knowing he must have borrowed it. His hair was slicked back and she could see the red scrape marks on his chin from a recent shave. He stood at attention, in the same manner as when he was helping Lady Summerset in and out of the motorcar.

His eyes widened when he saw her, and he cleared his throat. Turning stiffly, he opened the door of a staid green motorcar. Touched, she reached out and laid her fingers against his arm. "Thank you," she said simply.

The small gesture broke his tension and he smiled widely. "I borrowed the car from the gamekeeper. I didn't imagine you wanted to walk to Summerset."

She remembered the last time she had tried to walk to Buxton and how Lord Billingsly's laugh rang out in the crisp morning air. She shook her head to clear her thoughts. Shame on her. She shouldn't think of that now.

She glanced at Andrew's profile as they bumped down the driveway. His neck was red, as if he sensed her scrutiny. Unlike most men, he wore no hat, and his hair ruffled in the wind. It made him look vulnerable somehow, as if he had forgotten a piece of his armor.

He turned to her abruptly, as if he had just thought of something to say. She dropped her eyes, embarrassed at being caught staring.

"I hope you don't mind if we stop in at my parents' house first. One of the horses is doing poorly and my brothers are at a loss. I'm better with the animals than they are."

Prudence didn't show her surprise. She certainly hadn't prepared herself to meet his parents. But something about the pleading look in his eyes made her check her reaction. "Of course, that's fine. I'm just glad to be out of Summerset."

He nodded. "I don't like it much myself. Much too stuffy for me. I'd rather be out of doors."

"Would you like to be a farmer?" she asked, to be polite.

He nodded. "In a way. You see, I'd like to go to the veterinarian school up in London and after I've done my student training, I'd like to buy a small holding to farm while building a practice. But of course, there's always the question of money." He laughed a little, as if realizing he shouldn't have spoken of money.

Prudence noticed that while the upper classes rarely spoke of money, the lower classes had little shame about doing so and oftentimes seemed to have a more intuitive understanding of profit and loss, acceptable risk, and the rise and fall of the economy than those who ran the government. "I think that's a fine idea."

He shook his head. "Pipe dreams." His voice had taken on a harsher tone and Prudence realized that he was probably repeating something he had heard all his life. "I tried to save when I first started working at Summerset, but the family always needed something and I realized just how tough it would be." He suddenly pointed to the ruins of an old castle on the hill above them. "There's Hollingsworth Castle. Or what's left of it."

She turned to look, understanding that he wanted to change the subject.

They spoke of inconsequential things after that until they pulled onto a road that was more of a path than a road.

"Hang on. It's going to get bumpy."

Bumpy didn't even come close to describing the path that ran along a field on one side and a stand of trees on the other. Prudence thought her teeth were going to come right out of her head. They turned a corner and came upon a small stone cottage and a large, modern barn. She wondered how much of Andrew's carefully saved money had gone into constructing such a fine building.

In comparison, even the dimness of the cloudy afternoon couldn't hide the disrepair of the cottage. A corner of one of the windows had been broken and a piece of rag had been stuck in the hole to keep out the cold. It was small, far too small for the number of grubby children who came scampering out. They climbed onto Andrew after he got out of the car, as if he were a tree. A lesser man may have been embarrassed by such circumstances, but Andrew just gave her his wide, bashful smile. Prudence laughed, and suddenly she realized that she could develop feelings for him if she tried. An old man with a large, knobby head and a bent back appeared in the doorway, followed by a younger man who looked so much like Andrew, she knew he must be his brother, in spite of the meanness of his clothing.

She climbed out of the vehicle, realizing that he wouldn't be able to open the door for her. He glanced back and she saw that he was embarrassed through and through, trying to come up with some way to introduce them. Her heart once again swelled with compassion. The children, having spotted her, immediately hid behind their father and their grandfather.

Andrew made quick introductions. The two men bowed toward her awkwardly, as if the movement pained them. Then they hurried Andrew toward the barn.

"I'll only be a moment," Andrew called over his shoulder. He nodded toward her as if to tell her to mind her dress before disappearing into the barn.

Prudence stood awkwardly in the yard, wishing she hadn't gotten out of the car. Now what was she supposed to do? She smiled at the children, who were now inspecting the motorcar. There were two girls and a boy left. The other boy, obviously older than the rest, had trailed after the men into the barn. A brown-haired girl with a snub nose climbed up onto the running board in order to get a better view into the interior. Her thin brown coat looked too small to button up the front and Prudence knew she must be freezing.

"I don't think you should do that," Prudence said.

"I don't think you should do that," the girl mimicked. The other two children, who looked to be about three or four, with hollows in their still baby-round cheeks, tittered. The older one, made brave by her success, hopped off the motorcar and sidled over to Prudence. "Are you Uncle Andrew's sweetheart?" she asked.

Prudence shook her head. "I'm just a friend."

The girl cocked her head to one side. "Why are you dressed so posh, then? I think you're his sweetheart." Brazenly, the girl reached out and fingered the fine material of Prudence's dress.

The door opened behind her and Prudence turned. A tired woman stared out into the yard. The skirt of her ill-fitting green wincey was stained with barnyard muck. She kept sweeping her mousy brown hair back carelessly with the back of a flour-covered hand. With a start, Prudence realized that the woman couldn't be much older than she was.

"Get in here and leave the lady alone," the woman said, her eyes never leaving Prudence's.

The children scampered into the house and Prudence and the woman stared at each other for a long moment before the woman shut the door. Prudence's heart beat wildly in her chest before she climbed back into the vehicle. She didn't belong here. The children knew it, the men had known it, and the woman at the door had known it. Prudence was as alien at this farm as she was in the Grand Hall of Summerset.

So where did she belong? She wrapped her arms around herself to keep warm, wishing that Andrew would hurry. Resting her forehead against the cold glass of the window, she wondered whether she would really belong anywhere again. At home she had belonged, but looking back, she realized just how much Sir Philip had protected her from the snobbishness of his class. If they all went home, what would their lives be like? She shivered as she understood there would be no going back for her. Ro and Vic had their own lives, lives that, whether any of them wanted to admit it or not, could not include her. At least, not in the manner that they used to.

It was not a cheerful thought to realize that her family wasn't really her family and that the future she thought she would have—marriage to a suitable young man, running her own home somewhere close to Ro and Vic in Belgravia or Mayfair—simply wasn't an option. And Lord Billingsly, that wasn't an option either. Her mother must have known that. Why hadn't she said anything? Why hadn't she kept Prudence more separate instead of allowing her to think she was one of *them?* She must have known this time would come.

Then a thought hit her so hard, she drew in a quick breath.

She did know it would come. That's why she had left her so much money.

For a woman of Alice Tate's means, acquiring money like that would have taken a lifetime. Where had she gotten it? No matter what things her mother had kept hidden from her as she grew up, Prudence was sure that thievery was not one of them. She had gotten the money from somewhere, enough money for her daughter to buy herself almost any kind of reasonable home she wanted. Enough money to act as a buffer against living on the street. She would have to earn her own living, of course, but Prudence had been brought up skilled in a number of things and she could probably earn enough money from music lessons alone.

Sadness washed over her like a fine Cornwall mist. Even if the Buxton girls did make it back home, which Prudence was beginning to doubt, life wouldn't be the same and she needed to try to figure something out. Because being a lady's maid at a great estate was not an option for her—no matter how much loyalty and love she felt for Rowena and Victoria. She had the means to change her life, and she suddenly longed to do so.

Maybe it was time she quit putting off the inevitable. But inside she shivered, her fear of being out in the world all alone—for the first time in her life—wrapping itself around her like poison ivy.

She jumped when Andrew started the car. She'd been so deep in thought that she hadn't even heard the crank.

"I'm sorry it took so long," he said, climbing in next to her. "It was just the scours, but my dad refuses to use the modern way to get rid of it and instead insists on old wives' methods. They are generally a lot riskier and smellier." He laughed.

"That's all right." She smiled. "How did you learn so much about animals?"

"The local vet always let me watch and I sneaked over to his clinic whenever I had the chance. I think he would have taken me into his practice if he didn't have his own son to put through veterinary school."

They drove in silence for a few minutes, and Prudence relaxed, enjoying how comfortable he made her feel. "So why do you want to be both an animal doctor and a farmer? It seems like one would take up enough time," she said.

"And then some," he agreed. "But I love research as well, especially agricultural. I read a book a few years ago called *Agriculture, Science, and the Myth of Production* and it changed the way I looked at food production. My family was unwilling to try anything new that might make farming more efficient. I thought I could dabble in that while I worked as a vet." He bit his lips as he looked out the front window. "I know, pipe dreams."

"No, it's not," she assured him. "I've actually read some of Murcray's book. It's brilliant. Or what I read of it was."

He turned to look at her, startled, and almost veered off the road as a wheel got caught in a rut. He fought for several seconds before pulling the vehicle back up onto the road. "You what?"

"Did you think I couldn't read? *Sir Philip* kept a variety of books on hand, and Murcray was a contemporary of his."

He laughed. "I'm sorry. I've never even met a man who read that book, let alone a pretty girl."

Prudence couldn't help but smile at his use of the word "pretty," and his cheeks reddened when he realized what he'd said. He cleared his throat. "Sorry, we missed tea. We can have an early supper."

"That would be fine," she assured him. He glanced over at her and she noticed how nice his smile was. She imagined what her future would be like with this young man. It had to be better than being a lady's maid. Then she thought of the woman in the doorway and shuddered. No. It didn't have to be like that. She had some money. Surely that was enough to start a future with, even if it did mean she had to face that future alone. But still the image lingered.

The Yuletide had burst onto Summerset like fireworks at a jubilee. Boughs of velvet-laced holly wrapped around each of the thirty oak trees that lined the drive, and each of the black iron lampposts in the front of the house had a festive topknot of red ribbons and silver bells. London may have dressed itself up for the holidays in celebratory attire, but nothing could compare to the sheer opulence with which Summerset adorned herself.

Rowena stood at the window at the top of the hall, watching Elaine and Victoria walk arm in arm through the formal rose gardens. Rowena had expected Victoria to be more distraught and volatile as the holidays approached, but watching her now, giggling with her cousin, Rowena saw that even if Victoria didn't know it herself, she had stepped into life here at Summerset as easily as if she had been born to it.

As had she, Rowena realized in surprise. The kind of life Rowena and Victoria lived here, though very different from their city lifestyle, was almost as comfortable as slipping into an old dressing gown. But how long would the feeling last? How long before she and her sister would begin to chafe under such restrictions? The lounging around all day was abominable, as was the inexplicably strict division between the Buxtons and those who actually ran the household—the servants. But still . . . the history, the stories, the grandeur, and the elegance were intoxicating. And while she knew, as did her father and his contemporaries, that this way of life was dying out, must die out, she had to admit that she was suddenly saddened by the thought of its passing now that she'd had the opportunity to fully experience it.

As she stepped back from the hall window, her eyes caught those of her banished grandfather. Like Victoria, she barely remembered the old man who spent most of his time upstairs in the grandest stateroom. Just those rare occasions when the children would march, led by Colin, followed by her and Elaine, with baby Victoria carried by the nanny in the background, to give old Grandpapa a kiss good night. She wondered why they bothered at all, considering the mixed feelings she sensed in the adults during those moments.

The old earl had ruled the house with his mighty temper and the iron grip he had of everything that happened at Summerset. It must have been difficult, she thought, to watch old age encroach in such a way that left his physical abilities impaired but his mental acuity intact. To watch his control slip away and placed into the hands of someone he would always think of as inferior.

Then she heard a noise that drove all other thoughts out of her head. The sound of an engine, coming not from the road below but from somewhere out in the gray skies. She unlatched the window and pushed the leaded glass open, allowing a blast of wintry air to sweep the hallway clean of all mustiness. She poked her head out, craning her neck. There he was, coming up over the ridge. Jon didn't come every night, just often enough to let her know he was thinking about her, and the sound of the engine never failed to make her smile.

The plane soared closer and she clasped her hands to her chest as her heart soared with it. Below, the girls had stopped walking, and, shading their eyes against the thin, pale sunshine, they watched as the plane made a leisurely loop around the castle before making its way west once again.

More than anything Rowena wished she were sitting with Jon, following the sun to wherever it should lead them. She watched the aeroplane until her eyes could track it no longer and then she turned away, closing the window behind her.

Her thoughts suddenly shifted to Prudence. She still couldn't think of how to tell her the London house had been sold and that she and Victoria would be remaining at Summerset until they made other arrangements. *If* they made other arrangements. A lump rose in her throat. She would completely understand if Prudence didn't want to stay on, and perhaps they could look into other situations . . . just until she and Victoria made some kind of decision. She would tell her, of course, but maybe she would wait until all the festivities were over. Yuletide without their father was hard enough. She couldn't imagine what Vic would do if Prudence decided to leave as well.

Victoria sat at the top of a ladder, watching the antics of the others with the sort of superiority that came from being four feet taller than the rest of them. The arrival of Yuletide brought with it an ever-revolving list of guests all bent on making Rowena and Victoria forget that this would be their first Christmas without their father. It was all incredibly draining, and Victoria believed she would be much better off if they had just left her alone to make merry in her own way. She'd never been to Summerset for Christmas and knew she would have a good time if everyone would just stop coddling her and treat her like a grown woman.

Nanny Iris's cottage had also undergone a wonderful transformation, though of course not on this scale. Victoria had visited several times in the past month, and even though she knew there would be no lack of family to help the old woman usher in Christmas morning, she truly wished she could be one of them.

Right now, all Victoria wanted to do was sneak off to her secret room to study her office course and go through her *Botanist Quarterly Review*, which she discovered actually had advertisements for jobs and fellowships in the back matter. Some of them included opportunities to study certain types of flora and fauna in remote locations. She had typed up all sorts of pretend responses to these advertisements, wondering whether she ever would have the nerve to actually send one. Not that she had the qualifications anyway. She frowned and shoved that out of her mind. Where there was a will there was a way.

The room itself had received a kind of restoration since that first night when she had slipped in with her typewriter. She had done more cleaning, of course, so the musty smell was almost gone. What remained was merely a reminder of the past and it pleased her. She had plundered the other rooms for pillows, throws, screens, and decorations so that bric-a-brac erupted from every possible flat surface in a kind of haphazard gaiety that made her smile. African masks now shared the mantel along with ornate Oriental fans and small silver picture frames filled with ancestors long dead.

She wondered what Kit would think of it now.

She hung another ornament on the sixteen-foot tree that stood at the end of the Great Hall. Pretending not to, she studied Kit, who was talking to Aunt Charlotte and Sebastian's mother, the formidable Lady Billingsly. Kit was dressed formally in a dark, tailored waistcoat and jacket that fit his wide shoulders perfectly. He stood straight, a drink in one hand, his other hand tucked behind his back in a perfect gentleman's pose. Victoria knew it was all an act.

She knew it because whenever she caught him glancing her way, he would give her an audacious wink that made her blush. They hadn't spoken since the night when he had frightened her in her secret room, even though she'd gone there every night since he'd returned, half hoping he would show up.

Across the room, Rowena stood gazing out the window, barely noticing the festivities around her. Victoria noted that Rowena had become more reserved than ever, but it was more as though she was waiting for something to happen. But that was a lot like Ro, always waiting for something to happen rather than making it happen. She wondered whether it had anything to do with that flyboy she'd gone to tea with. The whole house was buzzing with the strange aeroplanes that had visited several times in the past few days. Elaine had finally wormed part of the story from her and declared it a lovely tale, but warned that her parents wouldn't feel the same way.

Victoria thought about confronting Rowena, but

since she had her own secrets, she left her sister alone. She wished her father were here. He'd know what to do.

Hurt rose within her again and she fumbled with a glass figurine. It slipped from her fingers and went hurtling down, shattering on the marble floor.

For a moment no one moved and then Aunt Charlotte spoke up. "I do hope that wasn't one of the Waterford crystal ornaments, my dear."

Victoria smiled weakly. "I'm sorry, Aunt Charlotte."

Her aunt sighed. "Never mind. That's what happens when you do the decorating yourself."

"It's all a part of the experience, Lady Summerset," Kit put in.

In reality the servants had already done most of the decorating and guests were allowed to add the trimmings, if they so desired.

A maid arrived in seconds to sweep up the mess. In moments she disappeared as noiselessly as she'd appeared. Victoria wondered what her name was. She sighed. It was strange to be living among an army of strangers.

"Allow me to assist you me, Miss Buxton." Kit climbed up the ladder Victoria was perched on and she nervously grabbed the seat to steady herself. She noticed his eyes glittering as he got nearer.

He was ridiculously close to her and slipped

one hand around her waist. "Don't worry. I won't let you fall."

She swallowed. Kit had the athletic body of someone who played on the cricket fields all through school and now rode, hunted, and played golf with the best of them. He handed her another ornament from the box she had balanced on her lap. "Go ahead."

Swallowing again, she leaned out to hang the ornament on the tree and his arm tightened. She shivered and he grinned at her as if knowing exactly what she was feeling. She had a strong urge to rap him on top of the head with her knuckles.

She heard the front door open and looked down the hall to see Cairns admitting more guests. The footmen were dispatched to take care of the newcomer's luggage while the guests were announced to the room by Cairns.

"Lady Summerset, may I present the Dowager Lucille, and her granddaughters, Lady Isabella and Lady Gertrude."

The new guests joined the party and there were curtsies, bows, and hand kissing. Elaine took the girls to one corner and persuaded a reluctant Rowena to join them. Victoria added another ornament to the tree. It was hard to breathe with Kit so close to her, and every time she looked down, his eyes were upon her.

"I think we should move the ladder, don't you?

We're getting quite a cluster in one spot." His voice belied a trace of humor and Victoria saw he was right. She had about twenty ornaments in the same small area.

"Don't worry," he whispered. "I don't think anyone will notice. They are far too busy flattering one another. Look."

He indicated the corner where her aunt Charlotte held court, and she saw he was right. The women all clustered together, fawning over Aunt Charlotte and Lady Edith Billingsly and gossiping about those who had yet to join the party. He took the box with him and Victoria carefully turned around and climbed down, very conscious that he had a view of her backside the whole time.

He pointed to the boxes still on the table. "Shall we continue our work? I think we make a good team."

She looked at him sharply. Was he making fun of her? It was so hard to tell. On the other hand, she did like spending time with him, more the fool she. "We may as well. The others certainly aren't going to finish it."

They worked for another half hour or so, ignoring the bell's continual ringing and the butler introductions. To Victoria, Summerset seemed more like an enchanted palace than a real stone-and-mortar home. Her father had always spurned Christmas at the abbey in order to spend the holiday in their London home, and though they always decorated and held parties, it was nothing on this scale.

Evergreen boughs encircled the Great Hall from the front door to the drawing room on the end. Huge bows of red velvet with gold thread gathered the boughs every five feet or so. Tall white beeswax candles stood on every available surface and hundreds of tiny silver snowflakes were strung across every arch, reflecting the candlelight, causing twinkles all over the walls and even glancing off the frescoes lining the hallway. The tree was one of a hundred that were being groomed inch by inch for generations of Buxton Christmases. The house itself had ten decorated Christmas trees. The one in the Great Hall, the one in the drawing room, one for the servants in the servants' hall, and one in each of the family's private bedrooms. Victoria hadn't even decorated hers yet, but she enjoyed the fresh citrusy scent that hung in the air.

"I have a surprise for you," Kit suddenly said close to her ear. "Can you get away in about twenty minutes?"

Victoria looked around the hall. About a hundred people now milled about the room, drinking wassail, port, and mulled wine. Her sister was in the corner with Elaine, Sebastian, Colin, and a half dozen other young people about their age. Victoria wondered whether they were the Cunning Coterie. Prudence, of course, hadn't been invited.

She gave him a quick nod. It was madness, of course, but no one would miss her, and after he'd practically ignored her for the past two days, she was curious as to what his surprise could be. Instinctively, she felt she shouldn't trust this strange young man, but when she remembered their hushed conversation in their secret room, she couldn't help but be intrigued.

"Meet me in the library," he murmured, and then sauntered away. Having signaled for one of the footmen standing at attention nearby to take away the ladder, she finished by hanging a few more ornaments near the bottom of the tree.

Then she went to the punch bowl, where a servant poured her a glass. She walked through the room, looking above the guests' heads so they wouldn't try to engage her in conversation. The women were lovely in their fine jewels and their gowns trimmed with feathers, fur, and crystals. Rowena wore a black lace dress with short sleeves made of cormorant feathers and had a matching black headdress sitting on her shining dark hair. A lump came to Victoria's throat and with difficulty she turned her eyes away from her sister's beauty.

The gentlemen, fine in their dark dress attire, were dressed to set off the gowns of their more extravagant, colorful wives. Her uncle stood on one side of the room, conversing with a group of distinguished-looking men. Occasionally, he and his wife would exchange strangely congratulatory glances, as if applauding each other on the success of the party. And so far the tree-trimming party was a success. After, there would be a twelve-course meal for the family and friends and then music in the music room. Tomorrow the serious festivities would begin with Summerset's renowned double ball. First, the Great Hall would be emptied of most of its furniture for the servants' ball. When the family had done their duty by their servants, they would retire to the fabulously decorated ballroom for their own ball, while the servants were allowed one more hour of dancing in the Great Hall. Not a minute more nor a minute less. No one dared challenge Lady Summerset's traditions. Many of the guests would leave the day after in order to be in their own homes for Christmas, but at least two dozen would be staying at Summerset until New Year's Eve.

Without seeming to hurry, Victoria moved gracefully to the stairwell and handed her cup to a servant who had been hired from town to supplement Summerset's own staff, many of whom were torn between readying themselves for the one night a year they were allowed to make merry and preparing for their own duties. Once she'd slipped out of the Great Hall without detection, she hurried through the darkened corridors to the library.

The library itself was a work of art, and few decorations were needed. Very little could improve upon the spectacular blue and white plasterwork of the walls and ceiling that was designed to frame a dozen classical Roman frescoes. The seating, tables, and cushions were all a neutral white, to emphasize the colors of the paintings. Victoria and Rowena spent little time here as children, even though they loved their own library at home. Though many of the books that lined the walls were quite good, they were mostly antique collectibles, not the sort that would fire the imagination of a child's heart.

On a low table in front of the white marble fireplace, Victoria noticed two large, leather-bound volumes. One of them had been left open, half on top of the other. She frowned and walked over to them. Things were not left out of place at Summerset. Once she saw what they were, however, she understood.

Like the others on the shelf, both oversized scrapbooks had the Summerset crest embossed on the dark, shining leather. They were separated by year and most were created one page at a time by loving mistresses, though many were created by servants when the lady of the house, such as Lady Summerset, had no taste for the task.

She'd seen books just like these on display

downstairs, laid out so people could look at Christmases past, as it were. The scrapbooks went back almost four hundred years and were considered the finest record of their kind in the United Kingdom.

She frowned and peered more closely at the dates. Why were these left here and not on display with the rest of them? Both were consecutive years, 1890 and 1891. Perhaps they were not considered old enough for display. She knelt next to the books, wondering whether she had stumbled upon someone's absentmindedness or someone's secret. The most important thing she'd learned about secrets was that you never knew when one was staring you in the face.

Coincidence or secret? She pulled the open book closer to her. Here was a picture of the entire Summerset staff and family, posed in front of the manor. She smiled as she spotted Cairns, who'd actually had hair twenty-three years ago. Mrs. Harper hadn't changed at all. She recognized many of the staff and wondered about people who would give their entire lives to serve another family instead of having one of their own. She read through the list of names written in minuscule letters to the right of the picture, along with their title. Many of the surnames were familiar and she wondered how many families, like hers, had been here since the very beginning of Summerset.

Then she saw *Iris Combes—Nanny,* and she bent her head closer to the picture. Victoria spotted Nanny Iris just to the left of the family, her rich, dark hair shining in the sun. She was flanked on the right by Victoria's grandmother, a small, quiet woman who had always reminded Victoria of a mother wren from her Beatrix Potter books. In the center of the photo, just to her grandmother's right, was the old earl himself. It must have been before the slow degradation of his body began, because he showed no sign of weakness, just a predatory arrogance that made Victoria shiver. His sons stood behind him in his proverbial shadow. Uncle Conrad appeared alone and beaten, but her father, recently married to his small, fairylike bride, beamed next to him. From the plumpness of her mother's face, she could tell that her mother was already pregnant with Ro. She ran her fingers along the side of the picture, wondering how different life might have been had her mother survived her birth. This wasn't the first picture she had seen of her mother, of course, but every new picture was a gift, for her mother always looked happy. But then, everyone agreed her mother had possessed a gift for happiness.

Blinking back the tears, she looked away. The last thing she wanted was for Kit to find her crying in front of an old scrapbook. Keeping her eyes resolutely away from her parents, she turned instead to Nanny Iris, who had her hands on the shoulders of a young girl who looked to be about three. Victoria's breath caught. Halpernia. The little girl whose passing the year Rowena was born crippled her father and forever changed her family. She had the Buxton hair, and no doubt her eyes were a sparkling green under the thick fringe of curls on her forehead. It was odd to think that Rowena, Elaine, Colin, and she would have an aunt only a few years older than themselves, had she lived.

Moving closer to the picture, she frowned. Who was Halpernia clinging to? It wasn't her mother, nor Nanny Iris, but a young woman who looked tantalizingly familiar. The answer came to her so swiftly, it caused a pain between her eyes. Prudence's mother! Her fingers ran down the right side of the book until she found a name that had been crossed out in such a way that the letters were completely illegible, but Victoria didn't need them. Prudence had several pictures of her mother displayed around the house in London, and Miss Tate had been an important part of Victoria's life. This was definitely Alice Tate.

She turned back to the photo. Alice wore a maid's uniform, but there was no doubt about the little girl's feelings for her. Why was this maid allowed to hold the hand of the proverbial princess of the house? Why was she standing so close to the family instead of back near the line of maids?

Victoria looked at the door, wondering where Kit was. Perhaps he had been detained? She needed to get back before she was missed, but before she left, she checked the other two books. After flipping through pages of christenings and births, she found the yearly staff and family picture and it was exactly what she suspected. Though there was a short, three-sentence entry concerning Halpernia's death, Alice Tate no longer appeared in the annual photograph.

She was putting the books away when a newspaper clipping fluttered out of the back of one of the books. Her heart raced as she realized what it was . . . an article on Halpernia's death. She looked in the back of both books, but it was the only one. She carefully folded the clipping again and stuck it down inside the top of her corset.

If Halpernia and Prudence's mother were somehow related, then Victoria was going to find out how. Prudence deserved some answers.

CHAPTER TWELVE

This would go a great deal faster if you would sit still," Prudence said the next afternoon. She kept the hairpins clenched between her teeth, which was a good thing because she was sorely tempted to stick one into Rowena's scalp. Rowena fidgeted, wiggled, and otherwise squirmed in her chair like a naughty child. Prudence had already helped her into a dark maroon lace gown with the black silk insets. Though the other women would be decked in their most brilliant dresses, the Buxton girls continued to honor their father by wearing only dark colors. Of course, everything looked lovely against Rowena's porcelain complexion and dark hair. Prudence tugged on a rebellious curl just enough to cause a sharp tinge of pain and Rowena glared at her in the mirror. "I just can't believe I have to change again. What would happen if I wore my tea gown to tea and to dinner? Would the meal be ruined? And how many parties do we have to have, anyway? It seems to take an infernal number of parties to celebrate one holiday."

"Someone's in a bad mood and pray remember, it wasn't my idea to come here." Prudence punctuated her words by jabbing a pin into the coiffure she was constructing.

Rowena lowered her eyes. "You would make a horrible lady's maid, Pru, you know that?"

Prudence snorted. Again, this wasn't her idea, but she didn't say it aloud. There were so many things she didn't say aloud to Rowena any longer. Prudence had vacillated for weeks between being furious with her friend and concerned for her, but now she was just furious. And resentful.

"Oh, would you two stop it?"

Victoria, whose hair was already finished, sat

on the edge of Rowena's bed, careful not to wrinkle her black silk gown with its customary Poiret Oriental lines. Black didn't become Victoria the way it did Rowena. It made her pale skin almost translucent, and her eyes even larger in her thin face. Even with carmine-colored lip rouge on her lips, Victoria still looked like a child playing dress-up.

Prudence looked at her and frowned. "What's wrong with you?" she asked bluntly. She was tired of playing the lady's maid while her friends got to dress up in fine clothes and eat delicacies that the entire kitchen had slaved over for the past week. Tonight was the first night she would get to dress nicely and here she was, making sure they were ready first. She wanted someone to fuss over her for a change.

"Nothing's wrong with me," Victoria snapped. "I'm just tired of listening to the two of you argue all the time. You sound like fishwives. I understand this situation is intolerable, but we need to make the best of it until Easter, when we can all go home. Right, Ro?"

Rowena paused a moment too long before saying, "Right."

"You're all done." Prudence dropped the combs and brushes carelessly on the dressing table. "Now I need to go get ready."

Victoria stood up. "Not so fast. How can you get ready without your dress?"

Prudence frowned, not quite understanding. "My dress?"

Rowena gave her a tentative smile and turned toward Victoria, who had sprung off the bed and scurried to the closet. "Victoria has a surprise for you."

"It's your turn to get ready. You have a dance tonight, too, you know." Victoria's voice, which just a few moments before had been petulant, now held a note of anticipation. She came back out of the closet holding a ball gown of a deep emerald-green silk. The lines of the dress were clearly Oriental inspired, with short kimono-style sleeves ending in gold tassels.

Prudence gasped. "Where did you get that? I would have remembered had we packed it."

Rowena smiled; it was a sad smile, but at least it was a smile. "I had it made up a couple of years ago in Paris but it was sent here by mistake." Rowena slid her fingers down the silk luxuriously. "I've never had a chance to wear it."

Prudence bit her lip. Would it be right to wear it with Sir Philip so recently . . .

"Don't even think of Papa!" Victoria said, so fiercely that Prudence jumped. "Papa would want you to be happy and look nice and go dancing. So stop it."

Rowena nodded, tears caught in her green eyes. "It's true, Prudence. Just wear the dress and be happy for a bit. Lord knows you deserve it."

Rowena's voice sounded weary and Prudence finally nodded.

Victoria clapped her hands and soon had Prudence standing at attention while she dressed her from head to toe.

Prudence could hardly believe it when she looked in the mirror. The green of the dress deepened the green of her own eyes, and the tight waist made her as slender as a reed. The girls had piled her hair into a mass of curls on top of her head and secured it with a peacock-green silk scarf tied like a tiara around her head. The ends of the scarf trailed down her back, which the cut of her dress left daringly bare to just under her shoulder blades. "What is the servants' ball like, do you know?" Prudence finally asked.

"I can tell you," Elaine said from the doorway. "I was wondering what was taking you both so long, now I know!"

The girls fell silent as they put finishing touches on Prudence's hair.

"Oh, please don't let me ruin your fun. Prudence looks positively beautiful." Elaine, stunning herself in plush pink lace, circled Prudence, her eyes wide with surprise.

"Thank you, miss," Prudence said rather stiffly.

"I'm serious! You're almost as pretty as Ro. You know what would be a deevie idea? If we snuck her into our ball with the rest of us, right under Mother's nose. She'd never be able to tell."

Elaine held up her hand as the protests rained down on her. "Fine, I won't, but it would be funny, you have to admit. The servants' balls are usually great fun. They start out formal, with Father dancing with Mrs. Harper, and Mother dancing with Cairns, and then the rest of us join in if we choose to. Most of the houseguests dance once or twice before retiring to the drawing room to wait for our supper. They do this to show how modern they are." Elaine snorted, then shrugged. "I don't know what happens after that, because we go to dinner to be served by the town servants and then the servants' ball ends about the time ours begins."

Victoria nodded. "I hear the Welbecks' servants' ball is so grand they have to hire fifty waiters from London just to fill in."

Elaine nodded. "That's why Mother has hers on the same day we have a ball for our guests. The orchestra will play for the servants in the Great Hall and then move to the ballroom for us." She shook her head, still looking at Prudence. Prudence was beginning to feel less like a young woman than a goose in a butcher's window. "I still can't get over how posh you look. I know I sound the snob, but you look more like Rowena's sister than Victoria does, really."

Prudence watched Victoria startle at this and then grow quiet, but Rowena laughed, a sad little laugh that made Prudence hurt. "We've heard that more than once. Father said it was because we spent so much time together."

"Are we ready? Is it time?" Victoria asked suddenly.

Impulsively, Prudence held out her arms to both Rowena and Victoria. She desperately wanted things to go back to the way they used to be. Victoria came to her, her blue eyes shining, but Rowena hesitated and her eyes avoided Prudence's. It was Elaine, unaware of the undercurrents in the room, who gaily linked arms with Prudence.

Rowena made a motion with her arm to the door and the girls left the room.

They were almost down the staircase when Rowena put her hand to her throat. "My locket. I forgot the locket Father gave me." She looked behind her at the girls, who still had their arms linked.

Irritated, Prudence pulled her arms from the other girls and took a step back. "You go on down, I'll just grab it and meet you there."

"Oh, I can get it," Rowena protested. "I didn't mean—"

"Don't be silly. I put it away last. I know right where it is." She hurried back to Rowena's room, feeling very much the maid, no matter how luxurious her gown.

After snatching up the locket, she headed downstairs, thoughtful.

"I was hoping I'd run into you."

Prudence startled as Lord Billingsly's deep voice sounded from behind her. The dark dinner jacket he wore sat in tailored perfection across his shoulders. His hair had been slicked back, but several unruly curls had sprung forward onto his forehead. His dark eyes smiled at her and then widened as they gave a surprised sweeping look over her dress and hair.

She felt her skin heat and she couldn't help but smile back at him.

"And why would that be, Lord Billingsly? You wish me to fetch you something, perhaps?" She kept her tone pert, trying not to show how his presence affected her pulse, now skittering in her throat.

His eyes flickered for a surprised moment, before a smile curved his mouth. "No. I have my own valet for that, as you well know. Why are you being difficult? Perhaps I was looking forward to chatting with you."

"Rule number one," Prudence answered.

His brows raised. "Pardon?"

"Rule number one is the reason I'm being difficult. Instead of being welcomed as a dear family friend or even as a respected stranger, I was handed a list of rules and shown to my room in the servants' quarters. Rule number one is never let your voice be heard by the ladies and gentlemen of the house. And rule number two: Answer politely when spoken to."

The moment the words came out of her mouth, she regretted them. He was being light and teasing as the occasion warranted—after all, it was a festive dance during which the classes mingled in an extraordinary way—and instead of taking advantage of it, she was being as prickly as a hedgehog.

For a moment it looked as if he wasn't going to speak, but then he nodded. "While I'm sorry for your treatment, I must say, I rather like that rule," he said.

Her head went back in surprise. "Excuse me?"

His lips twitched. "Rule number two, answer politely when spoken to, indicates a polite conversation, which is exactly what I had in mind. Are you looking forward to tonight's festivities, Miss Tate?"

He was giving her a way out of her surliness, and gratefully, she took it. "Indeed, I am, Lord Billingsly. Even the servants should have a good time now and then." There, she'd done it again. Her situation and position rankled and there was just no way to get around it.

He held out his arm for her to take. "I can see that polite conversation is going to be difficult this evening. Perhaps we would be better off just dancing."

Prudence drew in a deep breath and took his arm. "I would like that very much, Lord Billingsly."

His eyes, dark as coal, twinkled down at her and she tried to match his gaze, if only to show that he hadn't rattled her at all, even though his presence both thrilled and dismayed her.

His eyes softencd. "If we were to speak, instead of just dance, my number one concern is to find out how you're getting along, really. Are you being mistreated?"

She turned from him and began walking down the stairs, forcing him along with her. "And if I were, Lord Billingsly? Exactly what would you do about it? Call out Lord Summerset? Circumstances and birth have brought me to this situation, and I am dealing with it the best I can. I will stay with Rowena and Victoria until Easter, and then after that . . ." She faltered. Her mind blanked as they reached the last step of the staircase.

"And then after that? What are you going to do after that, Prudence?" His voice was low under the sound of merrymaking and she could hear a note of disquiet.

His use of her first name further confused her. They stared at each other, the moment spinning out between them for an eternity. She resisted the pull she felt toward him. In Sir Philip's house she might have been deluded into believing that all would be well. She might have teased him in return. She might have told him about the books she was reading, or her journals. She might have done a million things, but she wasn't in Sir Philip's house, she was at Summerset and it was a whole different world. An entire class system stood between them.

"Rowena! Don't let my dear boy make you late for the festivities. Whatever would your dear aunt say?"

Prudence twirled around toward the voice and lost her footing on the stair. Lord Billingsly caught her before she could fall, his arm going around her waist. She felt the heat linger for a moment as she steadied herself.

"Oh. You're not Rowena."

A small, older woman stood several steps above her, her hand holding a pair of pince-nez glasses to her face. Her elaborately dressed hair framed a pointed, inquisitive face, but the dark eyes that regarded Prudence were sharp and so much like Lord Billingsly's that she knew immediately who the woman was. Prudence dropped her eyes and studied the richly detailed carpeting between them. "No, my lady."

"Then who are you?" The woman's voice was a bit querulous.

This was a woman who didn't like to be taken by surprise. "My name is Prudence Tate, my lady." Prudence sank into a curtsy.

She spotted Victoria on the other side of the hall, waving as the orchestra swept into the first tune. She turned back to Lord Billingsly and his mother. "If you will excuse me. Victoria and Rowena are waiting."

She gave another curtsy. She knew she was being rude, but she absolutely didn't want to engage in small talk with Lady Billingsly, who was almost as frightening as Lady Summerset.

As Prudence made her way through the crowded room, she noticed that she raised a small commotion as she passed. Not among the wellborn, who had no idea who she was, but among the army of servants, most of whom were waiting for the traditional dances between the Lord and Lady and the housekeeper and butler to be finished so they could begin their own fun. They didn't even bother to whisper as she passed, speaking so that she could hear them: "Look at her putting on airs, acting like she's one of them." "Wait till Mrs. Harper sees her. She'll be out on her cheeky arse, mark my words!"

Mortified, she looked around and found herself surrounded by the people she worked with every day, dressed in their Sunday best outfits, a pretty collar or a new shirt the only indication that this evening was different than their half days off. Their eyes were filled with rancor, envy, and outright malice. Victoria and Rowena had dressed her up to make her happy, and instead she only felt like a traitor, a fool, and, more than ever, an outsider.

She reddened, then tilted her chin upward,

refusing to be cowed. They were judging her just as the gentry had, and she was jolly well tired of being judged. She focused instead on Vic and Ro's welcoming faces across the room. But the gauntlet continued with each step.

"You have to wonder what sort of duties one has to perform to get a dress such as that," someone said as she passed.

"I've heard she thinks she's so far above the other servants, she won't even use the servants' privy," one bawdy voice sniggered.

Prudence's fists clenched together and she felt the bite of her fingernails as they cut into her own flesh.

Then Susie, braver than Prudence ever knew she could be, shoved her way through the crowd and gave her a huge hug. "You look so fine! And look at me, thanks to you!"

She twirled, completely ignoring the people surrounding Prudence. As often happens with bullies who are being ignored, the crowd lost its momentum and dissipated. Prudence almost cried with relief.

"Well?" Susie asked, posing. She still wore her ill-fitted dark brown wincey skirt, but the blouse, made of fine linen, was perfectly tailored for her with deep ruffles at the neck and cuffs.

"You're welcome. It was the least I could do for Christmas, as you've been so nice to me." Prudence hugged the girl in return.

Susie was swept off to dance by a gardener, but before Prudence could reach her destination she was stopped by Andrew, whose grayish green eyes twinkled at her. "I was going to ask you to dance but you look so fine, I'm half afraid you'd break in my arms!"

Prudence pushed the words she'd heard from her mind. "I keep trying to reach Victoria and Rowena, but in this crowd I can't seem to get to them." When she looked over to where she'd last seen them, she noticed that Victoria was dancing with Kip, and Rowena was dancing with her cousin, Colin. Prudence threw up her hands in surrender. "I would love to dance with you, Mr. Wilkes, and I promise I won't break!"

He took her hand and Prudence noticed he was wearing the suit that was too small for him again.

"Rowena!" she called, as Rowena and Colin danced by. Rowena held out her hand and Prudence slipped her the locket.

"What was that?" Andrew asked, but Prudence just shook her head and indicated they should join the dancers. His arms slipped around her waist and she relaxed, feeling safer and more comfortable than she had all evening. She soon noticed how absorbed he seemed to be in counting and she smiled to herself. "It's more fun when you don't overthink it."

He grinned. "But perhaps more dangerous for you?"

"I told you before I wouldn't break."

The music stopped. "We were cheated on that dance, would you like to try another?" Andrew smiled and squeezed her hand a bit. "I promise not to break you."

Before she could open her mouth, someone came skidding to a stop next to them and Lord Billingsly broke in. "I'm afraid Miss Tate promised the second dance of the evening on her dance card to me." He nodded at Andrew, whose brows drew together in confusion. Taking advantage of his opponent's slow reaction, Lord Billingsly appropriated Prudence's hand from Andrew's and whirled her away.

"I certainly did not promise you the second dance, Lord Billingsly," she huffed, searching for Andrew over his shoulder. But then his hand cupped her waist, sending a shiver up her spine, and she forgot about Andrew, forgot about everything except trying to breathe.

"I knew if I didn't do something quickly, he was going to keep you for the rest of the evening and we couldn't have that. And please, call me Sebastian. I think we've known each other long enough that we could consider ourselves friends."

She tilted her head back and looked into his eyes, which for once weren't teasing her. They looked serious, as if they were asking her a question. She wished she could look into his eyes and give him the answer he wanted, but knew it was impossible. They would both be hurt by such a friendship. How could he understand? Until she had come to Summerset, she hadn't understood either. "I'm not sure what the point of that would be. A friendship between a lord and a lady's maid is frowned upon, even in these *enlightened* times."

"The point is that I like you and would like us to be friends. And you know that you aren't really a lady's maid, Prudence."

Prudence's cheeks flamed. He didn't know anything about her. Didn't know, for instance, that she was the illegitimate daughter of a servant girl. Maybe her father had been a groom, or perhaps a hall boy. She couldn't be sure. What did this young, handsome lord with his perfectly fitting suit and impeccable bloodline want with her? What would he say if he knew the truth?

"No, but I *am* the daughter of a servant." Prudence stopped dancing, her throat constricting. "A friendship between us would lead to no good at all, Lord Billingsly, and I am not interested in any trouble. If you will excuse me."

Just then there was a loud commotion at the other end of the hall and the music faltered for a moment before continuing. The dancers craned their heads to see what was going on. Prudence watched Cairns carting two struggling young men out of the room by their arms. As they made their way through the door, Prudence gasped when she saw that one of them was Andrew.

• • •

Lady Summerset glided through the crowd, her face fixed with an expression of nonchalant enjoyment. That was the look she intended and she pulled it off, in spite of the half dozen pressing emergencies that always occurred when throwing an event of this size. Her steadfast companions in keeping everything running smoothly during the double balls were Hortense, Mrs. Harper, and Cairns. All three knew that in spite of it being their night to have a good time, their duty came first. Lady Summerset could hire extra servants from town to serve dinner, but no one could take the places of those three. In fact, Lady Summerset was certain that if Cairns, Mrs. Harper, and Hortense had been in charge of the Boer War, it would have come to a much speedier conclusion.

The servants' ball was coming along splendidly, except for that one little difficulty concerning their footman and Sir Dalton's valet. But Cairns had taken care of that. He had just given her the report and surprise, surprise, it had concerned Prudence Tate. Lady Charlotte unfurled her ivory fan and fanned herself slowly, her eyes scanning the room.

It was the second time this evening that the girl's name had been brought up. She was becoming every bit the nuisance she'd feared, though for entirely different reasons. Her dear friend Edith had already come up to her and asked who Prudence was. Evidently, she'd found her son having a rather intense conversation with the lovely Prudence on the grand staircase. Having to tell her dear friend that Prudence was her nieces' lady's maid was one of the single most mortifying things she'd ever had to do. She and Edith had long cherished the hope that their two families would be united through marriage, and she was sure that, given time, Sebastian's and Elaine's friendship would blossom into something more. Until it did, every female was a potential threat, and if the daughter had the cunning and wiles of the mother . . .

Lady Summerset spotted Prudence standing with Victoria, Rowena, and Elaine and a few of the other girls in their set. They were watching the dancers and chatting. Only with discipline was she able to keep the slow-burning irritation she felt in her stomach from showing on her face. How dare the girl dress that way? If Lady Summerset hadn't known better, she would have taken the girl for aristocracy. There were very few servants, no matter how comely, no matter how fine the clothing, who could pass for gentry. Something in their language or speech would give them away. But you could introduce this girl to court and no one would know that her mother was a slatternly maid who'd had a child out of wedlock when she was barely old enough to wear long corsets.

The burn increased as the Duchess of Kent stopped to speak to the girls. Lady Summerset watched, incensed, as Prudence was introduced, gave a heartbreakingly perfect curtsy, and chatted with the Duchess as if she had a right to it all. The Duchess moved on and Lady Charlotte sauntered in that direction. There had to be a way to put a stop to that creature before she could cause any more mischief. She was stopped a few moments later when Lord Billingsly, accompanied by Lady Summerset's son and young Kittredge, descended upon the girls, laughing. In spite of several shakes of her dark head, Prudence was led out onto the dance floor by Lord Billingsly, who had glanced at no one else, not even the comely Lady Diana Manners, who had also joined the group.

Warning bells rang in Lady Summerset's head as she observed the couple dancing, their eyes full of each other. Glancing around the room, she spotted Hortense in the arms of Sir James McLeod, a retired commander of Her Majesty's Navy. Lady Summerset caught her eye and indicated that her presence was needed. If Hortense was displeased at her inconvenient summons, she gave no indication and was by her ladyship's side in moments.

"I need to speak to Prudence as soon as possible. Send her to the drawing room just before the bell is rung for supper. And please let Cairns know that I changed the seating arrangements. Put Elaine next to Lord Billingsly. Seat whoever was there next to Mr. Pettigrew, please."

That accomplished, she made her leisurely way through the Great Hall, chatting with her guests and asking her servants whether they were having a good time. Her servants assured her they were and whispered to one another, gratified that she'd remembered their names.

By the time Lady Summerset made her way to her lovely new drawing room, it was almost time for the bell to be rung for dinner, always a trying time, as the extra servants from town were bound to do something wrong, unlike her own servants, who served impeccably. She trailed her fingers along the satiny-smooth marble of the fireplace mantel, considering her next move. The fact that the girl was still here, after all the subtle attempts to force her out, indicated a tiresome stubbornness and loyalty. Two character traits that may be applauded in others but were rather an inconvenience in this case. Her continued presence at Summerset was not only the threat of a possible scandal but now it was also a risk to her daughter's happiness. Something must be done.

She heard Prudence enter the room behind her.

"You wished to see me, my lady?"

Lady Summerset turned to face Prudence and her stomach churned uneasily to see the Buxton

313

eyes staring back at her. She wished her own daughter had received those signature eyes instead of her own commonplace blue ones. But then Prudence lowered her eyes in a subservience Lady Summerset knew she didn't feel.

"Do you know why I asked you here? No, of course not," Lady Summerset continued without waiting for an answer. "You couldn't possibly know."

The girl's eyes shot up to Lady Summerset's face for a moment before she lowered them again—the only evidence of her surprise.

Perhaps Lady Summerset's greatest unacknowledged talent was her gift for cards. She was a skilled player in any game society chose to play that season, and her chief talent was the ability to both win *and lose* at will. It takes real skill to lose a game without arousing the suspicion of the other players. This skill came in very handy with Poor King Edward, who was a passionate and talentless card player. She knew exactly when and how each card should be played and it was time to play one now.

"I'm sure you are quite aware that you are not wanted here at Summerset." Prudence's head came up and she paled. Lady Summerset continued. "Don't take it personally, my dear, because it really has nothing to do with you, but rather the whole situation."

The girl made no attempt at subservience now.

314

She kept her eyes trained on Lady Summerset in a way that was rather unnerving. "Exactly what would it take for you to leave, I wonder?"

"Excuse me?"

Lady Summerset held in an impatient breath. "I suppose you are staying on because of your loyalty to Victoria and Rowena, and that is commendable, but surely you can see now that it's not necessary? This is their home and they are among family. I know their upbringing was unconventional, but surely you can see that this is the life they were born to and it's a life that you definitely were *not* born to?"

"Isn't it?" the girl asked, rather saucily. "I'm the daughter of a maid and I am here as a lady's maid. You might say this is exactly what I was born for."

Lady Summerset had an urge to slap her but smiled instead. "You misunderstand me. Yes, your mother was a maid, but you were not raised to be in service. And really, your presence here is making both Victoria and Rowena unhappy, though in different ways."

She watched the girl's face carefully and saw that her words had hit home. She pressed her advantage. "I'm not unkind. I am simply of the school that believes like should stick with like, and I am afraid your continued presence in my home will only serve to upset my nieces further." She paused to let her words sink in. "So what would you need in order to leave comfortably?"

Prudence pressed her hands together until her knuckles were white. "You are offering me money?"

Lady Summerset's mouth pursed together with distaste. How like the young to bring up money. "I'm offering you . . . assistance."

Prudence cleared her throat. "I am here because Rowena and Victoria want me here. They need me to be with them and their father would want us to be together. I will leave when they no longer need me."

Prudence turned to leave, but Lady Summerset grabbed hold of her arm. "So you would stay even if doing so is hurting the girls you profess to love?"

Prudence remained stonily silent.

"My offer is still good when you come to your senses."

Prudence shook Lady Summerset's hand off her arm and once again, Lady Summerset wished for the old days when one could strike a servant with no consequences. Prudence whisked out of the room, her head held high.

The dinner bell sounded and Lady Summerset took a moment to compose herself. Then she placed a smile on her face and went to join her guests.

CHAPTER
THIRTEEN

Rowena threw herself into having fun at the servants' ball. She gossiped with the girls, gushed over her cousin's impromptu plans for a skating party tomorrow, danced with every young man who asked her, and even participated in the planning of the evening's prank. During dinner, she flirted sweetly with the old deaf major to her right and listened intently to the woman on her left, whose reigning passion was in the care and breeding of corgis.

And none of it did a damn bit of good. The world stayed drab and cold, and inside, where there should be feelings and thoughts and ideas, there was emptiness. What was wrong with her? For something had to be wrong. Young women didn't just stop feeling alive because their father died. She knew her sister was in every bit as much pain as she was, but Victoria was still Victoria. She was still passionate and articulate and mercurial in her emotions. Rowena didn't feel like the same girl at all. Of course, she'd never been as spirited as Vic. Maybe her father's death had just revealed to Rowena her true character . . . she was a boring, cold, listless woman without passions or original ideas, who was destined to grow old without having really lived.

She shook her head, impatient with her gloomy thoughts. How morbid she could be for heaven's sake!

Elaine stealthily passed her a flask and Rowena shrugged. Might as well. She still had another ball to make it through. Now that the servants' ball was over, the rest of the orchestra had joined their companions who had played earlier and they'd reconvened in the grand ballroom, where the family ball was to begin. She took a short pull on the flask, sputtered, and passed it back to Elaine.

"What is that?" she asked. "It's so sweet!"

"Black cherry brandy. Kit brought it. Isn't it wretched? We're putting it in the punch and we'll see if anyone notices."

"Someone will notice all right. It's horrid." But it warmed its way down her chest and into her stomach and Rowena felt herself relaxing ever so slightly.

She spotted Victoria standing near the doorway next to Kit, who had suddenly become her sister's shadow. At first she'd been concerned about such a suave young man taking an interest in her little sister, but as far as she could tell he seemed far more smitten than Victoria was. Poor fellow. He'll soon find out that Victoria still looks at men as simply deeper-voiced playmates.

"This is my favorite part of Christmas," Elaine said, linking her arms with Rowena's. "No matter how boring the balls are, it's almost worth it to see the ballroom look this way."

Rowena agreed. Though the ballroom had been wired for electricity, for this occasion the room had been lit with the soft, flattering glow of hundreds of candles from the low-hanging crystal chandeliers and dozens of gold and ivory Chinese lanterns, all of which were reflected in the large gilt mirrors lining one wall. Rowena knew that this year the giant Christmas tree in the corner had been strung with thousands of electric fairy lights, which would be turned on at the designated moment. They were still rare enough in country homes as to cause a sensation.

The corners of her mouth twitched. Of course, no one but the Coterie knew just how much of a sensation the lighting of the Christmas tree was going to cause.

Small white and gold chairs with ivory brocade cushions were scattered in little groups under enormous potted palms to give the ladies and gentlemen a place to rest when they tired of dancing. The chairs and sofas had been specially designed for the room in the 1700s by Thomas Chippendale so they would fit perfectly under the mirrors. The dance floor itself was a work of art, each inlaid piece of wood brought over, log by log, from South America, back during the colonial period. It gleamed with the care that only the attention of a half dozen servants working for a week could impart.

She spotted Aunt Charlotte near the punch bowl, regal in a rose-colored lace ball gown with sleeves that puffed out softly at the shoulders. A shimmering tiara sat on her head and a diamond choker glittered at her neck. She and Sebastian's mother were chatting with a blue-haired princess from Austria. Her uncle was speaking to a Turkish diplomat near the orchestra with some men from the House of Lords. Her cousin Colin and Sebastian stood with Kit and Victoria, watching the orchestra warm up after their hour-long break and reconfiguration. The only person who wasn't here was Prudence, but of course, she wouldn't be here. She hadn't been invited.

Pain and guilt stabbed at her stomach. Funny how those emotions could always be felt, no matter how big the void inside of her was.

Then the orchestra started up and Colin claimed her before anyone else had a chance to. Rowena enjoyed dancing, and if dancing could drown out the pain she felt or the thoughts that hummed about her mind like useless bees, then she would dance until the sun came up.

The orchestra turned out to be quite good, and played classical tunes as well as the more modern, piano-driven tunes such as "Glow Worm," "Moonstruck," and the "Lily of Laguna" that Victoria loved so much. She danced mostly with Colin, whose keen sense of humor, open admiration, and undemanding conversation made him the most agreeable of her dance partners. Too many of the other young men wanted to flirt with her or impress her with their pedigree. After her father's industriousness and his passion about his work, these young men, who did nothing, seemed lifeless and insipid. And none of them could come close to holding a candle to Jon, whose love of flying made him the most compelling man she'd ever met. She wondered whether he liked to dance. She closed her eyes and imagined that it was Jon's arms around her, whirling her about the dance floor. For a moment her breathing shortened, until the music stopped and she realized it was just her cousin.

Sebastian claimed her moments later. She didn't mind dancing with Sebastian, either, because she suspected his interest lay elsewhere and he had other motives besides wanting to dance with her.

The music hadn't played four bars before she was proven right. "Why isn't Prudence here?"

His voice was flat and Rowena stiffened in his arms. What had Prudence told him? That Rowena was the horrible sister who had stuck her in a servant's role and then left her there? What could she say? That the accusations were true but she hadn't meant any of it, so sorry? They had gone halfway around the dance floor before she finally responded. "My aunt would not welcome Prudence here."

"And you don't find that unconscionable?"

"What would you have me do about it?" she flared. She glanced around to see whether anyone had heard her. Lowering her voice, she continued. "The only way I could get my uncle to accept the idea of Prudence coming with us was to tell him she was our lady's maid."

"You could have left her in London." His voice was accusatory and she winced.

"To do what? Uncle Conrad wanted to sell our London home."

"He *wanted* to sell your home? He doesn't now?"

Rowena bit her lip. She did not want anyone else to know that the house had been let out until she had a chance to tell Prudence. Prudence already felt betrayed. If she found out . . . "That's not what I meant. I'm sure he is just as eager to sell our home as he was then, even though I have begged him not to. Besides, Lord Billingsly, what is your interest in all of this?" Rowena turned the tables on him, desperate to dodge this line of questioning.

He stared over her shoulder, his jaw set and his mouth firm. For several moments they whirled in silence as the "Blue Danube" played. There were so many dancers reflected in the mirror, twirling in so many brilliant colors, that it almost looked as if they were dancing inside a kaleidoscope.

"Would you believe my interest is impersonal in nature, or perhaps I merely have an unexplained interest in the treatment of servants?"

Rowena tilted her head back to get a better look at his face. The sense of humor she had noticed before revealed itself now in the curving of his lips, but the smile didn't quite reach his eyes, which held sadness in their dark depths. She shook her head. "No, I actually wouldn't believe either of those things."

"I didn't think you would." He drew in a deep breath before speaking again. "The truth is, I have found Miss Tate captivating beyond all normal reason and have since the first time I laid eyes on her. I dearly wish to get to know her better. Unfortunately, circumstances being what they are, I'm not sure that is possible, and at the end of every encounter I end up feeling either foolish or like a cad."

Rowena's heart constricted. She'd had no idea what events she would put into play by her careless bargain with her uncle. But what other choice did she have? "Prudence is special. Far too special to be put in the position I have unwittingly placed her in."

"Then why did you?"

His voice was as short as the question and Rowena pulled her hand from his just as the music ended. She sensed his frustration and was sorry for it, but honestly, she couldn't be held responsible for one more person's misery.

"We were losing our home on top of just having lost our father. Should we then lose our sister, as well?" She whirled around to leave but he caught her by the arm.

"But isn't that exactly what you've done? Haven't you lost her just as surely as you lost your father?"

She jerked her arm out of his hand and stalked off, tears stinging at her eyes.

A bell sounded and her aunt Charlotte stood near the orchestra and clapped her gloved hands softly. When the crowd quieted, she gave a gentle smile that belied the steel underneath the lady-like exterior. "I would like to personally thank everyone for coming. My husband and I feel so blessed to have so many wonderful friends. It's now time to light the Buxton family Christmas tree. Please help yourself to a glass of champagne and my husband will make a toast. There will be a buffet at the far corner of the room after, and of course, the dancing will go on for hours yet."

Rowena wanted to sneak out of the ballroom and go hide in her room, but she couldn't possibly do it now. She had committed to be involved in the prank and she couldn't back out. She took a deep breath and, as nonchalantly as possible, slipped a handful of firecrackers from the miniature velvet bag she wore attached to her wrist. Victoria, Elaine, and several other young women did the same thing. If anyone noticed the little velvet pouches the young women carried on their wrists as they used to carry dance cards, they no doubt thought it a new fashion. The pouches were Elaine's idea. They not only allowed them to sneak in a large number of firecrackers, but they also let the women take an active part in the prank. And to think Elaine used to be such a starchy young miss.

There was a flurry of activity as everyone snatched fluted crystal glasses from the servants circulating in and out of the crowd. Not looking her in the eye, Sebastian passed her quite close and bumped her gently as she passed him the firecrackers.

As Lord Summerset began speaking, the young men of the Coterie began moving casually to different points around the room. Elaine had been correct—there were so many candles about the room that lighting the firecrackers wasn't a problem.

Rowena's uncle came to stand next to his wife and slipped a hand about her waist. They stood together, tall and statuesque, regal in their bearing and mien. Together they were a shining example of privileged British aristocracy. "As my wife says, Providence has seen fit to bless us with so many good friends to celebrate the Yuletide season with," Lord Summerset began. "Let us forget all our cares, such as the labor movement"—he paused as many of the men laughed—"and enjoy ourselves. A toast to all that is good about our fair country." He held up his glass and everyone held up their glasses before drinking.

Rowena clutched her champagne glass but didn't raise it to her lips. As everyone took a sip from his or her glass, the multicolored lights on the eighteen-foot tree lit up in a rainbow of brilliant colors. There was a gasp of appreciation from the crowd moments before an earsplitting snapping and popping sounded from all corners of the room.

In spite of having braced herself for it, Rowena still jumped and several women screamed. One old woman fainted as a thick smoke wafted through the room. For a few moments the noise was deafening and then it waned after the last of the firecrackers died down and the crowd realized what had happened. Only someone was still in hysterics.

Everyone turned toward the balcony to where a cluster of servants stood, watching the ball. Prudence, still in her finery, stood with her arms about Susie, whose screams slowly subsided into a terrified whimper.

Rowena stared at Prudence and her stomach plummeted, for the look on Prudence's face was unlike anything Rowena had ever seen from her typically amiable friend. Two high spots of color stood out on her cheeks, and determination sprang from the set of her fine jaw and the slashing line of her mouth. Even from far away Rowena could see the fire in Prudence's eyes as they blazed out at someone in the crowd. Rowena gave a quick prayer of thanks that the look wasn't aimed at her. Then she followed Prudence's gaze and with a shiver of deep apprehension realized the person Prudence was staring at with such scorn was staring back at her, just as fiercely.

Aunt Charlotte.

The next morning, Rowena sorted through the pile of ice skates, searching for a pair that looked as if they might be close to her size. She'd been tentatively enthusiastic about the impromptu skating party her cousin had thrown together, thinking it would be a good way to get away from the house, but now she wondered why she had bothered to come at all. Victoria had skated away with Kit the moment he arrived, and though Rowena had at first worried about her sister's breathing, she noticed the young man being uncharacteristically accommodating of his charge by skating slowly and taking plenty of breaks. Rowena smiled as she watched her sister. She looked ethereal today in a peacock-blue fur-trimmed cloak she'd borrowed from Elaine.

She'd been surprised that Aunt Charlotte had let them all come out to the frozen pond unchaperoned, but after the prank last night, her aunt no doubt realized that the young people needed an outing that would expend their energy, as well as keep them out of her hair as she entertained her other guests. If her aunt only knew, Rowena thought, watching as one of the girls passed cigarettes to the others. Smoking in public! Judging from the way everyone acted, it wasn't the first time.

Rowena finally found a pair of skates that would fit and sat on a nearby log to put them on. The last time she had gone skating, Prudence had accompanied her and they had helped each other with their skates. This morning, Prudence hadn't even shown up to help her dress, which at first had irritated her and then made her cheeks burn with shame. They'd never had to tell each other their whereabouts at home. The thought of home made her want to throw her skates to the ground. Their personal items were no doubt being packed and shipped to them as she sat wrestling with a stupid skate, and she still hadn't gotten the nerve to tell Victoria that they couldn't go home, let alone Prudence.

She finally stood up and took a couple of hesitant steps onto the ice, wondering whether she still remembered how to skate. There were several ponds either on or adjacent to Summerset property, but this was the only one wide enough and shallow enough to freeze all the way across on a regular basis. The Buxtons and others from town could skate here almost every year. In the summer, it was mostly a frog pond for young boys to play in.

Thinking of Prudence made her remember the look her aunt and Prudence had exchanged the night before. Worry tensed her neck and shoulders. Prudence had no idea what their aunt was capable of. You did not want to be on her bad side.

Colin clapped his hands, interrupting her thoughts. "Coterie!" he called before skating up to her and performing a sliding stop that sprayed snow all over the hem of her dress. She was about to protest, but the smile he gave her was so cheeky, she couldn't scold him. She envied him his simple happiness, even though she knew that as he was being groomed for a life he didn't really want, he couldn't possibly be as happy as he acted.

The others skated over, some with more skill than others. She'd met them all last night of course, but couldn't for the life of her remember their names. The one young woman she had really enjoyed, Lady Diana, had left with her parents this morning for, in her words, death by a deadly dull royal reception in London. There were about twelve of them in all, including all four Buxtons and their friends. Ages ranged from Kit, the eldest at twenty-six, to Victoria, who was eighteen. Rowena knew without asking that all were wealthy, highborn as well as high-spirited, and working very hard at thumbing their noses at established society while at the same time enjoying the privilege it afforded them.

Colin cleared his throat and Kit solicitously handed him a flask. Colin took a long drink and nodded in gratitude. "Thank you, my good man. Now, you've all met our cousins, the honorable Rowena and Victoria. They wish to be considered for entrance into our humble club."

One of the young women, a brassy blonde with bold Slavic features, laughed. "And when has a Buxton ever been involved in anything humble? And of course they can join. It's not as though we have an admittance committee."

Elaine laughed and held up her thumb and forefinger about an inch apart. "Not even an itty-bitty committee, Daphne?"

"God save me from a committee," Kit muttered. Victoria grinned up at him and Rowena frowned. It wasn't that she didn't want Vic to be happy, but there was something about Kit that was so cynical. Rowena wasn't sure that he could really be happy with anyone, let alone her excitable, imaginative little sister.

"Death by committee?" Victoria asked.

"Surely it wouldn't take death to become one of us, as none of us are dead. But I'm finding the whole thing rather moot. You're either Coterie material or you are not." Daphne shrugged.

"But exactly what makes up Coterie material?" Rowena was finally roused enough to ask. "Seems to me the entrance requirements are rather vague."

Sebastian laughed. "I think the whole club is rather vague."

A horn of a motorcar blared behind them and they turned to see a Buxton vehicle arrive, carrying several servants. Another one chugged past them and parked on the other side of the pond.

After exiting the car, two of the servants went to the back of the vehicle and pulled out several large baskets from the rear seat. Another brought out a folding table and began setting up what appeared to be a hot luncheon. Andrew approached Colin and stood at attention. "Excuse me, sir. Your mother sent us with refreshments."

Colin waved his hand. "But I thought we had brought refreshments?" He peered into a small basket that had been sitting on the bank. "Elaine, all you brought was hot chocolate and spirits?"

Elaine shook her muff at him. "You said we should rough it."

Andrew stood at attention, waiting to be dismissed so he could help the others set up their food. Rowena frowned, noticing a cut above one eye and a bruise across his brow bone. Had he been in a fight?

While Colin and his friend verbally sparred

over the definition of "roughing it," Andrew stood, waiting to be dismissed.

"Thank you, Andrew. That will be all," Rowena said, unable to bear his awkward, erect stance any longer. The footman gave her a nod of gratitude and hurried up the bank to the auto.

Colin looked at the decanter in his hand. "Well, as long as it's out, let's drink to the new members."

Victoria's face fell. "What? No pledging of blood or secret initiation?"

"You can always jump down a rabbit hole," Kit drawled next to her, and again, Rowena saw the complicit smiles they gave each other. Was there something more than just an innocent flirtation going on between them, something she should know about? Not for the first time she felt the overwhelming responsibility her father's death had created for her. Why did she still feel so unequal to the challenge?

"No blood as yet," Sebastian said, speaking for the first time. "The opium dens all come later."

Everyone laughed as the servants picked their way down the bank with trays piled high with sandwiches. Rowena twitched her shoulders, out of place and out of sorts. The servants had brought chairs for the ladies and set them up on the edge of the ice. Victoria sat down and patted the chair next to her.

"Come eat with me, Ro. Aren't you famished?"

From across the pond where the other vehicle had stopped came a loud hooting. The others, busy with their food and flasks, took no notice, but when Rowena glanced over, she saw the servants all looking over at their group and laughing. Rowena flushed, watching the servants weaving in and out of the skaters, serving them their tea and hot chocolate. She supposed they did look like a bunch of pampered children instead of a group of adults who were perfectly capable of packing, serving, and eating their own food.

Her eyes narrowed as she spotted a redheaded man looking her way. It couldn't be Jon, could it? Her heart pounded. Though she'd sent him a note thanking him for a lovely afternoon, she hadn't heard back from him except for the nightly visits of his plane.

He was sitting on a rock and watching his companions skate. Every once in a while she heard him call out to his friends, and the sound of his voice sent her pulse racing. Without thinking, she set her half-eaten sandwich back on the silver salver, much to Andrew's surprise.

"Sorry," she muttered, before skating off. Halfway across the pond she almost changed her mind and turned back, but his companions had noticed her beeline across the ice and had correctly surmised that she was headed for them. They came together as a group surrounding Jon, who looked more handsome than ever with the cold adding color into his high cheekbones and his unruly dark red hair all askew as if he'd just taken off a cap. A flickering of his eyes was the only surprise he showed as she approached.

She came to a careful stop in front of him and gave all the young men a nervous smile. As loud and unruly as they were before, they had lapsed into a group as bashful as choirboys, though they all looked to be in their midtwenties.

"Hello, Jonathon. How is your ankle?"

Four pairs of eyes widened at the use of Jonathon's name and the others turned toward him accusingly. His cheeks grew even redder under their scrutiny. "It's much better, thank you. Though not quite up to ice-skating standards, mind you."

"And how do you know my rascally brother, miss?"

Startled, Rowena turned toward the young man who had spoken. Yes, there was a certain resemblance, especially about the eyes. He stared at her boldly and she raised her brows. "You might say he fell right into my lap," she answered tartly.

Jonathon laughed and stood up carefully. He took her arm as if to claim ownership and Rowena blushed, rather liking the sensation. "Gentlemen, may I present to you one of the New Women. Don't cross her, as she's liable to take you down a notch or two with her very sharp and emancipated tongue."

There was a guffaw among the men and Jonathon's brother stepped forward.

The man's eyes swept over her in appreciation, and Rowena was glad she'd dressed sensibly for the occasion. Instead of wearing fur as the other girls had, she had donned a slim-skirted, blue-ribbed skating suit and matching cap and dark blue wool gloves and scarf. A sensible, no-nonsense dress, though trousers would be far more sensible for skating than a skirt could ever be.

"If this is the New Woman, I wonder why I ever bothered with the old ones," Jon's brother said. "And would this New Woman have a name?"

Jon tensed next to her and his grip on her arm tightened. "Actually, she does. George, may I present to you the Honorable Rowena Buxton? Rowena, this is my older brother, George. Don't mind him, I got all the manners in the family."

But the good humor of the party had fallen away with the mention of her name. If she thought Jon had reacted poorly to her last name, that was nothing compared to the chill emanating from his brother.

"A Buxton, eh, baby brother? Reaching a bit above yourself, aren't you?"

Rowena winced, but Jon's hand released her arm and then he pulled her close, his arm over her shoulders protectively. "You don't even know her, and if you did, you would be ashamed of yourself. Come, Rowena, let's go for a walk, shall we?"

Mutely, she nodded; they turned their backs on the group and walked away carefully, as she was on skates and he was wearing shoes and limping.

"I apologize for my brother. I'm afraid he can be a bit of a pill."

She glanced at him, but he was staring straight ahead, his jawline set and his lips pressed together. "I take it there is no love lost between our families. Would you mind telling me why?"

He looked over at her, surprised. "You mean, you don't know?"

She shook her head. "You have to remember, I was not brought up here. I only came for the summers, and even then there were so many social events, we rarely spent time together as a family. So I was not really privy to anything that may have happened."

He shook his head. "It probably never came up because your uncle treads on the lower classes as a regular thing. No doubt he didn't spend more than five minutes thinking about it altogether. Only as much time as he needed to tell his army of solicitors what he wanted and how to get it. They did all the dirty work, while he went hunting or riding or whatever it is he does when not choking the life out of his tenants."

She stopped, stricken by the bitterness in his voice. Part of her felt she should defend her

336

uncle, but how could she defend him? Jon was probably right.

He saw her face and took a deep breath. "I'm sorry. The Wellses become a bit overwrought on the topic of Conrad Buxton. But it really has nothing to do with you."

His voice was uncertain as he added that last part and Rowena began moving again. "No, it does not," she said firmly. "My father left Summerset for Oxford when he was nineteen and never looked back. If my uncle did something to hurt your family, I am very sorry."

"Your apologies couldn't possibly put a dent into the wrong that has been done, but I do thank you for the sentiment. You see, I hold your uncle responsible for my father's death."

Rowena gasped, placing one hand over her open mouth. They stopped moving and she turned toward him. Her skates added several inches to her height so that he was only an inch or so taller than she was. His eyes, so close to the color of the sky they had flown through together, seemed very close to her own, and her pulse raced. "I'm so very sorry for your loss, but I don't think my uncle . . ." Her voice stopped as he placed a gentle hand over her mouth.

"Listen before you make judgments. I don't make these accusations lightly, but neither are they up for debate. Understood?"

She nodded and they continued moving, he

337

walking and she gliding along next to him.

"The Wellses and the Buxtons had been friends for a very long time, since the War of the Roses, actually. A young page named Wells saved the life of the son from Summerset. Lord Summerset knighted him and gave him a large piece of his estate in reward. It was a prime piece of land and they made a good living from it. So even though I'm not of noble blood, I am considered gentry." He gave her a wry smile, but Rowena couldn't smile back. The pit of her stomach was in knots as she anticipated what she was going to hear about her family.

"Over time, the friendship between the two families waned a bit as the Buxtons amassed a fortune and the Wellses sat, happy and satisfied with their big stone home and the decent living the farm afforded them. They made enough money to give their sons and daughters a good start and they were always involved in the civic life of the town."

"It sounds like a good life," she ventured, but Jon was so caught up in his story, he didn't even seem to hear her.

"My father was a bit of a dreamer and had more ambition than the Wellses who came before him, and he became convinced that there was a seam of coal near the old quarry. He must have had some reason for believing it was so, because he hired an expert to assay the property."

"And they found coal?" Rowena knew without being told how the story would end. The only part that puzzled her was how on earth her uncle could possibly be responsible for his father's death.

"They found coal," Jon agreed. "It wasn't a great deal. Not nearly what they have in the north or in Wales, but it was of very good quality and enough to make a small fortune for the Wells family. Only the Wells family will never see the profit from that coal. In a classic Buxton maneuver, Lord Summerset brought up an old property line dispute, and of course the courts settled in your uncle's favor."

A cramp of misery settled between Rowena's eyes. "I'm so sorry," she said softly.

"That isn't the worst of it," he continued. Rowena wanted to put her hands over her ears to stop the words, but felt she ought to listen. "My father was so convinced that things had changed, that the courts couldn't be bought by wealth and privilege, that he fought them. Hard. When it became more and more clear that he wouldn't win, he grew bitter and angry and in the process emptied the family coffers of all our money. When it finally ended, we'd lost almost everything and barely had enough money to keep the property solvent. And of course, the Buxtons added more money to their already fat wallets while my family teetered on the edge of bankruptcy. When my father finally came to his senses and realized what he had done, he took a gun, walked out to the old stone quarry where the new coal mine was already in production, and shot himself in the head. And that, my dear Rowena, is why the Wellses can't abide the Buxtons."

Sometime during the last few minutes of his story they had stopped walking. Rowena's legs were shaking as she tried to understand the horrible story she had just heard. And the sad truth was, he was probably right about her uncle. The business that had ruined a family probably sat on his desk for several days and then had been dispatched with due speed and into the hands of the lawyers. "Get me that property," her uncle had probably said, and the lawyers had done it. And it's not as though the Buxtons needed the money. While other great families teetered on the edge of disaster, the Buxtons had a talent for making money, and each earl had added to instead of taking away from the family fortune.

Turning to him, she took his hands into hers. The calluses between his thumb and forefinger caught on the soft wool of her glove. She'd never felt that on a man's hands before. She was sure her uncle had never had them, nor any of the young men who frolicked on the other side of the pond. "I'm sorry from the bottom of my heart that happened to your family. I can say nothing that can make up for any of it. Just know that I care that it happened and I am sorry. I do hope that what happened in the past won't affect the friendship you and I have."

Their faces were so close she could see little flecks of green in the blue. Just as she lost herself in the wide blue of the sky, she could lose herself in the blue of his eyes.

He smiled down at her. "Others have offered their sympathies, but nothing has ever soothed as much as those words coming from your lips. Thank you, Rowena. And no, let's not let it affect our friendship." His head bent and for a fraction of a second, his lips brushed across hers. It had only been for a moment, but her mouth missed the heat of his the second he withdrew. Startled, she pulled back and looked around. Victoria and Elaine were staring out across the pond toward her and she wondered whether they had seen. Had she really just been kissed? It was so quick, it was like it hadn't happened at all, and yet her lips still tingled from the contact.

He laughed at her bewilderment and she pulled her hands out of his. What on earth should she do now? She had just been kissed. In public. And she liked it. The teasing light of his eyes told her he suspected that she liked it.

"Would you like to fly with me again?" he asked as she pulled away.

She hesitated, her heart pounding. She should say no. After that little scene she should certainly say no. "Yes," she said breathlessly, skating away. "Oh, yes." And she went back to her party, his laughter ringing in her ears.

The sun was just setting and the last of the light, coupled with the light of the moon reflecting off the snow, made the unused portions of the house gleam strangely. Victoria smelled the fire even without the light shining through the open door. Part of her resented his entering her room without her, but that was silly. She knew he would be here. At the skating party today, he had told her he had been detained the last time and he wished to renew their rendezvous. For a moment she thought to tell him to go hang, just to see his reaction, but then she remembered what she had discovered about Prudence's mother. She had a feeling that Kit, much like she, knew all sorts of things he wasn't supposed to know. At any rate, he might be able to point her in the right direction.

She entered the room quietly. At first it seemed empty, but then she spotted him standing in front of a perfectly shaped evergreen tree. He lit the last candle as she watched. Along with the light glowing from the fire, it created a lovely and festive atmosphere.

He heard her swift intake of breath and turned toward her, smiling. "Happy Christmas," he said simply.

She clapped her hands with delight and his smile grew. "Oh, it's beautiful. How did you manage?"

"It wasn't easy," he admitted. "I had one of the servants cut down the tree and take it to my room. I've been pilfering decorations from your aunt Charlotte's stash and have been hiding them in the room across the hall for the last couple of days. I was terribly worried we would run into each other in the hall and you would demand to know what I was doing."

He looked delighted that his secret had been a success and it was the first time she had ever seen him without the bored, haughty look he always affected. He was much improved without it.

She came and stood by him and they both stared at the tree. A silence descended for a moment until she slipped her arm into his. "Thank you so much. This is the nicest surprise anyone could have given me. The trees in the rest of the house are lovely, of course, but our holidays at home were never as grand as here and this tree in this little room is absolutely perfect . . . it reminds me of home."

He laid his hand on hers. "I'm so very glad. The first Christmas after my father passed away was the most difficult. After that it gets easier, though it's never the same."

"Were you very close to your father?"

"Not exceedingly. I don't think any little

English aristocrats are close to their parents. We're all raised by nannies and governesses and sent away to school at eight or nine. But he loved me and I loved him, in our own fashion. I sense this wasn't the same way with your father."

She shook her head, staring hard at the candles flickering on the tree. "No. We were all very close. We were raised much differently. My father had very radical ideas on child rearing and we spent most of our time together as a family." She stopped talking, unable to go on, and Kit patted her hand.

"I didn't bring you here to make you sad, and I have another surprise for you."

She raised an eyebrow. "More surprises?"

He nodded, looking more like a naughty boy than a bored aristocrat. He pointed to the bottom of the tree and she stooped for a better look. A velvet jewelry box wrapped in a silver ribbon sat underneath. "And I didn't bring you anything," she murmured.

He laughed and handed her the box. "Christmas is about giving, not getting."

She looked up into his blue eyes, surprised. "That's a decidedly sentimental sentiment, Mr. Kittredge."

"I have them on occasion. But don't tell anyone."

She untied the ribbon carefully to give her heart time to slow. Her breath caught as she stared at the small cameo necklace inside. The disk was shining onyx against which the dainty ivory profile of a woman glowed softly. It hung on a chain of delicate filigreed silver. "It's lovely," she breathed, lifting it out of the box.

"I'm glad you like it."

"Thank you for my gift. And the tree."

He glanced sideways at her, a half smile curving his lips. "You're very welcome. Sometimes I surprise even myself."

She tilted her head so she could see his face. He was staring at her, his eyes serious. "But there is something we must discuss," he said.

She nodded, matching his seriousness with the same sincerity.

"I have been wrestling with this for the past several days. I enjoy your company. I enjoy your company very much. I don't think I've ever met a woman who was so easy and stimulating to be around. You are one of the least boring people I know."

He paused as if puzzled by the turn of events and Victoria drew back, alarmed. Good God. What was he getting at? He wasn't trying to propose, was he? For that would change everything . . .

"I wish us to be friends. Good friends, actually, but I am afraid that it might give people ideas that I was interested in you for reasons other than friendship, which is not at all the case as I am not interested in marriage."

She rocked back on her heels and resisted the urge to laugh. He took himself so seriously! At least he wasn't asking her to marry him, which would be outrageous. "Pardon me while I attempt to understand . . . you are afraid people may receive the wrong impression?"

Here he nodded and looked so uncomfortable that a thought struck her. "You're afraid *I* shall receive the wrong impression."

He shifted again and refused to meet her eye. She pinched his arm, hard, and his eyes flew open. "Hey!"

"If we are to be chums, then you have to tell the truth. You were afraid that I would get the wrong impression, weren't you?"

He nodded, his mouth turned downward.

"And even though I told you that I didn't want to get married, that left no impression what-soever? You didn't believe me at all?"

It was almost amusing to see a gentleman so tall trying to shrink himself. "Well, not exactly . . ."

She stuck a finger in his face. "You thought that just because I'm a woman that I would *have* to want to get married." She shook her head. His face was evidence enough. "Now that we're friends, you need to remember that almost everything you think you know about women is going to be turned on its ear. Understood?"

He looked down at her small hand and then

grinned. "How old did you say you were?" he asked, marveling.

"Now I have something I need from you and this is to be in the strictest confidence. Can I trust you?"

He nodded, his blue eyes quizzical. "I don't take friendships lightly, as you will find out."

"Excellent. Read this, please, and tell me what you think."

His brow furrowed as he took the newspaper clipping. She waited until he read it through. "Why do you think they had an inquiry concerning Halpernia's death?" she finally asked. "Do you think there was something not right about it?"

He shook his head. "They always do for a drowning. They ruled it as accidental."

She nodded. "I saw that. I just get this feeling that there is something more." She took back the clipping and made up her mind. "I need you to come with me. I know someone who may have the answers. Will you come?"

He put out his hand and smiled at her. "Right now, my dear, I would follow you down a rabbit hole."

She nodded. "You may not feel that way by the time we're done."

CHAPTER
FOURTEEN

Prudence walked carefully along the frozen track back to Summerset, not wanting to slip and fall. She knew she could have asked Andrew to take her to town and back, but after the ball a few nights past, she wasn't quite sure what to say to him.

Her cheeks flamed again as she thought of the reason he and one of the gardeners had a scuffle during the ball. The man had actually said aloud that Lord Billingsly must be the toff who had bought Prudence's green dress and that it didn't take a schoolmaster to figure out why. Who knew that such a muddle would come of a simple ball gown? And fancy Andrew sticking up for her virtue that way. She had no idea how to express her thanks and her embarrassment, which was why she had chosen to walk to town today instead of asking for a ride. Rumor had it that Andrew and the gardener had each lost a week's pay over the skirmish.

Well, she supposed she would have to deal with that sooner or later. She had enough on her mind today without including Andrew. Her cousin had been among the townspeople who had worked at Summerset the night of the ball. He had given her the news that the family had wanted to meet her.

The only stipulation was that she not mention Alice's name to Gran. Apparently, Prudence's mother was a favorite and the heartbreak had almost killed the old woman. So Prudence had spent the morning with Wesley and his parents and Gran, who had taken residence at her son's house until she was back on her feet again.

Her heart warmed again as she thought of meeting her family. She'd felt such a void since they'd moved to Summerset and she'd lost her sisters that she'd never thought she would feel that warm connectedness again.

At first the reunion had been awkward as they struggled to find things to say that didn't involve Alice, but after they began eating lunch and stopped trying so hard, the conversation had taken wing and Prudence ended up having a pleasant time. Her uncle had her mother's eyes and the same wide smile and she had warmed to him immediately. It wasn't like family time, but it was a start and she knew they truly meant it when they extended an invitation to come by any time.

Which was a relief actually. Prudence wasn't exactly sure what she was might do, but living at Summerset was quickly becoming unbearable, and though part of her still wished that things would go back to the way they were come Easter, she knew in her heart that nothing would ever be the same. It was time for her to stop being such a coward and start making plans for herself. Now that Lady Summerset had made her true feelings known, Prudence knew it was only a matter of time before things came to a head.

Prudence hurried around to the servants' entrance. She hadn't told the girls she was leaving again this morning and was anxious to check on Victoria, who had seemed strained when she had last seen her. A large delivery wagon stood in front of the door, but Prudence didn't think it remarkable. With a house full of guests, the amount of food they ran through each day was staggering.

She nodded to a housemaid in the hallway and bid the cook a cheery good afternoon. It had been two days since the ball and she had been careful to behave in exactly the same manner as she always had. Not that it mattered. They would never accept her into their folds.

"You'd best get upstairs to help your young mistresses," Hortense's voice came from behind her.

Hortense had been cool toward Prudence since the servants' ball, though Prudence wasn't much surprised after discovering her ladyship's animosity toward her. She only wondered why it was that Hortense had been kind to her in the first place. "And why is that?" Prudence asked.

"Their belongings arrived from London while you were gadding about town and my lady is fit to be tied. Imagine having the entire contents of a house show up on your doorstep when you have a manor full of guests!"

"It isn't an entire houseful," one of the footmen said, coming in the door carrying a trunk. "Just their personal effects and such."

"Whose personal effects?" Prudence asked, the beginnings of unease prickling down her arms.

"Your mistresses', of course," Hortense sniffed. "A good lady's maid would know these things."

"I'm not a lady's maid," Prudence snapped, unbuttoning her coat. She hurried up the stairs and out into the Great Hall. Most of the guests had already retired to their rooms to rest and bathe before dinner or were playing cards in the drawing room. Prudence didn't bother with the servants' stairs, instead going right up the main staircase—the quickest way to Rowena's room.

"Prudence!" Lord Billingsly called behind her, but she didn't stop, couldn't stop. In her heart, she knew the truth, but needed to hear it from Rowena.

The entire room was filled with trunks and a few pieces of furniture. Prudence recognized the pretty dressing table Sir Philip had bought for Rowena on one of his trips to France and a small gleaming rocker that had belonged to Ro and Vic's mother.

Rowena stood in the middle of her green and gold room, panic playing across her pretty features. Victoria stood across from her, her hands clasped and her fingers twisting tightly. "Just what is going on?" Victoria's voice was high and thready, a sign that she would lose her breath if she didn't calm down.

"That's what I would like to know," Prudence asked, her voice far calmer than the tumultuous panic on the inside.

Rowena blanched. "I'm so sorry. I didn't want anyone to find out this way."

Victoria stamped a foot. "Find out what? If you don't tell me right now . . ."

Automatically, Prudence went over to Vic and laid a calming hand on her shoulder. "You need to breathe, Vic. Close your eyes and take a few small breaths. We'll find out what is going on but you need to breathe." She rubbed Vic's shoulders in small circles until the girl nodded and did as she was told. The moment Victoria's eyes closed, Prudence's own gaze swept to Rowena. Their eyes caught and held. Pain glimmered in the depths of Rowena's eyes. But there was something more, which hurt Prudence more than anything. Shame.

Victoria's color returned and her eyes flew open. "You let him sell our home. You let him sell it and you didn't even have the courtesy to tell us." She put her hand over her mouth and sobbed.

"No. No, I didn't. Uncle didn't sell the house, he just let it. It's still ours. He says we may decide what we want to do with it."

The words were right, but Prudence noticed that Rowena didn't come toward them, didn't move in with a reassuring hug.

"Good. Then let's move back," Victoria said. "Let's not wait. We can unlet it."

Rowena said nothing. Bitterness welled up inside Prudence and came out in a laugh so hostile; it caused both of the other girls to startle. "No, we can't. He let it for an extended length of time, didn't he? Otherwise you would have told us."

Victoria's head swiveled back to her sister. "How long has our home been let? How long do we have until we can *decide?*"

Rowena looked down at the ground as if the answer were written in the new carpeting. "Seven years," she finally said.

"Seven years?" Victoria shouted. "Seven years?"

Tears, more in anger at her sister's betrayal than in grief at losing the house, began rolling down Prudence's face. "When were you going to tell us? How long were you going to let me play at being your maid? Did you enjoy that? Do you realize what I've gone through? What I have done because you said everything was going to be just fine?" She stopped and shut her eyes as the room spun around. She took a deep breath and opened them again. "I trusted you."

"I'm sorry, Pru. I didn't mean . . ."

But Prudence had had enough. She had given

everything and more to show these women her love and gratitude. She considered them family. But this proved that they could never be family. A real sister wouldn't have done this to her.

Her fists clenched by her side. "Your father would be so ashamed of you."

She whirled around to see Elaine standing white-faced in the doorway. Behind her, Sebastian's eyes were full of both shock and compassion. When she swept past them and back down the stairs, no one tried to stop her. She hurried out the front door, not knowing where she was going, only that she had to get out of the house.

Once outside, she ran down the drive until a hitch in her side forced her to stop. There was no way she could run far enough anyway. Then she leaned against one of the old oaks and sobbed.

Everything rose up and attacked her from all sides. Sir Philip's death, her mother's betrayal, her own illegitimacy, her treatment at the hands of the staff and the family because of who she was, and worst of all, Rowena's duplicity, the final blow.

Why hadn't Rowena just told her that they had no home to go back to? Even if Rowena would have had to tell her that she, Prudence, would have to find a different home or situation. They could have figured it out together, as they did everything, but no, Rowena was too selfish or too weak or too something to tell her the truth, and by lying she'd let Prudence live in an intolerable situation. She'd slept without heat, had lived and worked without dignity, had had tricks played on her by others, and just two nights ago someone had called her a tart. Her cheeks burned at the thought.

Prudence sniffled and dried her face on her sleeve. Her coat was still open and she had lost her hat at some point. She buttoned up her coat and looked back toward Summerset. Darkness was coming on quickly, and Prudence knew she would have to go back. She couldn't stay out here all night. She had to get her things and make a plan.

"I think you lost this."

Disoriented, she turned until she located Sebastian walking toward her, carrying her black beret.

She tried to smile but the effort was too much, and in the end she just took the hat and pulled it down over her head.

"Are you all right?" he asked her softly.

She shrugged. "As good as I can be. I'll be fine." She tilted her chin up. "I'll be fine," she repeated more firmly. "I'm just going to have to find another situation until I decide where I want to go and what I want to do."

He cleared his throat. "Will you be going back to the house or would you like me to drive you somewhere?"

She thought briefly of Wesley and her family but put the thought out of her head. No. The relationship was too new. She could stay at the inn, but she had little money with her, and the banks would be closed until after Christmas. No doubt, the inn would be filled for the holiday and she wasn't sure Summerset even possessed another hotel.

"I'll have to go back," she admitted. "At least for now."

He took her arm and they walked slowly back toward the house. "May I make a suggestion? This would be far more appropriate and seemly coming from my mother, but under the circumstances—I do know of a position that may be just what you are looking for."

She glanced sideways at him but he was staring straight ahead. "And what would that be?"

"My cousin's best friend is an invalid. She had a riding accident when she was a girl and as a result is bound to a wheelchair. She also has occasional breathing problems, similar to Victoria's. She is a bit older than I am and quite lively. I believe you would like her."

"I'm not a nurse, Sebastian," she said, then blushed at the use of his first name. It just seemed so natural.

Sensitively, he ignored it and continued. "She has a nurse who attends to her physical needs. She is hoping to engage a companion to travel to

Spain and Italy for the rest of the winter. My cousin used to be her companion until she was married last fall. It may be the perfect position for you while you sort something else out."

He was right. It would be.

"There's another thing that makes it perfect." He stopped walking and turned to her. His eyes shone mysteriously in the darkness. "It means you won't disappear and I will get to see you again."

Her heart thudded in her chest and for a moment she thought that perhaps he was going to kiss her, but then he turned away and began walking again. It was as if he sensed that she was too fragile for even one more emotional incident. She swallowed. "How soon would you be able to contact them?"

"Cara is staying with my cousin for the holidays. I will send a note directly."

"Thank you," she said simply.

He nodded. And they walked in silence toward what was left of Prudence's old life.

Victoria sat across from her aunt and uncle in the study, wondering whether they had seated her in this chair on purpose. The graceful Queen Anne chair they had indicated for her to take was just tall enough so that her feet did not reach the floor. It took everything she had not to swing them like a petulant child and put herself at a distinct disadvantage.

Her aunt, still in her flowing lace tea gown, spoke first while her uncle looked on, both benevolent and disapproving. Victoria couldn't wait to reveal what she knew. She wondered how long it would take for their expressions to change.

"Victoria, we have guests. I find it extremely discourteous of you and your sister to indulge in a screaming match in the hallway. And then to demand a meeting with your uncle and me." Here Aunt Charlotte shrugged helplessly. "It borders on rude."

Victoria considered her words. She wished Kit could be with her. He had been the perfect companion to take to Nanny Iris's yesterday. She'd been close to breaking down when Nanny Iris had told her the truth, but Kit stayed calm and was able to quiet her almost like Prudence used to do. But Victoria knew this was something she had to do alone. Originally, she had planned on telling Rowena and then confronting their aunt and uncle together, but after today she didn't know whether she would ever be able to trust Ro again.

"I am sorry if our argument embarrassed you, Auntie," she said. "But you must understand the shock Prudence and I felt to discover that we were not going home at Easter and indeed that we didn't have a home to go back to. And that is part of why I need to speak to you now."

Her aunt's pretty features remained both aggravated and disturbed. "Don't concern yourself with such things, my dear. You will be staying with us in Belgravia for the season. It's much larger and will accommodate all of us, as well as guests."

Her uncle finally spoke: "That is precisely what I told Rowena. It's not as if I didn't take your and your sister's wishes in mind. I didn't sell the home; I just let it out until you and your sister are in a better position to make such decisions. Even though it belongs to the estate, I did that as a courtesy, as that is where you both grew up and where you were closest to your father. And I'm sorry if it's old-fashioned, but it is impossible for you two to live there on your own at your age."

Victoria wanted to protest his last point, but she wouldn't let herself become distracted. Arguing with her uncle about women's suffrage and rights would not attain her objective. "While I don't agree with your decision, it would be pointless to argue about something that is already done."

"And yet that is exactly what you and your sister were doing and at the top of your voices, I might add," Aunt Charlotte said, her face twisting wryly.

"But it's not why I insisted that I meet with you both," Victoria put in quickly. She must get this out or she might lose her nerve, and she did not wish to lose her nerve. The reason they were in this mess in the first place was because her sister had lost her nerve. Or maybe Rowena didn't have any nerve to begin with.

"And why did you insist on meeting with us?" Uncle Conrad consulted his pocket watch as if she were keeping him from an important meeting.

"I have come to discuss Prudence with you." Her aunt waved her hand as if there were nothing to discuss, and her uncle shook his head in disgust. "Or rather Prudence's mother."

The hand waving and head shaking stopped.

Victoria took a deep, careful breath even though she felt herself shaking inside, as if she were having her own personal earthquake. "I would like to discuss Prudence's position in this family, or rather, why she is living in the servants' quarters when that is the farthest place from where she should actually be."

Her uncle stood, but Aunt Charlotte's eyes never wavered from Victoria's face. Victoria tried to meet her gaze, but her aunt's will and character were too strong and Victoria finally turned her eyes to her uncle.

"I don't know what you are talking about," he said, but his neck, slowly turning the color of a ripe tomato, gave lie to his words.

"She knows," her aunt finally said. "The child knows." Aunt Charlotte turned to her husband and patted his hand. "Let me deal with this, darling. Victoria is family, it will be fine."

Victoria watched relief spread over her uncle's features. "Thank you, my dear. I will see you before dinner in the drawing room?"

Aunt Charlotte nodded. "Of course. I sat that American, Mr. Danworth, next to you for dinner as you requested. You'll be able to talk horses all through the meal now."

"Thank you, my dear." The Earl inclined his head at both Victoria and his wife and left the room.

Victoria wanted to scream. Here she was sitting on a secret that could destroy the Buxton family and they were talking about the seating chart!

Victoria settled back in the chair and readied herself to face down her aunt. The way Prudence was being treated—and lied to—was completely unjust. Victoria could gain strength from the notion that she was fighting for what was right. If she couldn't save her father's home, at least she could defend her sister.

Lady Summerset sat perfectly upright in her chair and took her young niece's measure. While Rowena was far more beautiful—and less fragile—she'd apparently misjudged just how much steely resolve this particular child possessed. It no doubt came from being infirm so much of her young life. If you were sickly, you either overcame it or it overcame you. It gave one a sense of strength. And the chit certainly had more pluck and strength of character than her own daughter, who only cared for having a good time with that group of friends of hers, the

Coterie or whatever it was they called themselves. No, Elaine was a darling girl and would make a good match, but she would never be a ruler within society.

But who would have thought that little Victoria with the peculiar passions and big eyes would be staring her down as if she could actually win this little skirmish?

Would she have pulled such a stunt at eighteen? Challenging those with authority? She certainly maneuvered and manipulated those with control, but rarely challenged them directly. Lady Summerset thought of the suffragettes in prison, starving themselves for the vote. So many of this new generation of young women had no qualms about defying authority face to face.

But would it achieve their objective?

Letting Victoria stew a bit, Lady Summerset arose from her chair and walked over to her husband's desk. Taking out a piece of paper, she scribbled something quickly on it and then rang the bell board. Victoria looked on, puzzled and a bit apprehensive. Good. When the servant arrived she handed him the piece of paper. "Please give this to Hortense, immediately. Thank you."

Taking her time, Lady Summerset sat back down in the chair and settled the folds of her lace dress around her. Then she gazed at her niece, unperturbed. "I asked your uncle to leave because some of the things we are going to discuss are a bit delicate for a girl such as yourself to be talking about in front of a man."

"Really, Auntie. I'm almost nineteen."

"Still. I don't care what modern manners say, sensibilities demand certain decorum. Now, why don't we come straight to the point? What do you think you know and what do you want of it?"

Victoria tilted her chin. "I know who Prudence's father is."

"And how is it you know the answer to a question that only God knows the real answer to?" Lady Summerset asked quietly.

Victoria faltered but only for a moment. "You know, when my suspicions were first raised, I thought perhaps Uncle Conrad was her father or worse." Here Victoria closed her eyes for a moment, but then took a deep breath and continued. "Or worse, perhaps my own father. But it wasn't either one of them, was it?"

Lady Summerset had a biting retort on the tip of her tongue, but she knew how much it must cost the child to even consider her own father, so she held it in. "No, it was not."

Victoria looked down at the ground, and Lady Summerset felt a pang of pity for her. Life was so much more painful for those who faced it head-on.

"My grandfather was some kind of monster, wasn't he?" Victoria said.

Lady Summerset gave a surprised laugh. "A monster? Hardly. He was a man who had certain tastes and had the power to get what he wanted. I'm sorry to put it so bluntly, but as you said, you're *almost nineteen*."

"But if it was against her will?" Victoria cried out.

"Who knows if it was? We weren't there, we don't know."

"So you're not denying that the former Earl of Summerset is Prudence's father?"

There was a cry at the door where Hortense stood with Prudence by her side. Prudence was as white as a sheet. Victoria rushed to her side and she and Hortense helped Prudence into the chair next to Victoria's.

"You may leave us now, Hortense. Please have hot tea waiting in my boudoir. And have my bath drawn, please."

Hortense disappeared while Victoria knelt down next to Prudence, rubbing her hands. The girl looked as if she was going to faint.

"I'm sorry, Prudence. I was going to tell you after I spoke to my aunt."

Prudence just shook her head.

Lady Summerset watched both of them. There was no doubt the family resemblance was strong in Prudence, which was one of the reasons Philip had listened to her pleas and not brought her back to Summerset. What a fool he was to rescue the girl's mother like that and raise the child as family. As if she had a right to it all! She shook her head. No matter what her husband and brother-in-law told her, the girl had no rights whatsoever.

But even at that, she wasn't an unfeeling person. There would be a respectable resolution to the issue. There would have to be. They had kept the scandal at bay for too long to have it exposed by two foolish young girls. She brought her attention back to the matter at hand.

"I don't understand," Prudence finally said.

"Victoria? Don't you think you should be the one to tell her?" she said.

Victoria stood, still holding Prudence's hand in hers. "I went to Nanny Iris with my suspicions last night and she told me the truth."

Prudence looked around, confused. "Nanny Iris? Sir Philip and the Earl's old nanny? What would she have to do with anything?"

Before Victoria could answer, Lady Summerset shook her head. "Perhaps the story should be told by someone who knows all the facts."

"Nanny Iris had enough facts that the family paid her off handsomely," Victoria flared.

"Sit down, Victoria," Lady Summerset snapped. "You forget, this isn't just Prudence's story, it's Halpernia's, as well. This isn't just a family scandal. It's a tragedy, so let's conduct ourselves accordingly." Victoria fell quiet. Lady Summerset looked at Prudence. "You know who Halpernia was?"

Prudence nodded.

Lady Summerset stood and poured herself a glass of brandy from the crystal decanter her husband kept on his desk. She took one sip and then another while the girls watched her silently. No wonder he enjoyed his brandy so well. It really did calm the nerves.

"Victoria is right, Prudence. As far as we know, you are the daughter of the late Earl of Summerset, Harold Xavier Conrad Buxton. Your mother was a maid here during that time. He took a liking to her and as happens, she soon found herself with child." Victoria tried to interrupt, but Lady Summerset held up her hand. "No, I will not speculate on whether the interlude was forced or mutual. That hardly has any bearings on the current situation anyway."

"That's because it's not your mother, Lady Summerset, nor the story of your birth."

Prudence's voice was tight and bitter, and Lady Summerset had an urge to slap her.

"Your mother wasn't the only one," Victoria broke in. "There was more than one town girl and one of them even killed herself!"

"Enough!" Lady Summerset snapped. She looked at the glass in her hand and then took another sip. "Let's not stray too far from the story at hand. What may or may not have happened with other young women has no bearing on Prudence's mother, or Halpernia for that matter."

Victoria subsided and Lady Summerset went on. "Alice and Nanny Iris were quite close and Nanny Iris tutored the girl when they were done with their duties. Little Halpernia took a liking to Alice, and when Nanny Iris had an afternoon off, Halpernia wanted no one else but Alice to care for her. Once, when they were out walking . . ." Here she paused and wasn't sure she would be able to go on. She and Conrad had been out walking with little Colin that morning and heard the cries. She'd never wanted to speak of these things again, and now here she was being forced to. She took a deep breath and continued, resolutely. "No one knows exactly what happened, but somehow Alice neglected her duties while with the Earl, and little Halpernia drowned in the pond."

Prudence gasped and Victoria drew closer to her.

"So girls, what do you think the family did after that? Lady Margaret, the Earl's wife, had a nervous breakdown. The Earl never quite got over it and had his first stroke nine months later. They pensioned off Nanny Iris generously, as her services were no longer needed. Alice was discharged, of course. She would have been let go anyway, as soon as her condition became public knowledge."

"Of course," Prudence said, her voice bitter.

"What would you have them do? Decorate her for finding the body?" Lady Summerset snapped. Prudence looked away. "Philip had recently married and left for London. Knowing that your mother was expecting a child, he hired a private investigator and found her in dire straits, so he spoke to his wife and they offered her a position in their household. I'm sure he felt some obligation to you as you were his half sister. The rest you know."

Lady Summerset folded her hands across the top of her dress and waited.

Victoria was the first to speak. "So knowing all of that, why did you try to make her into a servant? She is a Buxton! She's my aunt!"

Prudence leapt to her feet, her eyes flashing. "No, I'm not! I'm living proof of both a scandal and a tragedy. I'm the bastard child of either a shameful situation or a vicious attack. My mother was the reason your real aunt died. Why would anyone, except your father, who was the kindest person in the world, welcome me into his arms and home? According to your class, I am worse than a nobody!"

"But we don't believe that!" Victoria cried out.

"It doesn't matter what you believe, Vic. That's the way the world works. They didn't want me here, so they made it unbearable for me to be here."

Silence descended upon the group. The ancient clock behind them was the only sound in the study besides the slight wheezing of Victoria breathing.

Lady Summerset finally cleared her throat. "I think when Victoria came to me this evening, she wanted to have her story confirmed and she had some grand idea that you would somehow be accepted into the family so she wouldn't have to worry about losing you, but that's not going to happen, is it, Prudence?"

Prudence stood in front of Lady Summerset. The girl was still wearing her fine walking suit from that afternoon. Her Buxton breeding and genteel upbringing showed in her perfect carriage and the fine set of her head. Pity, really.

"No," she spat out. "I have been lied to, betrayed, and treated abysmally. Why on earth would I ever want to be a Buxton and align myself with your kind?"

"Prudence! Stop!" Victoria cried.

Lady Summerset nodded. This was exactly the type of response she expected. "I'm not an unfeeling woman. If you require some kind of money, we would be more than happy to . . ."

Prudence shook her head. Her set jaw and clenched fists showed just how difficult it was for the girl to keep herself under control. Lady Summerset respected that. She'd felt the same way on more than one occasion.

She tried again. "Tomorrow is Christmas, but I am sure if I called the inn . . ."

"That won't be necessary," Prudence said. "I have family in town."

Lady Summerset inclined her head and Prudence left the room without a backward glance.

"Prudence!" Victoria cried out again. "Wait!"

Lady Summerset caught hold of Victoria's arm before she could run after her friend. "Give her some time. Think of the shocks the girl has had today."

"But she needs me!" Victoria said.

Lady Summerset sighed. How like the young to act like they could change everything. Victoria would be crushed by Prudence's departure, but she would accept it. One of the advantages of youth was the ability to accept the unacceptable. She gathered the girl gently into her arms. How long had it been since she had held her own daughter like this? Before finishing school, surely. "Your friend needs to be alone now. Give her a day or so and then go to her. You will be more help to her once you both have calmed down. She'll feel differently then, surely."

Prudence wouldn't and Lady Summerset knew it, but she let Victoria cry, brokenhearted, in her arms, wondering whether Hortense would ever be able to get the tearstains out of her lace.

EPILOGUE

The repetitive rattle of the train would have lulled Prudence to sleep if she had been able to sleep, but considering that she hadn't slept for the past five nights, there was little chance she would do so now.

At least she wasn't alone.

In hindsight, she was glad she'd asked Victoria to attend the wedding. If anyone was innocent in all this, it was Vic, who only wanted Prudence to move from her attic room to Vic's room. Victoria, who had received all of her father's sweet idealism, but little of his wisdom. Victoria, who thought that if only she could prove that Prudence was indeed a Buxton, her aunt and uncle would relent and accept Prudence as a member of the family.

And Victoria wondered why the other girls treated her like an imaginative child.

Of course, Victoria's presence only served to remind Prudence of Rowena's absence. But she didn't want to think about Rowena right now. Maybe never, but definitely not right now.

Prudence wished to forget she was a Buxton, to forget that she had the same blood as the people who treated others as if they were only a means to an end. Who would pay servants to quiet the death of a child or the ruin of a young woman?

Unbidden, Rowena's pretty features came to mind and Prudence's heart squeezed painfully, as it always did when she thought of the young woman who had been like her sister. She wanted to forget she had the same blood as someone who would betray a loved one because telling the truth was too hard or inconvenient.

She thought of her mother and the pain in her heart increased. And she especially wanted to forget she had the same blood as a man who evidently would not take no for an answer when it came to young women.

Prudence had had much time to dig further for information about her family this past week while staying at the inn. Her cousin helped her uncover other rumors about the former earl, a man people hated so much that by the end of his life he daren't set foot in town. No wonder the current Earl of Summerset spent so much money putting a wing on the new hospital and improving things for his tenants.

Compensation.

Restlessly, Prudence settled more comfortably in her seat. The man next to her stirred and she froze, not wanting to wake him. God knows he hadn't gotten enough sleep either this past week. She smiled tenderly. A good man. He was a good man and even if she wasn't sure about her feelings right now, she knew she would learn to love him.

He had been by her side the moment he'd heard of the ruckus and had refused to leave. He didn't care about scandal or class or even what his family thought. Only her.

She stared at the bouquet she still carried. Yes, she'd been right to invite Vic. Somehow Victoria had known that Prudence wouldn't think of flowers, or any of the other little touches that go along with marriages that had more than five days of planning. So Vic had gathered her favorites from the conservatory and made a bouquet for her.

"I know it's heavy on *Gardenia jasminoides*, but the conservatory didn't have much of a selection," Victoria had said, her lower lip drooping.

It had been the only time all day Prudence had felt like breaking down. But in the end, she had remained dry-eyed throughout the little ceremony that was attended only by Victoria, Susie, Wesley and his parents, and Cook on Prudence's side and his brother and sister-in-law and father on the groom's side.

Andrew stirred again and hesitantly Prudence reached out and patted his shoulder. His eyes flickered open and smiled at her before closing again. The night he had come to her she had told him almost everything, including her parentage. She didn't tell him about the job Lord Sebastian offered her because in her mind and heart that was no longer an option. Her cheeks heated as she remembered her cowardice. She hadn't even faced Sebastian with her decision not to take the job, but instead sent him a little note, thanking him for his kindness. She said nothing in her note about Andrew.

She may not have known exactly where she belonged, but she knew where she didn't belong and that was with the Buxtons, the Billingslys, the Kittredges, or any of the other families of the upper social class. No. That life would not be her life. She wanted nothing to do with them. Any of them.

Instead, she would move to Devon and after hard work and sacrifice, she would be the wife of a farmer veterinarian and it would be a good and happy life, one worthy of the man who had raised her. And if she missed the family and home she grew up with?

Prudence took a deep breath and let it out slowly. Well, then she would just have to make her own family. Her own home. That was all.

AUTHOR'S NOTE

Every writer of historical fiction comes up against the question of how far to bend history to accommodate plot and how far to bend plot to accommodate history. For this project, I had an amazing historical researcher and fact checker, Evangeline Holland (www.edwardian promenade.com), who was quick to let me know when I had strayed too far. Then I had to make the decision of plot versus history. Most of the time, history won out. I dearly wanted to keep the details of the book as close to La Belle Époque as possible, but there were times when the story itself came first. For instance, the funeral customs set in the first and second chapters of the book more closely resemble modern American customs than they do Edwardian customs, but here story trumped history. (You can read more about the funeral customs of the Victorians and Edwardians at Evangeline's great site.)

Besides Edwardian Promenade, I had many wonderful historical resources, both primary and secondary, to help me on my way. But I apologize in advance for any historical inaccuracies contained within the book and claim each mistake as my own and not the responsibility of my incredible fact-checker or resources.

NONFICTION RESOURCES

The Perfect Summer: England 1911, Just Before the Storm by Juliet Nicolson

Manners and Rules of Good Society: An Etiquette Classic by Anonymous

Victorian and Edwardian Fashions from "*La Mode Illustrée*"

The Opulent Eye by Nicholas Cooper

Below Stairs by Margaret Powell

The World of Downton Abbey by Jessica Fellowes

Victorian and Edwardian Fashion: A Photographic Survey by Alison Gernsheim

FICTION RESOURCES

A Room with a View by E. M. Forster

Howards End by E. M. Forster

The Edwardians by Vita Sackville West

The House at Riverton by Kate Morton

ABOUT THE AUTHOR

T. J. BROWN is passionate about books, writing, history, dachshunds, and mojitos. If she could go back in time, she would have traveled back to England, 1910, Paris, 1927 or Haight-Ashbury, 1967. She resides in the burbs of Portlandia, where she appreciates the weirdness, the micro-breweries, hoodies, Voodoo Donuts, and the rain.

READERS GROUP GUIDE

SUMMERSET ABBEY
T. J. BROWN

Though her mother worked as a governess in the London home of Sir Philip, second son of the Earl of Summerset, Prudence Tate was raised as a sister to Sir Philip's own daughters, Rowena and Victoria. The three girls believe their bond to be stronger than any blood ties, but when Sir Philip dies, their relationship changes forever.

Forced to move from London to the sweeping grounds of Summerset Abbey where their aunt and uncle reside, it is suddenly clear to Rowena and Victoria that not everyone welcomes Prudence into the high-society world they now inhabit. Instead of being seen as their equal, Prudence is relegated to the position of their lady's maid, and as each day passes the divide between them grows larger. Rowena, the elder, cannot deal with the responsibilities now placed on her shoulders, while Victoria struggles to be seen as something more than a sickly child. And Prudence, shocked by her treatment and stung by the attitudes of those around her, realizes that solving the mystery of her past might be the only way to find herself a future beyond the ever-present specter of class expectations that haunts all three girls.

QUESTIONS AND TOPICS
FOR DISCUSSION

1. Though the terms of Sir Philip's will were perfectly normal for the time period, what did you think about his decision to place the future of his daughters in the hands of the Earl? Were you surprised that he left no allowance for Prudence? Do you think he did this because he expected the situation to turn out differently, that he believed his brother and daughters would look out for her?

2. Throughout the book, Victoria makes certain observations about secrets. For example, she reflects that "The only secrets [she] enjoyed were her own" (pg. 34), and that "The most important thing she'd learned about secrets is that you never knew when one was staring you in the face" (pg. 291). Do you agree with her observations? Many of the characters including Victoria carry their own secrets, some trivial, some life-altering. Do you think they would've been better off sharing those secrets with each other from the beginning? Do you feel secrets push people apart?

3. What did you think of Rowena's first betrayal, the decision not to tell Prudence of the Earl's condition for her accompanying them to Summerset? Do you think it was

selfish or that, in that moment, she had no other choice? What about by the end? What might you have done in her shoes?

4. Think about how Victoria's sickness defines her as a character: How does it shape how others see her? How does it shape how she sees herself? Do you agree with Prudence's assessment at the end that she had "all of her father's sweet idealism, but little of his wisdom" (pg. 371)?

5. At Summerset, Prudence finds herself straddling worlds in a way she had never experienced before, unable to truly fit into one place or the other. How does this inform her decisions? Do you think she ever judges anyone unfairly, as unfairly judged as she is? How does she reconcile her duty to Rowena and Victoria with her bewilderment at being relegated to the maids' quarters?

6. Though much of the story follows Prudence, we also get to see chapters from Rowena and Victoria's perspective. How did that influence your view of each of the girls and their separate motivations? If you could ask the author to insert a chapter from another character's point of view, who would it be and why?

7. Though Lady Summerset can be seen as the main antagonist of the novel, her motivations are complicated. Consider a woman's

position at the time, and the choices (or lack thereof) she had regarding her future. In that sense, do you think she was doing the best she could to protect herself and her own family, even if it meant hurting Prudence?

8. Similarly, at one point, Rowena rages against their circumstances, reflecting that "she was as trapped as a fox in a hole. Trapped by her responsibilities, trapped by her social status, trapped by being a woman. Her uncle possessed all the power and she possessed none" (pg. 77). Discuss how this statement applies to all the women, regardless of social stratum. Ultimately, is it the Earl who has all the power?

9. Many of the young men in the book feel equally constrained, albeit in different ways. Consider the varying attitudes and actions of the male characters such as Kit, Sebastian, Andrew, and Jon, and how those attitudes and actions define their relationships with the women around them.

10. The young women of Summerset have their own ideas about what the future should hold for them. What are the differing views held by Prudence, Rowena, Victoria, Elaine, and even characters like Susie and Katie? Were you surprised by their attitude toward women of the previous generation (such as Lady Summerset)?

11. Do you believe Elaine knew the truth about Alice, and Prudence's birthright? Why or why not?

12. A question that many of the younger characters struggle with (regardless of class) is whether privilege (or lack thereof) that we are born with is privilege we truly deserve; or, put another way, what rights can or should be decreed by birth and what rights should we earn? At one point Rowena wonders whether, by loving Summerset and the way of life there, she and Victoria are per-petuating the problem between classes, as symbolized by Prudence. What do you think?

13. Before Rowena goes up in the plane with Jon, Mr. Dirkes tells her "Adapt or die!" Do you think this is what each girl was doing over the course of the story, in her own way? Is this a motto you would live by?

14. How do you see Rowena's story turning out? Victoria's?

15. Were you surprised when Prudence chose Andrew in the end? Who did you think would be better suited for her, him or Sebastian? Do you feel that, by denying her attraction to Sebastian, Prudence took the easy way out, in a manner of speaking? Or do you think she made the only logical choice?

16. At the very end Prudence notes, "She would just have to make her own family. Her own

home." What was your reaction to this ending? Do you think that the families and homes we grow up with aren't really families of our own making?

ENHANCE YOUR BOOK CLUB

1. Elaine and the rest of the Cunning Coterie fancy American cocktails such as the gin sling. Follow the recipe at http://cocktails.about.com/od/ginrecipes/r/gin_sling.htm and treat your club to a cocktail hour.

2. Have a viewing party of the popular PBS series *Downton Abbey* or a similar upstairs/downstairs type film such as *Gosford Park*. If *Summerset Abbey* was made into a movie, who would you cast?

3. Read a nonfiction account of life during this time such as *Lady Almina and the Real Downton Abbey: The Lost Legacy of Highclere Castle* by the Countess of Carnarvon or *Below Stairs* by Margaret Powell. Compare these accounts to the novel.

4. Learn more about author T. J. Brown and the women of Summerset by visiting her website, tjbrownbooks.com.

Center Point Large Print
600 Brooks Road / PO Box 1
Thorndike ME 04986-0001 USA

(207) 568-3717

US & Canada:
1 800 929-9108
www.centerpointlargeprint.com